Summer HEAT

ALSO BY JILL SANDERS

The Wildflowers Series

Summer Nights

The Pride Series

Finding Pride
Discovering Pride
Returning Pride
Lasting Pride
Serving Pride
Red Hot Christmas
My Sweet Valentine
Return to Me
Rescue Me

The Secret Series

Secret Seduction
Secret Pleasure
Secret Guardian
Secret Passions
Secret Identity
Secret Sauce

The West Series

Loving Lauren
Taming Alex
Holding Haley
Missy's Moment
Breaking Travis
Roping Ryan
Wild Bride
Corey's Catch
Tessa's Turn

Haven, Montana Series

Closer to You
Never Let Go
Holding On

The Grayton Series

Last Resort
Someday Beach
Rip Current
In Too Deep
Swept Away
High Tide

Lucky Series

Unlucky in Love
Sweet Resolve
Best of Luck
A Little Luck

Silver Cove Series

Silver Lining
French Kiss
Happy Accident
Hidden Charm
A Silver Cove Christmas

Entangled Series: Paranormal Romance

The Awakening
The Beckoning
The Ascension

Pride, Oregon Series

A Dash of Love
My Kind of Love
Season of Love
Tis the Season
Dare to Love
Where I Belong

Stand-Alone Novel

Twisted Rock

JILL SANDERS

This is a work of fiction. Names, characters, organizations, places, events, and incidents are either products of the author's imagination or are used fictitiously.

Published by Montlake Romance, Seattle
www.apub.com

ISBN-13: 9781542015226
ISBN-10: 1542015227

Cover design by Vivian Monir

Cover photography by Wander Aguiar Photography

Printed in the United States of America

Summer HEAT

PROLOGUE

Elle Saunders stood on the white sand as the bright orange of the sunset turned to a soft, warm pink. Gently cradling the case made of stone to her chest, she sighed deeply. It was time.

Taking a few steps into the clear, warm waters of the Gulf of Mexico, she opened the lid and released her last hold on the only man she'd ever loved. The only man who had given her everything.

"Goodbye, Grandpa Joe." She held in tears as his ashes floated and danced in the soft breeze and sparkled in the dying sunlight before disappearing from view as the sun slipped over the horizon.

Walking back to her Jeep in the dark felt like reentering a gray, drab world full of mundane tasks, but life went on. After all, she'd dealt with it before, having lost her mother at a young age.

Before she could climb behind the wheel of her Jeep, however, her phone buzzed in her pocket.

Seeing the picture on the screen that she'd snapped of Hannah Rodgers at camp one summer years ago, she smiled and answered it on the second ring.

"I just got back into town from my business trip and got your message. I'm at the airport now. How are you doing?" Hannah said before Elle could speak.

"I'm"—she leaned back against the old Jeep, letting the summer air warm her—"alive." How could she tell her friend in a quick check-in about the sadness that had overtaken her? How she'd almost let her depression consume her over the past few weeks? It was the truth—she was alive, and grateful for it—but sadness threatened to fill every pore in her being.

"I've called everyone else. They'll be there by tomorrow," Hannah added.

Elle nodded, not trusting her voice at this point. She'd stood on the beach for the past two hours, telling herself that she was now all alone in the world.

But here was a reminder that she wasn't.

The Wildflowers, or so the five ten-year-olds who'd come together at summer camp had called themselves. Five girls from diverse backgrounds, different family situations, who had formed a bond stronger than that shared by most sisters.

"We're here for you," Hannah said. "We knew he was sick, but . . . you didn't tell us that he was this sick."

Elle leaned her head back on the Jeep, wishing she could go back in time. "I—I didn't think he was this bad. I should have known you guys would want to say goodbye."

"Elle, you're the person we should have been there for. Not your grandfather," Hannah said as the speakers in the airport called out in the background. "That's my flight. I'll be there in a few hours. I've rented a car, so don't worry about picking me up. I've still got the keys to the house. Go home, open a bottle of wine. I'll see you soon." There was a pause. "Elle, we love you. You're our sister, even if you sometimes forget it."

"Thanks," she managed before Hannah hung up. She hadn't realized tears were blocking her vision until she turned on the Jeep's lights and noticed that everything was fuzzy.

Leaning her head on the steering wheel, she cried for the first time since finding her grandfather yesterday morning.

The weight she'd felt the last day and a half from coping with the loss had been heavy. Her first instinct had been to call her friends for support. But she would need to manage this part by herself and to deal with losing the man who had given up everything to raise her.

Now, however, after releasing his ashes into the clear waters near the place he had loved the most, she needed her friends to lean on.

When she parked her Jeep back in front of the big house in the small town of Pelican Point, she was slightly surprised to see her grandfather's longtime friend and lawyer, Bob Collins, sitting on the front porch, swinging and smoking a cigar.

"Thought you'd taken off on us." Bob stilled the porch swing as she sat next to him and rested her head on his massive shoulder. He wrapped a meaty arm around her, and she settled in comfortably next to him. The man was the same age as her grandfather had been, but where her grandfather had been tall and skinny, Bob was thick and muscular, since he still lifted weights down at the local gym. She was pretty sure the man had been doing that for so long that stopping the routine would probably kill him.

"No," she whispered. "I just turned Joe loose."

Bob was silent. "He sure loved you like his own. When he lost Emma . . ." Bob paused. "Well, you know, the only thing that saved him from going over the edge was you." Bob glanced down at her and brushed a strand of hair away from her face, then placed a tender kiss on her forehead. "I'd better get home—you know how Carolyn is." He started to get up, and his eyes narrowed. "Don't tell her I was smoking."

"Never," she promised, smiling since she knew that Bob's wife probably already sensed he was smoking those rich Cuban cigars somewhere.

"I put some papers on the table for you." He nodded toward the screen door.

"Papers?" She stood up. She hardly ever locked the front door anymore. There wasn't any need, since everyone in Pelican Point knew where the hide-a-key was anyway.

"It's probably no surprise to you what Joe had and that he'd left it all to you, but it may come as a surprise that he left one stipulation." He had one foot on the top stair as he looked back at her. "He doesn't want you to be alone in life. Nor do I." He winked at her. "Those friends of yours, what do you call them?"

"The Wildflowers." She smiled as Bob chuckled.

"Fitting. I watched the bunch of you sprout up like weeds, or, um . . ." He cleared his throat. "Like wildflowers, I mean. Anyway, if you have any questions, you know where to find me." He turned and disappeared into the darkness.

After a few minutes in the night air to clear her head, she walked into the house. Glancing around the massive place, she hugged her arms around herself and tried not to dwell on the emptiness she felt.

He'd been gone less than two full days, yet she wondered how long it would take everything to sink in. The loneliness, the loss, and the pain.

Sitting at the table, she pulled open the large tan envelope Bob had left and looked over her grandfather's will.

He'd left her everything—the house, the cars, the money in his bank accounts—but once she got to the part about the camp, she stopped and read that section over and over.

For the next few hours, she calculated, crunched numbers, and plotted as she reread.

When a car pulled up outside, she felt her heart jump, then instantly realized she couldn't tell her friend until they were all together. Grandpa Joe had been smart; it would be all or nothing going into the future.

Like a tornado, she gathered up the papers and shoved them in the downstairs closet, then went to greet Hannah at the door.

Before she could speak, she was gathered into her smaller friend's arms as more tears flowed.

Even after a long chat and several glasses of wine, she found it hard to sleep that night. She was too excited and nervous to settle down and rest. Not to mention the sinking feeling she had knowing that her grandfather was gone.

When she picked Zoey Rowlett up at the airport the following day, she almost blurted her plans out right then. Instead, she asked about her friend's softball injury.

Later that night, Zoey's sister, Scarlett, arrived. Aubrey, sweet Aubrey, was the last to shuffle into the house.

Maybe it was because Zoey and Scarlett had each other, and Hannah was . . . well, Hannah: strong willed, stubborn, and more of a spitfire than Aubrey Smith, who had the fiery hair that usually signaled that nature. Instead, Aubrey was shy, timid, and soft spoken, which had Elle wanting to protect her more than any of her other friends.

Still, after dinner, she suggested they all head out to the camp for an evening swim. She wanted them to be surrounded by what it was they would be fighting for. Where their future could be.

Maybe it was floating in the pool surrounded by the night or the third glass of wine she had been sipping, but by the time she finally worked up the courage to spring her idea on the others, she had convinced herself that there was no other future. It was this or nothing, in her mind.

River Camp simply had to be reopened, and she wanted—no, *needed*—her friends by her side. It had been over ten years since she'd first bumped into Hannah on these very grounds. She'd been going to the camp for as long as she could remember, but that year had been different. That year was the first year she had lived there. The year after her mother's brutal death, which had been quickly blamed on her father.

With her dad in jail and her mother gone, she had been welcomed into her grandpa Joe's arms with a long hug as the older man cried uncontrollably. Over the years, she would never see him shed a tear again. He claimed it was because he'd lost part of his heart when his only daughter had been killed.

That first year in Pelican Point, the kids had made fun of her in school. She'd been the butt of every joke, the girl everyone picked on. After all, she was the daughter of a murderer. Then, that summer, she'd met Hannah, Zoey, Scarlett, and Aubrey, and things had changed. Everything had changed.

She could be whomever she wanted with these new friends. So, she chose outgoing, popular, and being a girl who knew what she wanted in life. All the things she wasn't inside. But she'd played the part well enough that soon after that first summer camp, she became all of it and more, and not just to herself but to everyone else.

Who really cared what the local kids thought anyway? Less than a year after her mother's death, Rodney Whitfield's father had drunkenly driven his pickup truck into the front of the local grocery store and paralyzed a tourist. Her own family issues were quickly forgotten in town after that.

Now, she was Elle Saunders, the girl whose grandfather owned River Camp and would someday take over the elite summer camp for privileged girls.

Today, focusing on her friends in the main swimming pool, Elle couldn't count the number of times the five of them had sneaked in and enjoyed an evening swim together. All the fun they'd had together filled her memories more than the recent loss she held deep in the dark corners of her heart.

Zoey's long hair had blonde highlights at the tips, while her sister's remained dark with streaks. If she hadn't known them for ten years, Elle would have had a hard time telling them apart in the dark with their hair pushed back and wet. Of course, Zoey currently had her injured knee hoisted up on the pool steps and was rubbing it with her hands.

Hannah's blonde hair was like her own: long and thick. But whenever Hannah went somewhere, she always looked like she had a team of stylists, while Elle looked like a child had fixed her up. Even now, Elle probably looked like a drowned rat, while Hannah sat across from her like a photo shoot from a magazine.

Aubrey was always stunning, with her slate-blue eyes and her vibrant red hair. Her porcelain skin made Elle wish she could resemble her the most.

The five of them were having a blast in the water, and Elle knew it was time to tell everyone her ideas. After all, Hannah and Aubrey were due to fly out in less than two days. Both of them had jobs, lives back in cities. Scarlett and Zoey had their mother to take care of. That thought wrenched that empty spot in Elle's heart, so she built up her courage.

"I'm going to miss this place," Zoey said, shaking Elle out of her thoughts.

"What's going to happen to the camp?" Hannah asked.

Elle swam closer as she tried to think of the right words to say.

"That's kind of why I wanted us to be here," she said, looking over the water toward the dying sun. She wished those earlier shared times would never end. "Remember our first night here?"

She'd been thinking about it since she'd read her grandfather's will.

Zoey accused her of changing the subject, which she often did when she felt uncomfortable. It warmed her to know that they knew her so well, and she held in a laugh. Finally, after attempting to stall again, Elle just blurted it out.

"What do you think of opening the camp again?"

She was met with silence—actual crickets chirped in the background.

"You're going to open the camp back up to young girls?" Scarlett finally asked.

"No." She shook her head. "I'm thinking of turning it into a camp for retirees: you know . . . snowbirds." She laid out her plans quickly and knew that she was spewing words at them.

When she accidentally said the word *we* instead of *I*, Aubrey shocked her by jumping in.

"I'm in."

Everyone must have been shocked too, since Aubrey was, of the five of them, the most stable one in the group.

She felt her entire body shake with the extra adrenaline as, one by one, her four best friends—no, four *sisters*—answered her pleas for help.

CHAPTER ONE

One year later . . .

She'd been right. There was no way she could have opened River Camp back up without her friends' help. Since that night at the pool, all five of them had worked more than they ever had in their lives.

Elle had discovered something new about herself: she had a knack for organization and a head for business. She'd pushed herself harder than even she believed she could.

Still, by the time the camp was almost ready to open back up, she hadn't realized a full year had passed without her so much as spending a weekend by herself.

Work with her friends wasn't so much work as a common goal. She hadn't missed much over the year—at least she hadn't thought she had until she'd laid eyes on the three brothers Zoey had just greeted.

Watching them swagger toward the front doors of the main camp building from the third-floor apartment window had turned on a switch she'd long forgotten.

Even her latest ex-boyfriend, Jeff, hadn't caused that switch to flicker—not once over the yearlong relationship. After the first part of the new relationship had worn off, the only thing that had remained between her and Jeff was the memory of the abuse she'd survived at his hands.

"Wow, would you look at them," Aubrey said next to her. Elle had returned to the apartment she shared with her friends to change into a fresh T-shirt after snagging hers on a nail. When she'd walked in, Aubrey had been in the process of changing into dry tennis shoes since she had stepped into a puddle of mud and soaked her right foot and shoe. Now, she stood next to her, still holding one shoe in her hand. "Who called in the eye candy?"

Elle chuckled slightly, until the man with the long hair glanced up and his hazel eyes met hers, full force. She felt her knees buckle, and she fell backward, landing on her butt. She thought she saw him laugh up at her, but one minute she was looking out the window, and the next she was quite literally knocked on her ass.

"Are you okay?" Aubrey rushed over and helped her up.

She was so embarrassed. She blamed her old flip-flops and crawled away from the window while pulling them off her feet, and she tossed them toward the front door. Then she snuggled on the sofa and relaxed back against the cushions, wondering what the three men were doing there. Prospective employees? Lord knows they needed them.

She told Aubrey that her feet and back were hurting from the long day she'd had and that she just needed a rest.

Of course, Aubrey used that moment to get on the walkie-talkie that each of them carried around.

"Zoey, whoever they are, deal with them. I'm stuck helping Hannah for the next hour." She flipped off the radio and tucked it in her back pocket.

"Liar." Elle narrowed her eyes at her friend.

Aubrey shrugged and glanced out the window one last time. "No, it's true. I'm supposed to meet Hannah"—she glanced at her watch—"later. I'd pay a million dollars, if I had it, to be a fly on the wall and watch Zoey deal with them." A sigh filled the room. "Besides, I'm not ready to handle more potential employees. Not at the going pay rate they're requesting anyway. I've interviewed so many people in the past weeks I'm pretty sure time is stuck in a loop and I'm in my own *Groundhog Day* hell interviewing people for the rest of time."

Elle knew the feeling. She herself had compared the last three weeks to her own version of repeating hell. The first wave of prospective employees had elated her. Then, after a dozen or so interviews, she'd been over the entire experience.

"Maybe these three will be the last for a while," Aubrey said, walking away from the window.

"I doubt it. We still need"—she thought over the list in her head and groaned—"more. But, for now, they may have to do if they're cheap enough. I'm beginning to feel as if potential employees should walk in with price tags on their foreheads so we can cut all the bull out and just tell them we can't afford to hire them. As it is, we already have several employees filling different roles."

"Including us." Aubrey sat across from her. "Not that I'm complaining." She held up her hands. "Being the director of counselors, as well as teaching tai chi and judo, is far better than being someone's secretary." She shivered.

"Still," Elle said, "you were working for your father."

"Even more reason to stay here," Aubrey finished.

"I thought things were going better between you two?"

Just then Hannah strolled in. She tossed a large backpack down at the door, flung herself down next to Aubrey, and closed her eyes.

"That bad?" Elle asked as Hannah toed off her tennis shoes. The fact that Hannah was covered in mud sent both Aubrey's and Elle's eyebrows skyward.

"Worse." She moaned. "How many days left before we open our doors?"

"Twenty-eight days, nine hours, and"—Elle glanced at her watch and calculated quickly—"twenty-two minutes."

Hannah groaned. "Do you think it will get better?"

"God! I hope so," Aubrey said. "My feet, my back, and my butt hurt."

Elle glanced over at her. "Your . . . butt?"

"I fell off of Jack yesterday," she answered, rubbing the spot. Jack was one of the seven horses they had purchased to fill the stables.

"Fell off or were bucked off?" Elle asked, already worrying that one of the older horses they had sprung for wasn't going to cut it.

"Fell," Aubrey insisted. "I'm not really up to speed on riding. It's more of Zoey and Scarlett's specialty, remember?"

"Right." She relaxed back.

"Besides, Carter assured me it was a . . . How did he put it? 'A rider error, not a horse one.' Who wants wine?" She got up and went to the fridge to pull out a bottle. All five of them occupied the three-bedroom apartment her grandfather had lived in during most of the summer months while he ran the summer camp.

"Don't you feel any remorse?" Elle asked Aubrey when she handed her a full plastic glass of red wine.

"For?" she asked, her red eyebrows going up slightly.

"Leaving Zoey with the three hunks?" she answered.

"Hunks?" Hannah's eyes opened, and she took her glass from Aubrey.

"No," Aubrey answered her. "Yes, three of them," she said to Hannah. "Think different, equally hot versions of Jason Momoa."

"Yum, we could use some eye candy around here." Hannah sipped her wine. "Did she hire them?"

"Not sure. Aub left Zoey to deal with them all by herself. We don't even know if they were applying for jobs." Elle thought about it. If they weren't, what were they doing there?

"Poor Zoey," Hannah added dryly. "I'm sure she can handle them," she said before leaning back again. "I'm sure she's going to hire them. We've all been lacking in the sex area."

"Speak for yourself," Aubrey chimed in, causing Elle and Hannah to turn to her.

"Who have you been sexing up with lately?" Elle asked her.

Aubrey shook her head. "This one guy named Noneya," she said with a smile. "None ya business."

"Spill." Elle set her glass down. Normally, when one of them hooked up, it was blatantly obvious by the glow she had.

Still, as Elle ran her eyes over her friend's face, she could tell Aubrey had been holding something back.

"Don't waste your time," Aub said and got up. "I'm going to run downstairs and see if Zoey needs my help." The fact that she left the room without another word reaffirmed she really wasn't going to talk about her sex life. Yet.

"Fine." Elle leaned back and frowned at the apartment door. "So, at least we know it can happen here. I mean, we've been here for a year, working full time with hardly any time off . . ." Her mind whirled. "Do you think it's Carter?" she asked Hannah.

"Dean?" Hannah speculated quickly.

"It can't be Brent. He's married," Elle added, thinking of the head waiter their celebrity chef, Isaac Andrews, had personally hired. "Besides, we're the wrong gender." She sighed, thinking of all the other employees they had hired in the past few weeks. "It has to be an employee. I mean, there's no one else around."

"Do you think that it's a long-distance thing?" she started to suggest, but just then Scarlett walked in, picked up the bottle of wine, and downed several gulps. Then used the back of her sleeve to wipe her face.

"Rough day, honey?" Hannah asked softly.

"I hate him." She groaned and flopped down on the sofa beside Elle.

"Who?" the two of them asked at the same time.

"Levi. Who else?"

Hannah and Elle turned to one another and said "Levi" at the same time.

"Naw, he's not Aubrey's type. Besides, are redheads attracted to one another?"

"What are you talking about?" Scarlett broke in and then took another swig of the wine like a pirate downing rum.

Levi was one of their first official hires. Elle had known her fellow local all her life. She'd attended school with him since she'd moved in with her grandfather.

Levi had been one of the only people in her grade she could remember being nice to her. Hence her hiring him on the spot when he'd pulled into the camp shortly after they began the renovations.

She had hired several locals to help with the renovations, including Aiden Stark, her second cousin, fresh from college with a degree in architecture.

Aiden's grandmother (Nancy) and Grandpa Joe were brother and sister. Nancy had died shortly after she'd given birth to Aiden's father.

Aiden was a couple of years older than Elle, and shortly after she'd moved in with Joe, Aiden had come to her defense during a football game. He'd lent her his jacket after someone had spilled a soda on her white shorts on purpose. He'd told her that she was his cousin and that he'd been keeping an eye out for her.

When she'd talked to him about the project, he'd jumped at the chance to work with her, and she'd immediately hired him to oversee the entire camp's construction.

The fact that Scarlett and Levi were butting heads threw her off. Levi was one of the nicest guys she'd ever met. He lived a few miles away with his grandmother, who had raised him ever since his mother had become addicted to drugs when he was born. She'd died of an overdose shortly after his seventh birthday—taking with her the secret of who had fathered Levi.

"What have you done?" Elle asked. She knew Scarlett too well to assume it was something Levi had done.

Her friend's eyes narrowed. "Why is it always my fault?"

The entire room went silent; then all at once, everyone burst into laughter.

"Fine." Scar threw up her hands. "I simply asked him to help me move some logs."

"Asked or demanded?" Hannah asked.

"Asked," Scar said in a tone that made it clear she was pissed. "I mean, what's the point of hiring muscle around here if we can't utilize it?"

"What logs?" Elle asked.

"The ones by the old barn," Scar answered.

"What?" Elle sat up. "Scar, those must weigh a ton each." Some of the logs were actually full trees that had been chopped down by Aiden's team when they were clearing the forest of anything that could possibly fall in a strong windstorm. They had plans to cut them up into smaller chunks and use them for firewood in a few of the cabins that had fireplaces. "You can't expect him to move those himself."

"I didn't," Scar said, taking another sip of the wine bottle. "Just the smaller ones. But he wanted to argue, and, well . . ." Her shoulders slumped. "Things got heated."

Hannah chuckled. "I'll deal with him and explain tomorrow."

"No." She shook her head. "It's my mess. I'll . . . go now." She got up but stopped when Zoey walked in, followed by Aubrey. The look in Zoey's eyes matched those of her sister's less than five minutes before.

"Oh no, who pissed you off?" Scar asked.

Zoey's eyes moved around the room. "I hope you're happy."

Elle glanced around and then pointed her thumb at her chest. "Me? What did I do?"

"Both of you." Zoey pointed to her and Aubrey, who had sat back down on the chair in the corner. "You left me alone to deal with Thor and his brothers."

"Who are we talking about?" Scar asked, sitting back down and handing her sister the half-empty wine bottle.

"But I was running a search online for the brothers—Owen, Dylan, and Liam Rhodes," Aubrey said.

"Yeah, and you left me alone with them." Zoey started pacing, hugging the wine bottle to her chest.

"Oooo-kay," Elle said slowly, but Zoey was on a roll.

"There was nothing in the system about them. What were they? Jerks?" Aubrey said.

"No, it's just . . ." Zoey bit her bottom lip. "How was I supposed to say no to them?"

"So . . ." Elle started, looking around the room. "You did hire them? Right?"

"Of course: I offered them the jobs, and they agreed to do multiple jobs around here for chicken-scratch pay. But"—Zoey wagged her finger—"whatever happens, it's all your fault."

CHAPTER TWO

Twenty days later . . .

It wasn't long after the brothers had moved into a bunk room on the second floor that Elle spotted them on the security cameras sneaking around the campgrounds at night.

Her first thought was to approach them; then she mentioned it to Zoey, who had an idea to watch them closely. Since it was coming down to the wire as they prepped for opening, she couldn't afford to lose three new employees—not at what they had agreed to be paid anyway. So they voted to wait.

For several nights, the five friends were glued to the computer screen watching the brothers move around the grounds like spies.

"They're looking for something specific," Zoey said one night. "But what?"

"We can't afford to fire them," Elle said, biting her bottom lip and thinking about the budget she'd gone over earlier that day. They would have just enough to get them through the first few months, if she watched their budget closely. "Not now. Who would we get to replace them? Besides, they're building that slide thing."

"Dry tube slide," Zoey added.

"Right." Elle nodded. She'd researched the slide after they had suggested it and figured it would be one more low-cost attraction they could add to the website. "So, what do we do?"

"Two can play at the game of spying," Zoey suggested as she outlined a plan where they would each take a brother to watch. Zoey's Google search had turned up too many hits to give them anything specific about the men. She had even tried different searches using some of the state-employee databases they had access to. Which hadn't shown her anything new.

Elle sighed at that knowledge—she showed up on the first page. Most of it was about her taking over the camp, but there were several articles about her past and her parents.

Elle's gaze tracked Liam as she thought about the plan. He was currently sidling around the boathouse, trying to look casual as he peeked inside the dark windows. "Good idea," she said finally. "Plus it gives us some time to figure out what they're doing here."

"I'll take Dylan," Zoey said, her eyes on that part of the computer screen where he was walking around the pool house.

"Then I've got Liam," Elle said.

"That leaves the oldest one, Owen," Scar chimed in, looking over at Hannah.

"Oh no." Hannah shook her head. "I'm not a spy."

Aubrey chuckled. "And Elle and Zoey are?"

"Zoey is more spy than me," Elle added with a smile, earning her a playful nudge from Zoey.

"You've got to do it—Aub and I are swamped," Scar said. "Aubrey has to train everyone, and besides, I have to leave soon to help Mom move."

Hannah sighed. "Fine, but I want it to go on record that I—"

"Yeah, yeah." Zoey waved her away. "So, let's talk details."

Days later, Elle was just finishing up helping Kimberly, Zoey and Scar's mother, move into the Wildflowers' old cabin—the River Cabin. She was tired, covered in a thin layer of sweat and dust, and wanting a shower and bed as she walked the dark pathway toward the main building.

When she stepped off the porch, a slight movement and sound at her back caught her attention.

Deciding to play cat and mouse with whoever it was, she started down the dimly lit trail as if unaware. She smiled slightly when she heard footsteps following her.

Just around the corner, she ducked behind one of her favorite trees along the pathway and waited.

Seeing the dark figure pass by her position slowly, she jumped out, thinking it was Zoey. After all, she was trying to catch her off guard since she wanted to pay her back for the dunking she had given her earlier that day on the docks. Instead, Liam turned to face her on the pathway, smiling as if she hadn't surprised him at all.

"What are you doing?" she asked as she turned away to hide her blush. She started marching down the path toward the main building as if she hadn't just jumped out of the bushes.

She had caught herself mumbling whenever she spoke to him and had decided the less she talked around him, the better. So, normally she bit her bottom lip and let everyone else do the talking. But she couldn't miss a chance to probe into their actions.

"Taking a walk," he answered as he fell in step with her.

"You and your brothers tend to take a lot of walks." She glanced over her shoulder at him.

"It's the number-one mode of transportation around the campgrounds. Besides," he started as they climbed the steps to the building, causing her to roll her eyes at his mansplaining, "it's not a crime."

"Is there a reason I keep finding you in the strangest places?" Elle asked once they were just outside her office door. Now that she could see him in the light, she had to admit: he was even better looking than she'd first thought.

His long dark hair framed his face in soft curls, brushing against the few days' stubble on his chin. Stubble that gave him a more dangerous appearance. Since the camp wasn't officially open yet, he was in his own clothes—a dark short-sleeved shirt that highlighted arms rippled with thick muscles. She could almost feel them wrapped around her body.

"Like I said, it's not a crime to go for a walk," Liam said, interrupting her thoughts.

Elle tilted her head slightly and looked at him in disbelief.

"This makes it four times in the past six days that I've seen you sneaking around after dark." She had kept track—after all, running into him was a highlight. Especially after a full year of being sex deprived.

"Sneaking?" Liam's voice rose. "If you consider an evening stroll sneaking, what are you going to do when guests start arriving and milling about?"

Elle remained quiet for a moment as she took him in. Yeah, being around him caused her brain cells to shrivel up.

"Why were you out near River Cabin?" she finally asked as she headed inside, with him following.

"I saw a light," Liam answered. "I thought someone might be messing with the place."

Elle's eyes narrowed, and she remembered all the demanding work she'd just done to help Kimberly move the rest of her belongings into her new home. Her hair had come loose from the braid she'd done earlier in the day. No doubt she probably looked like a dusty rat at the moment.

"No, no one is messing with the place. It's just private," she said.

"Someone's living there?" Liam asked.

"Yes," she answered quickly.

"Who?" he asked.

Elle shifted slightly, trying to figure out a way not to answer him. Coming up with nothing, she threw up her hands.

"Zoey and Scarlett's mother. Scarlett and Kimberly just got back from Jacksonville after selling their old home."

Liam went silent for a moment as he leaned against her desk. "Why keep it a secret?" he asked.

Elle turned back toward him with a gasp. "I'm not. It's just none of your business," she deflected. "Why are you and your brothers sneaking around anyway?"

"We don't sneak." Liam straightened up. Even though he was only a few inches taller than Elle, he seemed to tower over her.

"Still, either you keep getting lost, or . . ." she started.

"I enjoy evening walks in the great outdoors," he finished for her. "The three of us enjoy nature. It's one of the reasons we got jobs here."

"Either way"—she moved toward the office door—"I'd appreciate it if you didn't go sneaking around the River Cabin. We've allowed Kimberly to rent it from us as a private home. She's a very reclusive person and doesn't wish to be harassed," she added, even knowing it wasn't the truth. Kimberly was very outgoing. Sure, she'd been through a lot in life, but Zoey and Scar had gotten most of their spunk from their mother.

"I have never harassed anyone," Liam said after he'd moved toward the door. A slight smile flickered on his lips, and Elle seriously doubted that he'd leave any woman feeling less than . . . shaken by that body of his.

Elle's eyes narrowed as she thought about what else he could do with that body.

She shut the office door behind her, locked it, and turned back to him. "Feel free to walk the trails; just steer clear of River Cabin," she said before turning away from him.

"Will do," he added, falling into step with her again as she walked away. "What were you doing out there?"

"Helping." She started up the stairs.

"If you had asked, we could have lent a hand," he suggested.

"Next time I'll take that into consideration."

"After all, isn't that why you hired us?" He smiled when she tilted her head in question. "Muscle?" He raised his arm and flexed his biceps, and she about melted at the bulk of his muscles.

Without saying anything, she pivoted and rushed up the steps to her apartment. She could have sworn she heard him chuckling behind her.

The following day Elle stood back and watched the iron gates swing open at the end of the long dirt drive and felt as if the weight that had been on her chest since her grandfather had died was suddenly lifted.

For the next hour, cars, taxis, and even several airport vans surged through the gates. Elle watched her employees rush around and unload the cars, then load the golf carts and shuttle guests off to their individual cabins. She felt completely helpless, since it had been decided that the best place for her would be to take up a position at the main building in case she was needed.

She had a few small things to do, but for the most part, she stood around and watched other people work. Of course, she had run into the Rhodes brothers rushing around the grounds several times.

She'd tailed Liam the first week after they had moved onto campus, although she had tried to avoid actually speaking to him. Zoey and Hannah had filled her in on what they had learned from the other brothers. But, so far, she hadn't discovered anything about Liam by just watching him, other than he liked to take walks in the evenings, and he was good at building things.

Dylan, the middle brother, was a skilled zip line guide, which had filled a key role at the camp. Owen, the oldest one, was occupying several roles, including working as events camp counselor and helping Aiden out with some of the basic maintenance issues.

Liam was the youngest of the brothers, at twenty-two. He'd been put in charge of the woodshop and would be working behind the bar at the pool house with Britt, the bartender, when needed.

Every time his gaze traced her, her body did things without her approval, like her knees turning weak. She'd already fallen on her butt once because of him; she didn't want to embarrass herself further in front of him.

Of course, each time she'd bumped into him, she'd tried to hold herself together while speaking to him. But after . . .

She felt like a schoolgirl with a major crush, and it was beginning to become annoying.

She tried to fake a professional attitude, but since her favorite actor was Jason Momoa, and Liam was a dead ringer, she had a hard time not falling all over herself around him.

She'd never really had problems being around men before, nor anyone else, for that matter. After that first year of living with her grandfather, she'd adopted a persona of strength around others. There was just something about Liam that stripped that facade away. And it scared her.

That first day they had arrived on campus for work, she'd stood next to him while Zoey and Aubrey showed the brothers the ropes. She noticed his eyes were different from his brothers'.

The three of them were all tall, with curly dark hair and flawless olive skin, but where Owen and Dylan had darker brown eyes, Liam's light-hazel eyes almost glowed in the sunlight.

She had sucked in her breath, which sent those sexy eyes her way. But then she'd stopped breathing entirely as he evaluated her, the left side of his lip curving up. He could surely guess what he'd done to her pulse rate. But she had looked away quickly to stop herself from falling on her face at his feet. A few minutes later she invented an excuse to leave them.

The fact that the man didn't say a lot made her wonder about him even more. Did he feel the same way about her, or was he just shy?

She'd spoken to Dylan and Owen a few times now, running into them on the pathways or in the dining hall, but on the occasions she'd trailed Liam after their first meeting, he'd always been as terse as she was—only saying a handful of words. Which had her thinking about building up enough courage to try and get something out of him about the brothers' nightly activities.

Zoey hadn't stopped voicing her concerns about the brothers—something wasn't adding up with them. More than anyone, she was determined to get to the bottom of why the brothers were there.

Yet though Elle had listened to her friends' concerns, half the employees who worked for them could have easily gone elsewhere and made more than her camp could pay them. She was desperate to keep the people they had. Even if the men were out almost every night, she couldn't afford to let them go now.

Normally, her days were packed, and they would be again after day one. But for the opening day, she had been talked into sticking close to the main building. Which she was regretting.

Like a glorified flight attendant, she greeted the guests, directed them to check-in, and connected them with someone who would cart them to their cabins.

Not her grandfather's original proposal.

She itched to move around, to be useful. And as the day progressed, her frustration grew. By lunchtime, she was determined to step away and help in other ways. While wolfing down a sandwich with her friends, she asked them if they needed help.

"Come on, someone find something to get me out of babysitting the front desk." She almost groaned it.

"Elle, you run this place." Hannah laughed. "Do whatever you want. Go tell Julie you're going to take the next guest to their cabins. Remember, you're the boss now." She picked up her tray with a wink and then walked away.

Hannah was right. Elle was the boss. If she didn't want to stand around the lobby all day, she didn't have to.

After dumping her own food tray in the bin, she walked to the front desk to ask Julie, their full-time front desk manager, if she could help out. Instead, she found Liam standing there, flirting with Julie.

She took a moment to scan him when that gaze wasn't on her, and she appreciated the view.

His khaki shorts and camp shirt looked better on him than on anyone else. They made him appear more mountain man than anything.

Feeling the heat of frustration surface as she overheard their conversation, she cleared her throat and leaned on the counter.

"I'm sure there is something more important you could be doing than wasting Julie's time," she said.

She thought she'd been prepared, but when those hazel eyes turned toward her, her heart rate galloped.

"Just dropping off a sandwich." He nodded to the plate that sat in front of Julie. "Brent asked me to help out since he couldn't get away."

"Oh." She felt herself sag slightly. Now she felt bad and felt her face heat. Deciding to ignore him, she turned to Julie. "I think I'll take a few guests out to their cabins." She reached for a clipboard, unsure if she was even needed to help with the guests.

"Actually, Liam was just requesting that someone help him out at the pool bar. He and Britt are swamped." Julie shrugged. "If you have some time, everyone else is busy right now, boss."

Her eyes flicked back to Liam, and she held in a groan. "What's going on over there?"

"The first thing on everyone's minds once they check in is to hit the pool and drink," Liam said. "They've all shown up at once. We're in the weeds."

"It beats trotting back and forth with guests for the next few hours," Julie said, her eyes pleading with Elle.

It was true: playing waitress for the next few hours would beat standing around feeling useless. But working with Liam was something she hadn't prepared for yet.

She tried to think of any excuse to get out of it, but when his hazel eyes turned on her with a small challenge, she jerked up her chin.

"Guess I'll be at the pool bar. If anything else goes wrong . . ."

"I'll use this." Julie held up the walkie-talkie.

"Thank you." Elle turned on her heels and marched out of the main hallway.

"In a hurry?" Liam said, catching up with her just outside the main building.

She cocked an eyebrow at him and nodded. "You did say it was busy." She walked to the pathway that would lead them to the main pool house and patio area.

She had just stepped into the shade of the tall pine trees when he pulled her to a stop.

"No need to run. Britt can hold the fort until we get there." His smile had her knees going weak. At that moment, she realized she would have given him anything. *Anything*—and that thought scared her.

She'd been willing to give Jeff the same at one point in her life, and knowing how that ended straightened her back. Renewed anger filled her at the thought of falling into another trap like her past relationship.

"You're up to no good." She didn't know what had caused her to blurt it out, but she wanted to knock the sexy look off his face. Instead, her words seemed to set a glow into his eyes.

"We've always been up to no good." His joke bounced off her, but the crooked smile didn't. "It's one of our favorite pastimes."

His arm had dropped away from hers, and she took a step closer to him. "I have to admit that at first, I thought it was just Zoey being . . . overly protective. Now, however"—she tilted her head and ran her eyes over him—"I'm going to be keeping an eye on you." She knew she was already watching him, but letting him know it somehow made her feel stronger. She turned to go, but his next words stopped her.

"Good, because I've been keeping a close eye on you."

CHAPTER THREE

He knew his words had come out as a threat, and if he had to be honest with himself, he meant them. The woman who stood in front of him somehow had the appearance of a naive beauty, but he knew more than anyone that appearances couldn't be trusted.

"You've . . ." The shocked look on her face told him that his words had struck a nerve. "Why are *you* keeping an eye on *me*?" She moved closer to him.

He glanced over her shoulder as a group of guests in swim attire walked up the pathway. "Later, princess." He took her arm and started walking toward the pool house. He smiled when she jerked her arm free of his hold. Whatever he thought of his father's latest mistress, he was pleased that, unlike all the others his father had gone through, this one had a little fire to her.

For the next hour, he watched her deal with customers as if she was born for the job. She smiled, chatted, and delivered orders like she'd been doing so all her life.

He'd spent a summer working behind the bar at one of the resorts his father had dragged him to, just so he could hook up with women. It had done the job. That summer he'd not only learned how to tend a bar and become a man, but he'd also learned a few things about women that even his father probably didn't know.

Apparently, he still had it. By the time the dinner hour came around, he had at least five invitations and a few numbers tucked into his pockets. Which he quickly tossed into the trash can.

"You don't have to throw those out. I'm sure you earned each one." Elle surprised him. He turned to see her leaning against the bar top.

All the guests had returned to their cabins to prepare for their first dinner in the main hall. Now, the pool and the patio area were completely empty. He had finished cleaning the bar top and had loaded the last of the glasses into the dishwasher unit when he'd found and wadded up the numbers and tossed them.

"It's just not right." He shook his head and glanced down at the trash. "Women stuffing their numbers down some guy's pants. Married or otherwise."

"That 'some guy' was you. You can't tell me that you and your brothers have never . . . taken a married or otherwise woman up on her offer." She gazed at him as she stretched her back as if it hurt her. "Something tells me you've had a pocketful of numbers like that before."

"True." He moved over to wipe the bar top in front of her, even though it was already clean. He enjoyed being closer to her and knew that he wanted to keep as close an eye on her as he could. "Though I've never taken a married woman up on the offer."

"Never?" she asked, shifting to sit at the barstool.

"Would you take up a married man's offer?" he asked.

"No," she said without hesitation, and something deep inside him believed her.

"What about age?" he asked.

Her eyebrows shot up. "Shouldn't really matter, if it's just a hookup. Does it matter to you?" she asked.

He'd never really thought about it. But the fact was, the beauty sitting across from him was shacking up with his father, a man easily twenty years her senior.

"Don't you have a fancy dinner to get ready for?" he asked in lieu of an answer.

She sighed. "Yes. Where did you work before?" she asked, surprising him.

"Club Med," he answered and watched her blonde eyebrows shoot up.

"Florida?"

He shook his head. "Bahamas."

She whistled. "I bet you had a line of women there."

He smirked as he leaned on the bar, his hands spread on the wood top, caging her elbows between them. "Why so interested in my sex life?" He enjoyed the spark that was building in her blue eyes as she brushed off his comment.

"Curious," she said, waving her hand.

"About my sex life or . . . me?" He let his voice dip.

"Why not go back to Club Med?" she asked, as if unfazed. "There are a million of them."

He turned the question around. "Why turn a defunct privileged girls' summer camp into . . . whatever this is?"

"A snowbird retreat camp." She kneaded her hands. "You didn't answer my question."

"We wanted to stick close to home." It was the truth. About the only one he'd told her since first stepping onto the campgrounds.

Destin, Florida, had been their home for almost ten years now. Dylan had his own place just outside town, while Owen stuck closer to the downtown Destin building that the family owned.

Liam had taken advantage of a condo the family also owned—his for the moment.

"Why do I get the feeling there's more to that story?" she asked.

"Your turn. Why open this place back up?"

"It seemed the right thing to do." She stood up and glanced back at the clock. "Aren't you helping out at the bar in the main dining hall?"

"Yes." He shut the heavy wooden door that closed off the bar area to guests and locked the padlock. They made their way together back to the main building.

"This was your grandfather's place, right?" he asked.

"Yes," she answered without meeting his gaze.

He already knew almost everything about her, since he and his brothers had done their homework on her and the place. What they hadn't found out yet was how she had funded the remodel. Her grandfather hadn't been a wealthy man, and from the look of the camp, there had to have been a big investment to get the doors opened again.

"You must feel a little overwhelmed with all of the loans." It was a gamble, but he figured one way or the other, he could get her to confess something about her financial status.

"Loans?" She glanced over at him.

"Sure, I mean, this place will probably make your investment back soon enough, but . . ." He dropped off when she stopped walking and cut him a sharp look.

"I don't have any loans." She tilted her head. "Is this your way of asking me if your paycheck will clear?"

"No." He glanced around with a chuckle as the sky started to darken around them. The pathway lights flickered on. "Just making small talk."

It would have to stay at that, for now—he couldn't figure another way to get the information he wanted. After all, his brothers were searching for answers as well. Answers to the financial aspects of the camp while they searched for their father.

It had been a few months now since they had last heard from their father. Not that it wasn't normal for their old man to disappear, but this time, the family's money had gone too. So, the three of them had stepped away from their lives and poured everything they could into researching River Camp and Elle Saunders, whom they believed to be their father's last conquest.

Looking at the pretty blonde standing across from him in cream shorts, a camp logo shirt, and tennis shoes, he just couldn't see it. Not that she wasn't his father's type. She was, after all, twenty-one and beautiful. She could have easily walked off the cover of any magazine, even in that camp uniform.

But something just didn't fit. Which was why he'd suggested to his brothers that he would get closer to her and find out all he could. Well, technically, they had drawn straws. Where Dylan would look into the sisters, Zoey and Scarlett, and Owen would get close to Hannah and Aubrey, Liam only had to focus on Elle.

He had to admit, she was one of the best-looking jobs he'd ever had.

"I'm really starting to think there is something else that brought you to River Camp."

"Oh?" His eyebrows rose. "So what? We must be into espionage?" He nudged her shoulder. The fact that she was almost his height was an instant turn-on. He'd never before been with a woman who was as tall as she was. Most women tended to hit him midchest. Which was fine and all, but of course, he instantly wondered how it would feel having those long legs of hers wrapped around him.

"Something like that," she said, breaking into his thoughts. It took his sex-starved mind a split second to refocus on their conversation again.

"We're just three guys looking for work." The lie tasted foul, and he picked up the pace.

"We'll see," she said as they reached the main building. "Dinner is a formal affair. You'll need—"

"I've already got my monkey suit waiting for me," he broke in. "Brent saw to it." He stopped at the base of the stairs. "Smart hiring him—the man knows his business."

Her chin rose slightly. "Thanks." She turned to go up the stairs.

"Thanks for your help," he called after her, and she glanced back at him. "I would have been lost without you."

She nodded quickly, then climbed the last set of stairs. He had to admit that he watched her hips sway as she disappeared. Hell, who wouldn't have?

When he entered his rooms, his brothers were waiting for him.

"Find out anything new? I came up with nothing." He stripped off his clothes and tossed them on his small bunk.

"No, not since we talked on the beach," Owen replied.

"Haven't had time to do anything else than ask Elle a few questions, which was a dead end. Opening a camp is taking more time than I anticipated," he admitted.

"Has Ryan given you any more trouble?" Dylan asked him.

"Not since she pretty much threw herself at me earlier today as I was coming out of the dining hall," he answered.

Liam had run into Ryan, a waitress who worked in the main dining hall, as he took Julie her lunch before Elle had ended up joining them at the front desk.

Ryan had caught Dylan sneaking out of Elle's office a few nights back. She confirmed that she knew who the brothers were and threatened to expose them to Elle and the others if she didn't get what she wanted.

He'd been thankful he'd had his arms full of the receptionist's lunch when he'd encountered the thin brunette. She'd tried to wrap herself around him, but he held the tray between her body and his. The wild look in her eyes made it clear he had to tread carefully with her. Avoidance was the best policy in most cases like that.

To be honest, Ryan was one of the reasons he'd been thankful that Elle had helped at the pool bar. Some employees acted better around the boss.

"Well, I'm meeting Zoey after dinner. I'll let you know how it goes," Dylan said.

"I'm working behind the bar helping Britt out tonight. Maybe I'll be doing that every night." Liam held in a groan.

"It's your own fault. I told you, playing bartender to get laid has consequences." Owen chuckled as Liam buttoned his shirt.

"Shove it," he said and tucked his shirt in. "What about you? What have you found out?"

"Aubrey is tougher than she looks," he said, causing his brothers to stop getting ready. "She teaches judo."

"Yeah, so? Lots of people do," Dylan said.

"I stepped into the gym while she was practicing." He shivered. "I've never been afraid of a woman half my size before, but . . ." He shook his head. "Remind me not to piss her off."

"Okay." Dylan laughed. "What about Hannah?"

"I have a feeling she's been avoiding me," Owen answered.

"She's busy. They all are. Now that the camp is opened, it's going to be even harder to get time with them," Dylan said. "Liam, you've had free time to check out all the cabins prior to opening. Any signs of Dad?"

"None." He felt discouraged. "There's a cabin near the stream that I haven't checked out yet. When I got close to it, I ran into Zoey."

"Did she suspect you?"

"No, I pretended to be lost while walking." He shrugged.

He glanced down at his watch and hissed. Then he quickly pulled on the rest of his suit and dashed out the door. "Catch up with you after dinner."

He was trying to put on his tie just outside the dining hall doors when he bumped into someone. His hands gripped the woman's shoulders.

Looking up, for a moment he was thrown off kilter; then he smiled into Elle's blue eyes.

"Oops," he said, then joked, "We've got to stop meeting like this."

She reached up to fix her long hair and smiled. "It's bound to happen often." She glanced at the bow tie he was gripping in his fist. "Need help?"

Yes. He'd been about to toss the thing on the ground in frustration. "It's been a while since I've worn one of these."

She took the tie from him and reached up to wrap it around his neck. While she worked on tying it, she talked about how her grandfather had always pretended he needed her help. She'd always believed it was because he'd wanted her to feel useful.

She laughed at the memories, and he watched her face closely. Her blue eyes were set in concentration as she worked, which gave him plenty of time to appreciate her beauty. Her nose had a sharp point to the end of it, leading his eyes to her full pouty lips, which were painted a soft shade of pink now. Her eyes, accented with silver makeup, looked silver blue when her gaze met his.

She was almost done tying the tie when his eyes moved down to her dress, and he felt his breath catch in his chest.

The silver dress fit her like a glove. No, better than that, like a second layer of skin. The low-cut front showed off a view of the best-looking breasts he'd ever imagined.

"Wow," he managed to say when she stepped back. He realized now what had thrown him off about her. She was wearing a pair of high heels, which caused them to be the same height.

A slow smile blossomed across her face. "I'll take that as a compliment." She stopped as footsteps rushed toward them.

He held in an inward groan when he saw that Ryan was the source of the sound. Her waitress uniform had replaced the shorts and T-shirt she'd worn earlier that day, when she'd practically thrown herself at him.

"Oh." Ryan's smile grew when she noticed him. "There you are—I was hoping we'd run into each other again." She didn't stop until she was standing closer to him than Elle was. Her hand came up and brushed down his dinner jacket. "Maybe we can meet after dinner?" Her gaze turned to Elle. "That is, if it's okay with the boss that we have our own lives?"

Elle stepped back slightly, but then her eyes met his.

"Employees are allowed their own lives on their own time." She glanced down at a thin silver watch on her wrist. "However, right now, aren't you late for your shift?"

"Right." Ryan giggled, then ran her hand across his chest once more. "See you later." She disappeared through the staff door.

Elle's eyebrows rose. "You look like you'd rather swallow that tie whole than to have her touch you."

He shivered. "I don't tend to fall for the crazy ones. That's more my father's speed." He hadn't realized the words had escaped his lips until he heard her laugh. It was the first time he'd brought up his father with her. He'd debated bringing him up with her before: worried about it really. What if she was his father's mistress? What would he do? He knew that his thoughts of her would change instantly.

Did he want that? Did she already know? It wasn't as if he and his brothers didn't look like their old man. Had she already placed them and was just stringing him along?

"I didn't think she was all that bad. Just silly. But if you want, I can talk to Brent . . ." she began.

"No," he broke in and opened the staff entrance door for her. "I'm sure she's a fine employee, it's just . . ." He thought of the Ryan conversation with his brothers and decided to keep it to himself. "Nothing," he finished and watched as she walked past him.

Then he swallowed the rush of lust that caused his throat to go dry as he noticed the back of her dress. A thin string crisscrossed her bare back, holding the silver material low over her firm ass.

"May I say wow again?" he said as he stepped into the back hallway with her.

"Do you think it's too much?" she asked, glancing at herself in the small employee mirror hanging in the hallway with a motivational sign above it.

"No," he finally managed to say.

"Good, we figured it was important to have the guests feel like they're at a fancy party each night."

"You're going to wear that every night?" His brain went foggy, since most of his blood had traveled south.

"Not this particular dress," she said with a smile. "It looks like Britt needs your help." She motioned to the bartender he was helping for the night. The older woman was a stockier version of one of his nannies, and he had instantly liked her, which was why he had volunteered to help her out whenever he was available. He suspected that Britt was short for Britney but didn't dare ask her for fear of retribution.

"Yeah." He waved and held up a finger to signal that he needed a minute. "Listen, why don't we continue this conversation after dinner?"

He liked the look of surprise on Elle's face.

"I . . . I'll think about it." She turned quickly and disappeared behind the curtain of the stage area.

After meeting Britt at the bar, he took over the drink-order queue and spent most of his night refilling people's glasses.

He took a break shortly before nine and chatted with Dylan when he stopped by. He filled his brother in on running into Ryan again, how she'd practically attacked him.

"What does she want from us?" he asked Dylan.

"She claims she wants what we have."

"What? An absent father who's run off with the family's money?" he joked.

"Fame." Dylan sighed. "She thinks by being seen on one of our arms in high-society circles, some of the glory will rub off on her."

"That's crazy."

"I've seen worse," he said softly.

Liam leaned closer to his brother. "Have you found out anything more?"

"No, you?" Dylan asked.

Liam shook his head.

"All we can do is keep digging," Dylan said before leaving.

Liam tried to keep his focus on his job, but he found it hard every time Elle came into view.

When the dining hall started to empty, she made her way over to the bar, and he filled her order for a Coke as she leaned on the counter and waited.

"So?" he asked as he set the glass in front of her. "How about a walk after?"

She appeared to think about it and tilted her head to the side. "Like all those nighttime strolls your family seems to do? Sure. I'll walk with you back to the main building." She took a sip of her soda.

The dining hall was officially in the same main building, but employees entered off the back of the building, allowing them also to walk around the gravel pathway to the employee entrance of the main hall and then up to the staff rooms.

He was looking forward to that short walk with her, and the rest of his shift seemed to fly by.

After helping Britt clean up, he found Elle sitting at a table with Hannah. When she noticed him, she stood up and made her way across the room, as if she'd been waiting for him.

"All done for the night?" he asked. Hannah didn't greet him, he noticed, but simply watched them, eagle eyed.

"Yes." She gathered her things, and they left.

He held the door open for her, and when she stepped out, she shivered in the night air.

"It feels like rain," he said and draped his jacket over her shoulders. "We're supposed to have some tomorrow. The temperature always drops before a storm."

She smiled. "Whenever it dips below seventy, Floridians break out the sweaters and boots." She hugged his jacket to her. "How about a walk to the water? I could use some fresh air."

"Sure." He silently thanked his lucky stars and followed her down an empty pathway. Falling in step with her, he wondered why suddenly he felt like he was on his first date again.

"It must be nice having brothers. I always wanted a sibling."

"Parents didn't follow through?" Yet despite his casual small talk, he knew her grandfather had raised her after her mother's death, and that her father had been locked away for that crime of passion, or so the articles he could find on her mother's murder had said.

"No." She turned toward a small clearing where a large wooden bench swing sat. "She died too young."

"I'm sorry," he said, sitting next to her and pushing the swing slowly. "What happened to your father?"

She sighed and crossed her arms over her chest. A move he hadn't seen her make before but knew that most women did it when they felt uncomfortable.

"He wasn't around much."

"Abandoned you?" he asked, knowing he was pushing, but maybe he'd get an insight into why she'd shack up with his dad. That is, if she really had.

"You could say that. What about your family?" She could turn the tables easily enough.

"Mom died shortly after I was born. My dad is around . . . somewhere." He shrugged.

"Around?" she asked.

"He may or may not be going through a midlife crisis," he answered.

She turned slightly toward him, and the swinging stopped.

"Joe went through one of those once. I was fifteen and had been living with him for a few years already," she said.

"What did he do?" he asked, curious.

"He sold his old truck and bought a 1969 Camaro." She smiled.

He whistled. "Black?" He had to admit, as far as midlife crises went, it didn't sound too bad.

"You know it," she said. "He drove that car around for almost a year before selling it and buying back the old truck he had before."

"Why would he go and do a stupid thing like that?" he asked.

She chuckled. "It was hard to shuttle big supplies back and forth to the camp in a Camaro."

"Why not keep both?" he asked curiously, since he had both a truck and a souped-up car sitting in his parking garage at the moment. The question caused her eyebrows to go up slightly.

"The camp was his baby, his entire life. He put everything he had into it, even if he didn't have anything left to give." She relaxed back and started rocking again. "There were times he'd go without buying new pants, which he'd ripped working on rebuilding the docks, just so he could afford new lumber." She closed her eyes.

"You must miss him?" he said.

"It was strange: when my parents were around, I never felt like I was part of a family, until him and my Wildflowers."

"Wildflowers?" he asked. He remembered hearing someone else refer to the friends as such but didn't know where the name had come from.

"Zoey, Hannah, Scar, and Aub," she said absently. "We met here"—she glanced around again—"when I was ten. Shortly after . . . ever since, we've been family."

"Why the Wildflowers?" he asked.

"It was what we chose as a nickname for the five of us. We were in the same cabin when we met here." She smiled. "It fit us. We're all different, but . . ."

"Together you make a beautiful bunch." He nodded. "I get it."

"Did you go to college?" she asked out of the blue. When he didn't respond right away, she continued, "I did for a while. When I moved to Denver, I thought . . ."

He could tell she was trying to get more information about him and decided to turn the tables on her.

"You were in Denver?" he asked, hearing the nerves in her tone.

"Yes." Her voice changed. "For a while."

"What did you do there?"

"Nothing," she said after a bit.

"Job?" he asked.

"No, Jeff didn't really . . . no."

"Jeff? Ex-boyfriend?"

"Yes." She stood up, and he prompted her to pause, taking her hand in his. It was cold, and he pulled it into both of his and rubbed it between his own to warm it.

"I have a few exes in my closet too." He tried to sound casual and not so eager for her answer. After all, talking about her love life meant that she might open up to him about his father.

"Jeff was my last," she said, avoiding eye contact.

"Still have a thing for him?" His heart skipped as he thought about her being with only one other man. He wanted to ask her more, like why she didn't have a trail of broken hearts behind her, but the look in her eyes told him she wouldn't have answered him. Yet.

"No," she answered quickly and took a step back. "I burned that bridge." She shook her head.

"Bad experience?" he asked.

"You could say that. I guess I tend to fall for the same type my mother did." Her hand gripped his for a moment.

"Was he older?" he asked, wanting to get to know more.

Her eyes grew huge. "No, he was a law student. My age. He just was . . . well . . . controlling."

"First and last, huh?"

"Yes." She nodded. "My father was like minded." She had started walking down the pathway as she talked, and he followed her.

They came to a small clearing and were surprised to see an older couple standing in the pathway smoking a joint and laughing.

"Hey." The woman turned toward them, then surprised him by walking over and holding up the joint to him. "Care to join us?"

"Um, no, thanks." He glanced over at Elle, who had pasted on her professional smile.

"Are you sure?" The man moved closer and wrapped his arm around the woman Liam assumed was his wife. "If not, maybe you two would like to have some other fun?"

Liam instantly picked up on the man's meaning, since the guy was scanning Elle and that silk dress she was wearing.

Stepping between the two, he shook his head. "Thanks for the offer . . ." he started, but Elle stepped around him, her shoulders straight.

"Thank you, but no, we were just heading back. Please make sure you dispose of that properly. Wildfires are common this time of year."

"Will do," the woman added with a giggle, tangling with the man in an embrace as Liam pulled Elle back down the pathway.

CHAPTER FOUR

"Well, that was fun," she said nervously as they stepped into the light near the back door. It had taken her a few seconds to realize that she and Liam had just been invited to join a couple for not only pot but sex.

That kind of thing had never happened to her before.

Still, when the older man's eyes had locked on her breasts, she'd been thankful Liam had stepped between them.

"Something tells me that won't be the last time you get an offer like that." He held the door open for her.

She smiled slightly as she passed by him—she'd handled it the best way possible. With grace.

"Thanks for walking me back."

"Anytime," he added as she reached the main stairs, and she got the hint that he wasn't going to head up to bed just yet.

"I'll see you tomorrow." She started to move toward the next set of stairs, but he stopped her.

"Elle, I'll need my jacket for tomorrow night."

She glanced down at the large dinner jacket wrapped around her shoulders. She'd enjoyed the warmth and his musky scent the moment he'd laid it over her chilled skin. "Right." She smiled and pulled it off, instantly missing both the feel and the smell. "Night."

She started up the stairs again and could have sworn she heard him whisper "Wow" one more time.

"Looks like you had a good night," Hannah said from her spot on the sofa with a thick romance novel in her lap when Elle walked in. A glass of wine sat on the end table.

"Better than yours." Elle nodded to the still-almost-full glass.

"I always forget I pour wine when I lose myself in a really great book," she said, picking it up and downing half the glass.

"Is there murder?" Elle walked over and glanced at the cover.

"Yes." Hannah smiled. "So far three people have died. I think I might know who did it, but . . ."

Elle sat down on the sofa next to the chair. "If I were an author, I'd end up killing everyone by accident."

Hannah laughed. "That's what Stephen King does, and he's made millions from it."

Elle chuckled. "Dinner was a tremendous success."

"Yeah, I know." Hannah set the book down after placing a playing card to mark her spot in the book. Her friend had tons of bookmarks, but the ace of hearts had been her go-to for as long as Elle had known her. At one point Elle guessed that it had been given to her by her first boyfriend, but when she asked Hannah about it, a sad look filled her eyes, and Elle never asked her about it again.

"Where is everyone else?" she asked, pulling off her heels.

"Zoey had an evening ride scheduled."

Elle winced at Hannah's wording, remembering the couple they had bumped into, but shook it off when Hannah continued. "Scar had another group of people that wanted to go out as well, and I'm not sure where Aubrey is. She was wearing hiking boots."

"Do you think she's meeting the guy she's seeing?" Elle asked, putting her legs up on the worn coffee table. It was only a matter of time before it would have to be replaced.

"Could be." Hannah shrugged and sipped her wine as her eyes ran over Elle. "Why were you smiling as you walked in here?"

Elle was just about to tell her about the couple when the door opened, and Scarlett walked in. They watched her remove her riding boots, then sit down, propping her feet on the coffee table. It wobbled so much that she moved her feet immediately.

"So?" Hannah and Elle said at the same time.

"How was the group?" Elle asked.

"Okay." Scarlett rolled her shoulders. "I stopped by and had a chat with my mom after. She's going zip-lining tomorrow."

"Really?" Elle asked. "I'm starting to feel like it was a smart business move adding them."

"Agreed. Zoey is going to flip her lid when she finds out Mom's going, though," Scar added with a smirk.

Elle chuckled. "I'll bet you five bucks she tries to stop her."

"No one in this room would take that bet. Matter of fact, I'll bet you she tries to stop her before tomorrow," Hannah said dryly as she picked up her book again.

"On that note," Elle said, standing up, "I'm going to take a shower and head to bed. I have an early morning."

"Don't we all?" Scar stood up and followed her down the hallway. Zoey and Scar shared her grandfather's old room, and Hannah and Aubrey shared the guest room, while Elle had taken her old smaller room, still filled with childhood memories.

At least there were three bathrooms to the apartment, which meant she had an en suite all to herself. Thankfully. Not that she would have minded sharing with the others, but after almost a year of living with four other women, she'd heard plenty of yelling about bathroom time limits.

She had just crawled into bed when she heard Zoey storm in. Rolling over, she silently wished that she wouldn't be interrupted, but when her door cracked open, she turned back toward the light.

"I'm still awake," she said.

"Good." Zoey marched in and plopped down on her bed. "That man infuriates me."

"Dylan?"

"Who else?" Zoey tucked her legs under her like she was preparing to stay awhile, so Elle sat up and flipped on her lamp.

"What did he do this time?" She knew that since the brothers had moved onto campus, Zoey had on more than one occasion complained about the man.

"I'm pretty sure he has a thing going with one of the waitresses," Zoey started.

"Who?" Things were getting juicy now, so she pulled her legs up to her chest and eagerly waited for the gossip.

"Ryan." Zoey frowned. "I forget her last name."

"Kinsley," Elle provided for her. "The woman made a pass at Liam tonight while I was standing there." She chuckled. "The man looked scared."

Zoey remained silent for a moment. "Actually, now that I think about it, so did Dylan."

"Maybe there's something more we don't know, then?" she hinted.

It appeared that all the hot air had gone out of Zoey, and they sat there in silence for a moment.

"Other than that, how was your night?" Elle finally asked.

"Good."

Elle could tell Zoey was hiding something, but Elle didn't think she had the energy to find out what at the moment. "I'm tired," she said with a yawn.

"Oh." Zoey jumped up. "Yeah, me too. Have I mentioned lately that I'm so very happy you talked us into this?" She hugged her.

Elle chuckled. "Talked, blackmailed . . ." She waved her hands. "All the same."

Zoey laughed. "Night." She kissed her on the forehead. "Grandpa Joe would be proud."

"Don't make me cry," she said to Zoey's back as she shut the door.

The next morning, Elle was woken by not her alarm but her cell phone buzzing. She reached over and answered it on the third ring.

"You'd better get down to the smaller pool," Julie said without even a greeting.

"What?" Elle sat straight up as her eyes flew open. Thoughts of people falling and injuring themselves flashed in her mind.

"Apparently, there was a party last night, and . . . well, just get down there quickly."

"On my way." Elle hung up and dressed in record time.

She jogged down the path and came to a dead stop when she noticed the destruction.

Pool chairs were out of place, with several of the cushions actually floating or at the bottom of the pool. There was trash everywhere, and empty beer bottles and cans littered the side of the pool; a few even floated in the water, while some were stuck at the bottom of the deep end of the pool.

"What the . . ." She felt her heart beating hard in her temple and reached up to place a finger over it to stop the vein from bursting.

"Looks like there was a nice party." Damion stepped up beside her. "I came out here to clean the pool this morning and found it like this."

She'd hired Damion Wells, a local, to run all things water related. Including the pool maintenance, boat excursions, and repair as well as paddleboard, kayak, and canoe rentals.

He'd been a year older than her in school and had been one of the kids she'd bonded with, since he'd been bullied as well. Being the only black kid in their small school had made him an instant target to a select group of bullies.

"What happened?" She glanced around at the mess.

"Looks like a larger party," Damion said. "Maybe even an orgy." He nodded to a used condom floating in the water.

"Eww." She took a step back.

"The chemicals should take care of anything . . . in the water," he said with a chuckle, "but the rest . . ."

"I'll get the cleaning crew down here." She instantly wished to bleach the bottom of her shoes and turned away from the mess to dial the front office. After getting Julie to call in reinforcements, she asked her to get Zoey and the others so the Wildflowers could discuss the mess before breakfast. Something had to be done to ensure that this sort of thing didn't happen every night.

The smaller pool was farther away from the main buildings and most of the cabins. It sat near the bay side, which meant there could be a loud party going on every night without anyone hearing a thing.

It wasn't until Zoey arrived that she remembered the security cameras they had sprung for prior to opening up. Since they hadn't needed them during the refurbishment, she'd almost forgotten their use, beyond spying on the brothers' nightly excursions.

When Zoey and the others showed up, they followed her back to her office, where she booted up her computer and opened the camera software. Seeing the couples going at it in the water was one thing, but when Hannah mentioned that they were swapping partners, and Elle recognized the couple from last night, she gasped and quickly shut off her monitor.

"We're a high-end swingers camp." She groaned as the realization dawned on her. Her vision started graying, and she wondered if this would become a standard part of her life, dealing with . . . well, everyone else's sex life.

Zoey clasped her shoulders to comfort her. "Hey, maybe it's just a fluke?"

Hearing a low chuckle, everyone turned toward the office door at the same time. Elle had been so eager to watch the video that she had forgotten to close the door. She was mortified to see Dylan leaning against the doorframe. Closing her eyes, she silently wished to disappear into the background.

What if word got out to the other, nonswinging guests and the employees about the party? Or worse yet, what if the media somehow got ahold of this news? Having the camp labeled as a swing club could ruin them. She knew of a few neighborhoods farther south in Florida that had been labeled the STD capital of the States. That reputation had damaged the area. When she focused on the conversation again, Dylan was telling them that the likelihood of the party naturally occurring was low.

The memory of last night, of running into the couple, played over in her head as everyone chatted about the party.

She wasn't naive. She knew that opening the camp to a grown-up crowd would open the doors for all sorts of other . . . activities. She had just assumed that they would be done inside.

Which had her face heating even more when she thought about the possibility of having stumbled upon a different scene with Liam last night.

After a discussion of breakfast, Elle erased the footage and got up to follow everyone else to the dining hall. As she stepped into the hallway, she turned to see Dylan's hand brush up against Zoey's arm. Her friend's eyes changed from annoyed to full of lust in a flash. Narrowing her eyes, she watched as Zoey walked toward her.

"What was that all about?" Elle asked.

Zoey waved her question off. "Nothing."

But she could see it in Zoey's eyes: there was something more between her and Dylan. Did that mean that Zoey trusted Dylan? Or had her friend fallen into one of the brothers' traps? She had to admit that even she had a difficult time not falling for their charm.

Were Zoey and Dylan having sex? Had it gone that far? Then, an image of what she'd seen on the screen surfaced, and Elle decided that she was far better off not knowing all the details of everyone else's sex lives.

They held a short meeting while they all ate breakfast. They decided she would write a memo to display on the cabins' computer screens reminding guests to be respectful of camp property.

After leaving the dining hall, she disappeared into her office for a few hours and wrote, then rewrote, what she wanted to say in the announcement. On what seemed like the hundredth version, she stood up and rolled her shoulders. She stopped herself from throwing her keyboard across the room and paced instead.

"Problems?" Once again, she'd left her office door open, and she glanced over to see Liam in the doorway, watching her. He looked comfortable, as if he'd been standing there for a while. His dark hair was pushed back away from his face, and he was wearing his camp shirt and khaki work shorts with a pair of worn hiking boots. He looked damn sexy, and she was confident that he knew it.

It wasn't the first time she'd seen the muscles in his legs, but each time she did, she found it harder to avoid drooling over him. The white camp shirt clung to him, as if it was a size too small, but she knew it was just the muscles pressing against the material that gave the appearance. Besides, she doubted a larger shirt would hide the span of his chest, nor would she want it to.

"No." The frustration she'd felt growing in the last hour came out in her voice, causing his eyebrows to shoot up.

"Mm? Sounds like you have one." He moved closer to her. "I heard what happened at the pool."

She closed her eyes and took a few cleansing breaths. "What did you hear?"

"That there was a party at the smaller pool." He perched on the side of her desk as his gaze ran her full length. Instantly, she felt self-conscious and hid it by sitting back down behind her desk.

"Yes, well." She cleared her throat. "Is there something I can help you with?" She flipped her screen off, hiding the message she'd been trying to finish.

"No, I came to see if I could help you."

"Oh?" she asked.

"Yes. I heard there were a few damaged pool chairs?"

She noticed a slight dimple to the side of his mouth as he smiled. She knew that he didn't smile often, which made it all the more attractive. "There were."

"I talked to Aiden this morning and suggested that I run it by you before dragging them off to the woodshop for repairs. I was also thinking I could have a few others built. Some sturdier ones?"

Instantly her mind flashed a scene of being dragged off to bed by Liam. *Damn,* she thought. She was having a hard time staying focused around him. Taking another cleansing breath, she tried to focus instead on the budget and figured she could adjust a bit to allow for the costs.

"Give me an estimate for the new chairs. For now, do you have what you'll need to repair the damaged ones?"

"Yes." He drummed his fingers against her desk, as if in thought. "There are a few trees that Aiden's crew have chopped down. With what they cleared, I can have a few other chairs built. Maybe even some more swinging benches."

Her eyebrows shot up. She hadn't thought of reusing the wood from the trees they had cleared.

"Good." She opened her expense program. "I'll set aside some money for—"

"No need." He stood up. "The shop has everything we need. There shouldn't be any extra costs."

"Really?" She knew her chin had dropped, but the look he gave her had it closing quickly.

"Yeah, princess." He leaned in until he was a breath away. "Did you know that when you stress out"—he reached up and ran a finger down her forehead—"you get a little twitch right here?"

She was too shocked at the feeling of his skin against hers to even breathe. Before she had a chance to gain her wits, he stood up and moved toward the doorway.

"I'll have the lawn chairs fixed and back at the pool by tomorrow," he said over his shoulder. "Make sure you wear a coat tonight when you trail me. It's supposed to rain." He disappeared out her doorway, leaving her vibrating from his touch.

She tried to focus on the memo again and gave up. She pushed the button and had her last draft going out to her friends for their input and approval. She glanced at her watch and cringed when she realized she had only a few minutes before her first event of the day.

Aubrey was teaching tai chi and judo, both of which she was highly skilled in. Hannah and Zoey took on the yoga classes, while Elle had decided to host a beginner's ballet exercise class. She hadn't expected anyone to be interested, but three ladies had signed up for her first afternoon class.

Elle had attended ballet classes prior to her mother's death, and her grandfather had talked her into continuing her training until she'd hit high school.

Hardly a day went by when she didn't don her leotards and work through the basic moves.

She pulled her gym bag out from under her desk and made her way down the hallway. She still greeted the employees and guests she passed on her way. After all, just because she was in a state of irritation didn't mean she had the freedom to reflect it to others.

When she walked into the locker room, she was slightly surprised to see Ryan there in a pair of cutoffs and a skintight black tank top.

Since it was before the lunch rush in the dining room, she doubted the woman was due on shift yet. Employees used the locker rooms to change into their uniforms or to shower, since most of the bathrooms on the second floor were shared.

"Morning." She continued past the woman toward a free area but stopped when Ryan motioned for her to come closer.

"I wanted to talk to you," Ryan said in a low tone, looking around the room as if there were spies everywhere.

"Sure." Elle tried to hold in her annoyance at the delay as she tossed her bag down on the bench.

"It's about someone who works here," Ryan said, continuing to glance around as if she was nervous.

Elle suddenly feared someone had done something bad to Ryan. After all, the woman was acting jittery, which didn't correspond to how Elle had seen her all the other times. From what she knew of Ryan, the woman was self-confident, strong willed, and demanding. Had the guests in that pool incident tried to bring her into it too?

"We can meet in my office, if you want." Elle touched her arm, trying to reassure her.

"No." She waved off the suggestion, but her shoulders relaxed.

"Okay . . ." Elle sat on a bench and motioned for Ryan to do the same.

"Well, I'm concerned that this . . . employee is damaging the camp's reputation." Ryan's distaste sharpened her words.

"Oh?" Elle felt her spine straighten. She'd trusted everyone they had hired, so far. It was the guests who were causing problems.

Hannah had, through some miracle, hired the popular Isaac Andrews as head chef, and they relied on his judgment to pick his staff. Like Ryan herself, for example.

Everyone else on campus Elle, Aubrey, and Zoey had overseen hiring and vetting personally.

"Yes, I'm afraid she's giving the guests the wrong impression. I mean, I have personally seen her throwing herself at men." Ryan laid an offended hand over her chest.

"Go on, who is it?" Elle's head tilted. "I'll make sure this is dealt with, quietly."

Ryan took a deep breath. "I wouldn't normally say anything, and I understand that she's a friend of yours, but . . ." Elle's spine tightened even further. "Well, it's just gotten so bad that I can't keep it to myself. Something simply must be done."

"Ryan," Elle said in a low tone. Her patience had been stretched too far.

After glancing around the room again, Ryan leaned closer. "You see, I'm sure Zoey just needs a warning or something . . ."

As Ryan continued to talk, Elle scanned the woman's expression with a frown, really looking at her for the first time.

Zoey had told Elle about a few run-ins with her she'd had. She trusted her friend far more than she trusted the woman sitting beside her.

That thought sent a lightning bolt through her thoughts. She'd dealt with women like Ryan all her life—the spoiled child who bubbled just under the surface was obvious. Finally Ryan stopped talking.

"I understand your concerns and thank you for coming forward about them; however, I don't think you're quite up to date on the logistics of things around here. Zoey and her sister are both major shareholders in River Camp. Zoey herself plays a significant role in keeping this place open."

Elle watched the woman's expression change instantly, and if she hadn't been sitting down, she would have taken a step back at the anger that grew behind her dark lashes.

"She is?" Her lips thinned.

"Yes." Elle smiled and stood up. "So, you can rest assured that she is doing everything she can to represent the camp in the best light." She picked up her bag and walked into the changing area. She hoped her words would keep Ryan off Zoey's back for a while. After all, it appeared now that the woman definitely had it out for her friend.

She thought quickly of moving the woman into a different role, but the fact was, no matter what job she gave her, she would probably still run into Zoey. Especially since the camp couldn't afford to let her go at this time. There was a serious shortage of good waitstaff in the area. Especially cheap workers who were already trained.

After changing, she walked into the studio and started warming up. Already, she felt better as her muscles stretched and began to burn. She greeted the three guests who joined her for the class and started moving them through basic beginning moves, soon losing herself in the music.

More than half an hour later, she had a sheen of sweat over her skin and felt limber and loose. After showering and changing for lunch, she wasn't surprised to run into everyone in the employees' dining room. The skies had turned dark, and she knew that within the hour, rain would start to fall, which meant outdoor activities would come to a halt.

Zoey sat next to her and dug into her lunch. "So. Good memo." She nudged her elbow.

"Ugh." Elle had forgotten all about it.

"No, I agree. You have a way with words. Especially when it comes to uncomfortable topics like orgies." Hannah winked at her.

"Let's never speak of it again," Elle mumbled as she nibbled on her salad.

"What are we talking about?" Scar asked, sitting down.

"Orgies and sex," Hannah said smoothly.

"Who's having sex?" Scar asked, causing Zoey to choke on the sip of soup she'd just taken.

Every gaze turned to her.

"What?" Zoey said when she recovered. "Don't look at me. I haven't had any real fun in"—she looked thoughtful—"forever."

Scar's eyes narrowed as she looked at her sister. "There's something else . . ."

"Did you hear?" Aubrey rushed over and sat down. Elle noticed she didn't have a plate of food and pushed an apple in her friend's direction. Aubrey was always forgetting to eat.

"Eat first," she warned her.

Aubrey picked it up and took a bite but set it down again and continued.

"I was walking here and happened to overhear a few guests . . ." She paused with a hacking sound.

"Chew and breathe," Zoey added with a smile.

Aubrey stopped talking and chewed, her eyes narrowing in concentration. Once she swallowed the bite, she started again.

"We made the cover of *Florida Travel*." She pulled from under her butt a copy of the magazine, which she'd hidden from them as she rushed over.

"What!" The four of them jumped up, but Elle was fastest and snagged the magazine from Aubrey's hands first.

There, on the cover of the popular travel magazine, was a picture of the five of them standing in front of the gates of River Camp.

"We actually made the cover," she said under her breath. They had all been interviewed and had had a shoot, but she'd never dreamed they would actually make the cover.

"What does it say?" Hannah asked, trying to look over her shoulder.

"Did you read it?" Scar asked Aubrey.

"No, I thought . . . we needed to do this together. Go ahead." Aubrey shoved it toward Elle. "Do the honors."

"Just look at us . . ." Elle felt tears pool in her eyes as she ran a finger over the glossy magazine cover.

There the five of them stood, as different as they were, yet held together by one purpose. They were all wearing their camp shirts and shorts with their arms wrapped around one another, laughing at something Scar had said.

"Open the article." Aubrey nudged her arm. "It's on page fifteen."

With shaky fingers, she flipped open the magazine.

"Calling all snowbirds—*Tired of the same old boring vacation spots? Looking for some adventure with your own age group and a little excitement to boot? The newly opened River Camp adult resort promises to be just that. With over 100 acres of private land to roam including your very own secluded beach, there are over thirty individual cabins to choose from, not to mention a full array of games and exciting events to keep you busy during your stay—swimming pools, zip lines, horseback riding, sailboats, canoes, and kayaks. You'll never have a dull moment. But if you're looking for a more relaxing time, there are several fully stocked bars to enjoy as well as a gourmet dining experience that includes celebrity chef Isaac Andrews. With all this and more, River Camp promises to be the next 'Florida hot spot.' Book your private cabin today, before you lose your chance.*"

"We did it!" Elle screamed. "We made the list." She leaped out of her chair and hugged the other girls.

They had been in lots of other travel guides—smaller ones, including local papers—but they hadn't hit the big time. *Florida Travel* was the most frequent place snowbirds went to find out about new resorts.

For the rest of the day, nothing could hamper Elle's good mood. Even when she stepped out to the dark sky and rain, her smile never faltered.

She dashed back to her office and plowed through the budget and the stack of bills on her desk with a smile on her lips. Aubrey had brought back more than a few copies of the magazine for the cabins and public areas. Elle would frame one cover for her office.

For a moment, she wondered if the article would attract different types of people from those they'd had during their first few weeks. After all, given the previous damage, she was hoping to keep the clientele a little more . . . upscale. Even though they were pretty much a wilderness retreat, the prices and activities they offered were of the highest quality.

She took a few calls from vendors and had a meeting with Aiden later that afternoon about the progress of the new cabins they were building. Two of them were currently in the works. One was almost finished and just needed a fresh coat of paint and some finishing touches on the tile work in the bathroom, while the other was just a skeleton of a building.

"How far out are we to booking the first of the two?" she asked, opening her calendar program.

"Less than a month," he said. "Have you come up with names yet? I hate just calling them Thing One and Thing Two."

She chuckled as she thought about it but shook her head. "No, the names usually come to me when I walk through them. I'll try to swing by later this week and get the feel of the cabin."

"We're on budget for both cabins," he muttered, looking over his notes.

Elle had known Aiden most of her life, seeing as he was technically the only real family she had left.

Her second cousin was tall and tan, with sandy-blond hair, and his silver eyes promised any woman he looked at a good time, or so her friends had always said. He'd been easily one of the most popular boys in school, which had initially scared her off from getting too close to him. But, he'd ended up being one of the nicest friends she could have asked for, and besides all of that, he was extremely skilled at what he did.

"I'll have Julie add the cabin to our booking program for the following month." She made another note. "Was there anything else?" When Aiden didn't respond right away, she glanced up at him.

"There's been some . . . activities . . ." he started, and Elle held in a groan—thoughts of new orgies flashed through her mind. "I'm not sure, but I think someone's been breaking into some of the outbuildings. My men swear that they close up and lock the doors, but when they arrive the following mornings, things just aren't where they used to be."

"Were the locks broken?" she asked.

"No." He shook his head. "I've asked my employees to turn in all the extra keys floating around, and I'll replace the locks so I will be the only one who has the keys."

"Just put the backup in my office. Have you checked the cameras?"

"We haven't installed any in there yet," Aiden answered. "I can show you the best spots to put them in."

"Was anything missing?" she asked.

"No." He frowned. "That's the strange part."

"Okay." She thought about it. "Why not take the camera outside of the pool bar tonight and put it where you need it most. I'd like to find out who's messing with things." He nodded before he left.

She heard the thunder and rain increase a few minutes later as the room darkened. Flipping off the office lights, she decided to make some inside rounds to check on how everything was progressing. In the main dining room, she found a group of guests playing a round of bingo with Aubrey and joined in the fun for a while.

Then, taking her umbrella and jacket, she walked over to the pool bar and was surprised at how many people had crowded under the awning there.

By the time she had made it back into the main building, she was soaked and tired. She was going to skip dinner, since Hannah had assured her that she had things handled that evening, but an hour before the scheduled guest dinnertime, she ended up in the employee dining room beside Zoey and the three brothers. The other employees at the large table peeled off to their various duties as Hannah, Aubrey, and Scarlett joined them.

She had her standard few days off coming up. Since they all rotated their work schedules, each of them got two different days off a week.

She had plans of putting her feet up, reading a few books, and sleeping a lot.

She was busy daydreaming about the next two days when she heard Dylan offer to help Zoey out. Hiding a smile, she quickly became shocked when all three brothers offered to help with camp security. She glanced around the table.

"What's going on?"

Dylan jumped in. "What if one of you stumbled across another orgy in session?"

None of the brothers seemed phased, beyond having the desire to tease each other over that word. And she wasn't sure, but she thought Zoey had kicked Dylan under the table.

"Okay." She stood up as she broke into the mini-argument that had developed and took a deep breath. She needed time to think of how to handle this. So she arranged to have a meeting with the employees later that night and returned to her office to try to sort out her thoughts.

As she bade them farewell and made her way back to her office to write a speech for the meeting, Liam caught up with her at the doorway.

"So, you're okay with this?" Liam asked.

"What?" She glanced over at him. Her vision flickered with the migraine pulsing in her head.

"You need some rest." He stopped her just outside, under the overhang, as the rain fell around them. His hand rested on her shoulder. She didn't realize that he had started massaging her neck until she closed her eyes and moaned, leaning into his touch.

"What?" she asked, trying to keep her eyes open.

"Rest." He wrapped his arm around her and started walking her toward the doorway that led to the hallway of offices. "You look like you need it."

The feeling of his arm around her almost caused her to give in, but her mind flitted between all the things she had to do. She couldn't wait for the two days off from work that were coming up. At first, she hadn't thought she would take her days, but after Hannah had forced her to start taking them, she'd grown accustomed to having the time to herself.

She shook her head. "I have a speech . . ."

"You'll make something up." He opened the back door for them both. When he tried her office door, it was locked. He glanced over at her with his eyebrows up. She took out her key card, swiped it, and opened the door.

Instead of turning on the bright overhead lights, he closed the door behind them, sealing them in the darkness of the room. She followed him to the corner that held a small sofa.

"I have . . ." she started to say, but he nudged her down to the sofa. She had to admit: getting off her feet felt wonderful.

"Rest," he reminded her. "Clock out for half an hour." He turned her and continued to rub her shoulders, moving her until she was lying facedown on one of the soft pillows Hannah had purchased, and she was helpless to argue with him about it.

Closing her eyes, she enjoyed the feeling of his hands on her. She'd dreamed of what they would feel like running over her. Her dreams hadn't been this good. Before she knew it, she was fast asleep.

CHAPTER FIVE

Liam stood back and watched Elle finish her speech to the employees later that night. When she tried to slip out the back door after, he followed her.

He'd overheard her telling Hannah that she would take the next two days off of work. He was scheduled time off starting the following day as well and had decided to drive into town and check with Joel to ask if he'd heard from their father.

Joel had been working for the business for the past few years. Liam and his brothers believed the man was their father's illegitimate son, but they didn't have the proof. So, they kept their mouths shut, because they'd really started to like the guy after they'd made the extra effort to get to know him better.

As he stepped out into the cool night air, he noticed her hugging her arms around herself as she stood on the stoop watching the rain from under an awning that was normally occupied with smoking workers.

"Have a few days off?" Liam's voice caused her to jump slightly. "Looks like the nap helped," he said, looking deep into her eyes. They were blue, a nice soft color that reminded him of the waters off Jamaica on a warm day. Now, he could see they were clearer and more focused than before.

She had her hand over her heart and took a deep breath. "Yes, thank you." She turned her shoulders toward him.

It had almost killed him leaving her on the sofa fast asleep. She'd looked like the proverbial princess sleeping until her prince leaned in and . . . it had taken all his willpower to set her phone alarm so she wouldn't oversleep and then leave her alone to rest.

"Great speech." He removed his jacket again and wrapped it around her shoulders.

"Thanks," she said and slipped her arms into the sleeves. "I wasn't going to stay outside for long, but there's something soothing about the sound of rain." She took a deep breath.

They remained silent for a moment; then she turned toward him. "Yes." She shook her head. "I have the next few days off. If you need something . . ."

"I'm off starting tomorrow as well." He smiled. "Maybe we could do lunch?"

"Oh, I didn't . . ." She bit her bottom lip, and he watched the movement like his life depended on it. The simple innocent act was one of the most erotic things he'd seen to date. "I guess I haven't looked at your schedule."

He chuckled. "With so many employees, it's no wonder."

"We only have a little over a dozen." She rolled her shoulders. "We could use more, but . . ." She looked off into the darkness again.

"Give it time." He watched the rain with her. "Why don't you hire more?"

She glanced sideways at him. "It's not that easy."

"Sure, it is. You must have enough people applying."

"Yes, we do. Plenty." Her tone turned sharp, and she started to remove his jacket.

He thought about the tone and knew it must be a sore subject if she felt so touched by it. He knew the area was known for difficulty in keeping employees and wondered if she'd had problems before.

"Meet me for lunch tomorrow?" he broke in before she could say anything else.

"I . . . can't," she answered.

"Can't or won't?" He placed his hands on her shoulders and moved a step closer to her.

"Won't," she whispered.

"Is there someone else?" he asked, his eyes glued to hers, and he felt his heart skip. He didn't know what he was expecting. That she would confess to being with his father? To hiding him somewhere? To taking the family's money? Whatever it was, he hadn't expected what came next.

"No." She shook her head and stepped back. "There hasn't been for a long time. I can't afford . . . entanglements." She removed his jacket and handed it back to him. "Thank you, good night." She walked back into the building.

"Crash and burn." He heard the purr of a woman's voice and groaned inwardly when Ryan walked out of the darkness, a lit cigarette between her teeth. "I didn't know you three could ever be denied anything. Especially from a woman." She moved closer until the smoke from her cigarette blew in his face before she tossed it to the ground.

"Ryan." He tried to step around her, but she stopped him with a finger to the chest.

"Tell those brothers of yours I'm not a patient woman. I will leave here on the arm of one of you and be connected to good high-society contacts while being wined and dined, or"—she raised her hand to his face—"your little secret will be exposed." Her finger moved up and scraped his jawline. "You're lucky I like older men."

She chuckled as she left, and he felt a shiver run down his back.

The following day, he decided to do a little more legwork. Since he had some time off, he drove around the small town of Pelican Point and played tourist. He hung out in the small coffee shop and had breakfast in a corner booth. All the time hoping to see Elle walk in. Two hours of wasting time, but he had a good meal. Then he walked across the street and made his way down the row of small shops nearby and thought about spending some of his family's money.

He mentioned to the clerk that he worked at the camp and asked in a roundabout way about Elle and her grandfather. The woman seemed unbothered about telling a complete stranger everything she knew about Elle and her family.

Including a nasty rumor that Elle's father was up for parole soon. Which, of course, had him pulling out his cell phone and doing a quick search to see if it was true.

Once again, the only article he could find online mentioned her mother's death and her father's involvement but nothing about his release or even if he *could* be up for parole during his life sentence. As he drove through town, he noticed a small library and pulled into the parking lot.

Inside, he asked the clerk if they stocked old newspapers. She offered to help him search the catalog and was just about to show him to the section when he turned to see Elle stroll in.

He quickly made an excuse to the clerk and rushed over to Elle's side.

"Hey," he said, causing her to jump slightly. "Small towns. Gotta love 'em."

She frowned over at him and almost dropped the armful of books she'd been carrying. "What are you doing here?" she asked as she set the books down in the return bin.

"Same as you. I read," he joked with a smile.

"You don't live in town." She walked into the stacks. "There is no way Heidi would allow you a library card." She searched the first row, then moved quickly onto the next. He followed her easily enough.

"I don't need one to enjoy a local library." Her eyes flicked toward him, then back to the row of books.

He knew he was pushing it, but seeing the slight irritation on her face was totally worth it. Besides, maybe he could find out more answers directly from her instead of scanning old smelly newspapers or, worse, having to scroll through microfiche.

"So, what about some lunch?" he asked when she had a few books in her arms.

"It's ten in the morning," she said, not sparing him a glance.

"Brunch?" He shifted to block her, and her eyes finally locked with his. "What else do you have to do besides go through that stack of Mary Higgins Clark books?" His eyebrows shot up a little. "I would have expected something more in the Danielle Steel genre."

"I love all books," she said as her eyes narrowed at him. "Do you have a problem with Danielle Steel?"

He held up his hands. "No, a good book is a good book. I'm not book-ist." He tilted his head and thought about it. "Or is it genre-ist?"

When she giggled, he smiled. "Come on, do something with me."

Just then an older woman walked around the corner and gasped at them.

Liam's arm rested on Elle's shoulder. From their outward appearance, they were close: not too close, but close enough that running over his last words had him cringing.

"Well, really, Elle." The woman spun on her heels and marched away.

"Great, now Mrs. Willow thinks we're doing it."

He couldn't help it and chuckled. "What are you, in high school?"

"Shut up," she hissed and grabbed another book.

"Hi, Heidi." She smiled brightly as she approached the checkout counter. Heidi had directed him to the papers.

"Hi." Heidi nodded, then looked at him. "Did you want to know where the old newspapers are?"

His back teeth ground. “No, thanks.” But it was too late. Elle shot him a sideways glance.

He remained silent as she checked out her new stack of books and put them into a bag she had.

“So?” He tried to pick up the earlier light mood as they left the building.

She stopped just outside a white Jeep and ran her eyes over him. “I was going to head to the beach and read.” She motioned to the relevant supplies in the back of the Jeep.

“Perfect.” He clapped his hands together. “I’ll tag along.” He figured he could get her to open up about her past or say more about the business.

“You don’t have a towel or a chair,” she pointed out, but he had skirted her Jeep and jumped in. She’d removed the doors and windows, and he was looking forward to enjoying the wind on the drive to the beach.

“I’ll be fine. If you want, stop by the store on the way out of town. I’ll buy us some fixings for lunch.” He watched her climb in. “You know, to thank you for saving me from boredom on my day off.”

She sighed heavily, then started the Jeep.

It was fun walking through the store with her. He picked out a few French rolls along with turkey for sandwiches, then tossed in some hummus and guacamole and a bag of chips for fun. When he picked up a six-pack of Cokes, she reached for two bottles of water as well. He took the bottles from her and put them in the buggy.

“Anything else?” he asked.

“No.” She shook her head, and as they made their way to the checkout counter, he paid as Elle talked to an older man in line.

From what he could tell from the raised eyebrows and harrumph noises, the guy must have been an old family friend of her grandfather’s. Before it was his turn to pay, she explained that he was a friend who worked at the camp.

When she introduced him as Liam Rhodes, it threw him for a moment, and he felt like shit for lying to her. He'd completely forgotten about the fake name until he heard her saying it.

It was like everything came crashing down on him again. All the weight of searching for their father and the money that was missing. The possibility of losing the hold on the family business.

Not to mention the fact that the woman across from him was suspected to be his father's latest mistress. He spared a glance in her direction and just couldn't imagine it. Even though Elle was totally his father's type, he was beginning to doubt that his father was Elle's.

He kept his mouth shut as she drove across town and finally turned down a dirt road just outside of town.

"I don't know of any beaches this way," he said over the sound of the engine and wind.

"Public ones? There aren't any." She turned down another trail and smiled when the Jeep started bumping down a narrow muddy lane.

"Off-roading it?" He held on to the handle as the Jeep bounced down the lane, the mud flinging up over the hood turning the white Jeep a dull-brown color.

Glancing over, he felt his heart skip a beat when he noticed the look of pure enjoyment on Elle's face.

"I wouldn't have pegged you as someone who liked off-roading." He laughed when she purposely aimed the Jeep for a large mudhole.

"Joe used to take me out here. It's the reason I bought the Jeep." She slowed and then pulled into a small area that looked like someone had parked there often. "We hike from here." When she turned off the Jeep, he got out, and before she could grab anything, he tossed her beach chair over his shoulder, secured it with the strap, and gathered the bag of food and drinks he had purchased.

"Lead the way."

With a grin, she pulled out a beach bag and her book bag from the back seat, and he followed her through a narrow walking trail that opened up to a raised wooden walkway.

"Joe and a few of his buddies built it." She glanced over her shoulder.

"Who owns this land?" he asked, keeping in step with her now that he could walk beside her.

"Joe, no . . . I do. Now." She shrugged. "Still, his buddies and their families have been using it for as long as I can remember. There wasn't a Saturday in the summer growing up that I didn't hang out here. That or the camp's beach, whenever camp was in session."

The tree line cleared and opened to a small secluded white sandy beach. They unpacked what they'd brought from the Jeep onto the pristine sand. Since he hadn't dressed for the beach, he waited until she laid out a large towel, then set the supplies down and sat down to pull off his tennis shoes.

He was thankful he'd worn his shorts, which doubled as swim trunks. He pulled off his shirt, tossed it onto his shoes, and turned toward her. When he noticed the look that she was giving him, he frowned.

"What?" He glanced down at his chest, thinking there was something on it.

"Nothing." She flushed a pretty shade of pink and looked down.

He chuckled. "Sorry." His smile grew, and he had to admit, he puffed out his chest a little more.

It was hard to tell now, but at one time in his childhood, he'd been a skinny kid with arms like noodles.

"You should come with a warning label," she said before pulling off her tank top and slowly peeling off her white shorts. It was his turn to stare now.

"So should you." His wolf whistle set her laughing. As she sat down beside him, she pulled out a book and held it out.

"You said you can read." She handed it to him.

"I've read this one." He nodded to the one he'd been wanting. "That one I haven't yet."

She handed him the book and then pulled out a large foldable beach hat and put it on her head, then a pair of dark sunglasses.

"Why sit on the beach and read if you're going to cover yourself up completely?" He shifted to get a better look at her.

She leaned the sunglasses down and rolled her eyes at him, and he smiled.

"To keep the sun out of my eyes while I read." She shifted in the chair. "Are you sure you're going to be comfortable down there?"

He'd set up her chair next to the towel she'd laid out for him.

"Yup, perfectly fine," he answered and, to prove his point, opened the book.

Still, it was hard to read when the view was so amazing. He'd grown up in the Panhandle, and still he wasn't immune to its beauty.

So, instead of reading, he watched the shoreline and horizon.

They had been there less than half an hour when they heard another vehicle pull up. Moments later, a young couple walked out of the tree line and called out to her.

"Elle." The woman waved.

"Hi, Carrie." Elle waved back.

The couple approached them. "We knew you'd be here on your first official day off." Carrie hugged Elle, shooting Liam a questioning look over her shoulder. "Rob was pretty sure you'd forget to bring something to eat, so we packed extra."

The man set a large cooler down in the sand next to Elle's chair.

"Hi, Elle," Rob said, his eyes following what Carrie's had by looking at him in question.

"Carrie, Rob, this is Liam," Elle said easily. "He works at the camp."

"Nice to meet you." Then Carrie turned to Rob. "Can you get the chairs?" When Rob turned and disappeared back down the pathway, she said to Liam, "My brother." He shifted slightly under her regard.

"Carrie and Rob are Bob's kids," Elle continued, as if that explained everything. "The man I was talking to at the grocery store."

He could see the resemblance now. Carrie was pretty enough, with light-brown hair and pouty brown eyes, but next to Elle, she faded into the background. Rob was a younger version of his father.

"Dad told us that he ran into you and noticed when you turned down the drive, so we thought we'd head out here and hang with you today." Carrie glanced in his direction. "What he didn't tell us was that you already had a friend along."

Rob returned with the chairs, and he held in a chuckle when Carrie moved hers to beside Liam.

"What do you do at the camp?" she asked while Rob and Elle chatted.

"Well, I fill in behind the bar, and I run the woodworking shop."

"Oh." She scooted closer. "What kinds of things do you build?"

"Easy, sis," Rob said with a chuckle. "Sorry, Carrie doesn't know how to be subtle."

"You're just jealous," Carrie joked. "Rob here has dated every single man in the Panhandle." She rolled her eyes. "I swear, he's even stolen a few good ones from right underneath my nose."

"As if." Rob laughed. "I didn't have to steal anyone." Rob gave him a wink. "But don't worry: I can tell that even though you are one delicious piece of eye candy, you scream heterosexual."

"Uh, thanks, I think." He shrugged as Rob laughed.

As the talk turned toward a series of questions asked by Carrie aimed in his direction, Elle set her book down and pulled out her iPad. As far as he could tell, she was working on the camp's budget.

"I thought you were going to read?" he asked her after a moment of silence between Carrie's interrogation.

"I am reading." She nodded toward the iPad.

"Fiction?" he clarified.

Elle shrugged. "I had a few things to go over first."

"Never a day off for a business owner?"

"I'm sitting on a beach instead of at my desk." She smiled and glanced around. "This is a way better view."

"True," he answered; then Carrie asked him a few more questions and took his attention away.

"I'm heading in," he finally said, breaking the questioning. Placing his book down, he was surprised when Elle stood up as well.

"Me too, I need to cool off." She set her iPad down, then tossed her hat off, keeping the sunglasses on.

"Not me." Carrie finally relaxed back. "If I'm going to keep any hint of tan for the winter months, I need to be at least three shades darker than I am now."

She pulled on a dark pair of sunglasses and leaned her beach chair back all the way.

He walked with Elle toward the crystal-clear water and stepped in, then turned and watched her glide in beside him.

"Is there anything you don't do gracefully?" he joked. "You even get into the ocean like a princess." He reached down and splashed water her way. He could have sworn that her eyes had narrowed behind the sunglasses. "That was a compliment," he added and moved deeper into the water.

She followed him until they were in shoulder high.

"Why are you really here?" she asked after he'd dunked his head under to cool off.

Slicking back his hair, he realized he was probably due for a haircut. He hadn't tried to grow it longer, but it was almost the length where he could tie it back, if he didn't mind all the man-bun jokes he'd get. He'd had it longer in high school at one point, but in the past few years, he'd tried to keep it to just above his shoulders.

"I'm here, princess, because you asked me to come along with you today." He smiled, keeping his shoulders under the water. He wanted to pull her closer, but she surprised him by laughing, then ducking her head under and mimicking his move by pushing her long blonde hair away from her face.

He'd thought she'd been beautiful when she'd been all dolled up the other night, but seeing her face clean and glowing in the sunlight, he realized just how beautiful she really was.

"You and your brothers are keeping secrets," she said easily when she settled beside him in the water.

"Everyone has secrets." He had turned toward her, and when he felt his knee bump against her, he smiled. "I bet you have a few yourself."

She flipped her sunglasses up on her head as the slow sway of the waves edged them together. "Redirecting is a classic sign of hiding something."

"Using psychology on me?" He hadn't realized he'd reached for her until his palm was touching the soft skin on her back.

"Maybe . . ." It came out as a whisper.

"Did you take classes?" He noticed a darker look cross her face. "See, you have your own secrets." He nudged her closer until their bodies were rubbing against one another. He couldn't help it: at that moment, the only thing going through his mind was getting her closer, feeling her, being with her.

Forgotten fully was the plan of trying to find out if Elle knew anything about his father or even the idea that she might be or had at one point been one of his father's conquests.

Now, the only thing he could think about was the soft feel of her body next to his.

CHAPTER SIX

She was in trouble. Deep trouble. She'd sunk into the hazel pools of Liam's eyes and was drowning. His hands were running up and down on her back, causing little shivers to race through her body. Even with the warm water of the gulf surrounding her, she felt her body shudder under his touch.

She thought it had been a good idea to hint to Bob that he should pass on the information to his kids and invite them to the beach that day. She needed Carrie to run interference with Liam. Besides, she knew her friend had a way of asking a ton of questions without coming across as pushy. After all, she'd finished two years of law school before deciding she wanted to become a small business owner instead and returned home to open a small but successful boutique along the beach.

Carrie likely knew that if Elle asked for her help, it was most likely to protect the camp and their investment.

How different he was from her ex—not just in appearance but in attitude. Liam had taken her friend's questions in stride and had laughed and joked along with both Carrie and Rob.

Jeff had never liked any of her friends and had always made her feel bad whenever she wanted to be around anyone other than him. Not to mention that he'd been very outspoken about Rob's life choices.

When she'd met Jeff in class, she'd believed that since he was going to school for his law degree, he'd be more open minded. It wasn't until after they had started dating that she'd felt like he was boxing her in.

She didn't want to think about Jeff or the mess she'd left in Colorado. Nor did she want her past to be brought up while she was trying to get information out of Liam.

Liam had avoided a few of Carrie's questions by asking his own. Of course, Carrie, being totally enamored of a sexy male giving her attention, had fallen for his tricks. Elle was stronger than that.

Wasn't she?

"You never really said if you went to school." Her hands went automatically to his shoulders when a strong wave knocked her into him. His grip on her waist tightened, and then he settled with his arms around her.

"I went for a while." He shifted her and blocked the next wave with his body. "Did you study psychology?"

"Yes, what did you study?" she asked, turning the tables back on him quickly. After all, two could play at this game.

Seeing his smile, she knew he understood the match.

"History and marine biology."

That surprised her. "Those two usually don't mix."

After she was knocked into him, he shifted slightly again so that his back was to the oncoming waves. His wide shoulders shielded her from the onslaught of the coming water. She tried to keep from exploring his wide shoulders with her fingertips but found her hands moving on their own accord.

"History goes with anything. As one of my professors always used to say, 'One must know where one has been to know where one is going.'"

"And the marine biology?" she asked.

"At one point, I was thinking of moving to the Keys to help repair the coral reefs. I met my best friend there, Carl." He smiled. "I could go on about how the reefs are disappearing"—he took a deep breath, and his gaze landed on her lips—"but I'll save that lecture for another time. Why psychology?"

"I wanted to dig deeper into what would cause man to do what he does," she said, pushing off from him to wade back to shore. He stopped her with a hand on her arm.

"I know about your father," he said, his hand stroking her arm under the water.

"Then you understand," she said, searching his expression. Most everyone she'd met knew about her parents. What her father had done. It wasn't as if it was a big secret, since there were tons of local articles about it. It had been the first murder in the small town in more than a century. Which meant that it was a very popular topic.

"I didn't hear . . . specifics, just the basics of what happened. Did you find answers in your classes?"

"Not really." She looked toward the horizon to compose her thoughts. "Instead, I found more complications." She thought back to when she'd met Jeff in one of her classes and the wasted time she'd spent with him. "So, I moved back home."

"You mentioned a boyfriend. John?"

"Jeff," she answered, the smile she used to shut down conversations slipping. "He's the complication."

Liam went silent for a moment, and she felt as if she was under a magnifying glass once more.

Her friends had looked at her like he was now when she'd been dating Jeff, as well as every time that her skin had been bruised because of his temper.

"Something tells me that if I ever ran into the man, I'd walk away with busted knuckles." He pulled her closer again. The warmth of his body heated hers further under the waters.

"On the surface, everyone had seemed to like Jeff." Except her friends. She didn't know why she still defended the man. It irritated her. Maybe it was hard to admit one's mistakes.

"But?" He waited.

"But there was a darker side to him." She still remembered the last time he'd hit her. The feeling of the back of his hand against her cheek—the sound of it. How she had fallen and bruised her knees because he'd caught her off guard once again.

Squaring her shoulders, she slipped into the logical part of her past's history. "One in every three women will experience physical abuse by an intimate partner in her lifetime." She closed her eyes. "In men it's one in every four." She glanced toward Rob, who was busy talking to his sister, laughing happily. Her heart skipped at seeing the change in him since she'd returned home. He'd grown from a skinny, scared man to a confident one who didn't give two shits who hated him because of his lifestyle. "Maybe it's why we grew so close after I moved back. I convinced Rob to leave his then partner."

"Beautiful and caring," he said with a frown.

"Why do I get the feeling it's not what you expected?" she asked, seeing the distant look in his eyes.

"Like I said, I know about your parents." She saw the change in his eyes. The look so many else had given her over the years. The look of pity.

"It's not a secret," she said reluctantly.

"No, it has been mentioned in articles about you and the camp," he agreed. "What wasn't is how it affected you."

She glanced around for a moment and knew that he was wondering if she was going to continue talking. Maybe share something that none of the articles had mentioned. Even now, the subject was a sore one for her. What memories she had of her parents she wanted to hold inside.

"I was a child," she finally said. "My father killed my mother because he was—I don't know, a jealous man—who claimed she was having an affair, or maybe it was just another way to control her." She looked back at him. "I guess the apple . . . and all that."

"Hey." He took her hand in his. It was strong and full of callouses and yet somehow still smooth feeling and soft. "The difference is, you got out."

"Yeah." She exhaled. "There is that." She gave him a weak smile.

His eyes locked with hers, and for a moment, she thought he was going to lean in and kiss her. Then his hands dropped from her skin, and he shifted away quickly.

"You wanted a drink." He waited until she'd moved to the shore, and then they sat in silence until, eventually, more people showed up. "I thought you said this beach was private?"

She'd been a little surprised at the number of visitors, but she figured it made everything feel very organic. She knew that she was loved, and seeing her grandfather's friends show up to surround her on the beach proved it even further.

"It is. Only a handful of Joe's friends know about it." She smiled as a game of cornhole started.

"Want to play?" She nodded to the game.

"Sure." He stood, dusted the sand from his shorts, and held out his hand to help her up.

Later, when they got hungry, food was shared and passed around. He'd been handed a beer, which had signaled that her friends considered him on the approved list.

She'd been thankful her friends had shown up; she'd overheard him answering several questions from John, who used to be an interrogator for the CIA.

Afterward, Carrie, Rob, and everyone else trickled away a few at a time before sunset fell. And then they were alone on the stretch of beach once again.

"I think you set me up," Liam said, sitting in the sand next to her. They had just come back from cooling off in the water once more.

"Oh?" she asked, pulling her hair up into a messy bun. "How so?"

"John." He said the man's name as if that explained everything. "Come on, I know that man must have worked for the CIA at one point."

She laughed. "He did."

Liam snapped his fingers and pointed in her direction. "I knew it. If you wanted to find out more about me, all you have to do is ask." The smile on his face was pure cockiness. The fact that it suited him didn't even scare her.

"Okay, why are you and your brothers at River Camp?"

His smile slipped slightly, and he glanced out toward the water. "Work is work."

"Don't make me get John back here," she warned.

He surprised her by chuckling. "We used to live in the big house across the water."

"The one Reed Cooper lives in?" she asked, thinking of the handsome older man who had everyone in camp speculating that he was also some sort of spy.

Liam shrugged. "I don't know who owns it now, but, well, we heard about the camp opening again, and we were curious. Besides, we needed jobs."

"Is that why you're sneaking around at night?" She watched humor flash across his face. "We have cameras everywhere, remember?"

"We did agree to help out with security at night . . ." he started, but the look she gave him shut his mouth.

"You were sneaking around long before that conversation," she pointed out when he only chuckled, as if it was some sort of game.

"Evening walks. I take them all of the time—we've talked about this." Even though his tone was light, she noticed that he was avoiding her eyes. Then he turned to her. "How about we find someplace to eat dinner?" He shifted. "I'm starving."

"Changing the subject?"

"Just hungry," he said with a smile.

She had known that he was stalling but figured she could still learn more by just simply being around him. After all, that was why she hadn't followed her own plan for her days off to return home alone and have a glass of wine while finishing her book.

"Sure, we can eat at the Sunset Café." She stood up and stretched. Then she turned to start collecting her things, but he was there, gathering her towels and books.

He carried her beach bag and the chair back down the pathway toward the Jeep as the sun sank farther into the horizon.

"Why open the camp again? Why not sell the place and move on?" he asked as she started the Jeep back down the dirt lane.

"It was my grandfather's wish," she answered easily.

"But the thought of selling must have crossed your mind?" he asked, causing her to glance over at him.

"No." She shook her head. "Not once."

"Why snowbirds? Why not privileged girls? Like it used to be?"

She chuckled. "We thought adults would be easier than kids."

He smiled. "Seriously?"

She nodded and turned onto the main road. Mud and sand spit up from her rear tires as she sped toward town. She loved hearing it fly by and hit her wheel wells. Lived for the feeling of plowing her Jeep through the dirt.

"Something tells me you love mudding," he joked and glanced behind them at the trail of mud she'd left behind her.

"You don't?" she asked.

"I never really thought about it." He shrugged. "I've never owned a four-wheel drive."

"Never?" She shook her head. "Pity."

"I'll say this again—you didn't strike me as a dirt lover." He reached over and played with the strands of hair that had fallen out of her messy bun that she'd tied her hair up in for the ride back into town.

She laughed. She'd heard the same thing all her life. Even Jeff had acted appalled when she'd suggested they go up into the Colorado mountains with her Jeep.

"There has to be something you do that is out of the norm." She slowed the Jeep down as they entered town.

"No."

She glanced over at the tone in his voice. "You're lying."

She waited.

"I paint," he finally admitted.

"As in, oils and watercolors?" she asked, interested.

"Yeah," he shrugged, as if embarrassed.

"So you work with wood and paint?" She parked the Jeep in front of the café. "I can see that. It's not really out of the ordinary."

"It is." He turned away from her, and she got the hint that he was very self-conscious about his pastime.

"I'd like to see some of your stuff sometime."

"No." He shook his head. "It's private."

"Do your brothers know you paint?" she asked.

"I'm sure they do." He shrugged.

"But you haven't shared it with them?" She didn't know why she was poking him further, but she just had to know more.

"No." He looked so uncomfortable that she caved to the pity and decided to change the subject.

"I didn't tell my sisters . . ."

At his quick look, she smiled and added, "My friends. We consider ourselves family. Anyway, I didn't tell them about Jeff." She stilled as memories of the abuse she'd suffered surfaced. Jeff had built her up at first, made her feel warm and loved; then, after she'd committed to the relationship, he'd turned. Tearing her down and belittling her had been his goal, all while trying to control her every move. The embarrassment of what she'd allowed to happen had been so overwhelming. She still struggled with it today. "I hid what he did to me from them. It broke their hearts. I still haven't talked to them about it, not really."

"Being abused and being a painter are not even in the same field," he said as he reached his hand out and took hers.

"No, but family is family, and sharing who you are with them matters," she replied.

The fact that he remained silent told her that he was thinking about it, deeply.

"Food." She broke into his thoughts. "Come on, they have really great steak here." She jumped out of the Jeep and met him at the front door.

For the next hour, they ate and enjoyed the company of the local café. The fact that, once more, she was surrounded by people she'd known most of her life and that Liam was acting relaxed and comfortable had her more at ease around him.

Since the library where she'd bumped into him earlier sat directly across from the café, she figured they would go their separate ways after dinner.

Even as the conversation outlasted the setting sun, she had to admit that she'd never before laughed with or enjoyed being around someone as much as she had with Liam.

Her relationship with Jeff had been . . . strained. She'd been a different person around him. She'd been the person she'd thought she'd wanted to be instead of being herself. Still stuck in her make-believe self she'd created all those years ago.

After she left him, she swore no man would ever again get her to be anything other than who and what she was. She was determined to not even fake anything for herself. From now on, in life, Elle was going to be herself. One hundred percent.

Conversations after the meal continued with questions; he would ask one, and she'd follow up with her own questions.

By the time the café was closing, she figured she had as much information on Liam Rhodes as she was going to get in one day.

Not that she'd learned why they were at the camp, but she did get better insight into who he was. He really did love the outdoors as much as he claimed. Working with his hands had been something he'd always desired to do. He made it very clear that he wasn't the kind of guy who could put on a tie day after day and sit behind a desk.

The way he'd brought up the subject of her mother had even been different from how anyone else would have. She was used to being looked at with pity, but she hadn't seen any in his eyes as he'd talked to her. Instead, he'd watched her closely as if gauging her emotions, and when he'd seen that the subject was causing her pain, he'd changed it.

After paying the bill, which she had convinced him to allow them to split, they walked out of the front doors to the warmth of a Florida summer night.

"This was one of the things I missed in Colorado." She took a deep breath of the salt in the air.

"What?" he asked, crossing his arms over his chest.

"Walking out to the warmth." She took another breath. "I was in Colorado in the fall and winter months."

"Don't like the cold?" he asked easily.

"I enjoyed the snow"—she smiled—"from the comforts of the indoors as I sipped a glass of wine in front of a fireplace."

He chuckled. "We went skiing in the Alps once." He soon got lost in his story. As he told her about the family's ski trip, she picked up on the fact that he'd come from money. She doubted he knew he'd given anything away. Just knowing that his family had once lived in the massive mansion across from the camp had confirmed her speculations even further.

But the day had been long, and she had to hold back a few yawns as the night ran on. There wasn't any point in prodding any further. What she wanted was a long shower and her bed.

"You're dead on your feet." He'd stopped talking and had moved closer to her. When he rested his hand on her arm, she felt her body heat at the light touch.

"Sorry." She yawned again, covering her mouth with her hand. "Spending the day in the sun always does it to me."

He nodded and pulled her close. "Thanks for letting me tag along today." His eyes ran over her face, and she couldn't stop the heat from building. It had been far too long since a man had looked at her with desire. She had told herself that she wouldn't fall into traps again, but her body screamed for just a moment of enjoyment.

"It was fun," she admitted, her voice barely a whisper in the night air.

"I really want to kiss you," he said softly, his eyes going to her lips. "But you're my boss." He shifted. "I won't, unless you ask me."

She took in a breath as she imagined how his lips against hers would feel. She could see herself completely melting against him, letting him engulf her and consume her.

That thought scared her, causing her to take a step back.

"I better . . ." She broke off. "Thanks."

The fact that he had a smile on his lips told her that he wasn't offended.

She threw the Jeep into reverse and drove the two blocks to the house she called home.

She parked in front of the garage and sat in the Jeep for a while, hoping the cool night air would help with the heat pulsing through her veins from his simple touches.

She walked in the back kitchen door and shut herself into the empty house. As she leaned against the kitchen counter, her mind and her body screamed at her for the lost opportunity of enjoying a man once again.

CHAPTER SEVEN

By the time Liam was back at the campgrounds two days later, he'd hammered out the specifics as to Elle's past.

Her father, Mark Bronson, was rotting away in a Georgia state prison, serving a life sentence for the murder of Elle's mother, Emma Rose Bronson.

Once Elle had officially been handed over to Joe Saunders, the courts decided to allow Elle's name to be changed to protect her from the public, since the case had been very popular in the papers and on television, and she was a minor.

He recounted their conversation to his brothers. She hadn't told him anything new about her mother's death, but he'd seen the raw emotion it had stirred. He didn't figure it had anything to do with his father, but still, they went over everything they knew about her past as if it meant something. To him, it just meant that she'd suffered as a child. Then again, most everyone he knew had had some past misfortunes. Even he and his brothers had lost their mother and watched their prior closeness ebb.

Shortly after her death, Owen had graduated school and gone off to college. His older brother had always had the goal of taking over their father's business. Then Dylan had moved out of the house after he graduated and went off to pursue his own goals.

By the time Liam graduated high school, he'd realized the three of them had become more like acquaintances than brothers. Once he'd been out on his own, he'd realized that his entire sense of family safety had been a facade.

Sure, Dad had played the doting father figure when he'd been home. But the more Liam had thought about it, Owen had filled more of the father part than Leo had. Even Dylan had taken on some of the role.

Shortly after graduation, he'd moved away for his classes in the Keys, had met Carl and Candace, and had learned what real relationships felt like. Meeting his two best friends had changed the way he'd thought about family. Candace had shown him his fear of loving wholly and that he'd been afraid to open himself up to others. Carl's push for him to just be himself had given him a baseline for his own success.

The two of them had really given him something that he'd never believed he'd have outside his childhood.

At the camp it was almost as if the brothers had a second chance at closeness, especially having a shared goal, which allowed them to bond.

If nothing came of their time at River Camp, at least they had that. Maybe, once they left the place, they would be a little closer than before.

Later, during his first night back at work, the camp had a talent show in the main dining hall. He was asked to help with a few props some of the guests needed.

Shortly before the talent show, he ran into Elle. Just seeing her in a different elegant silver dress, this one shorter than the first dress, had him wanting her even more. The skirt of the dress flared out so that when she moved just right, her sexy tan legs were exposed. His heart rate spiked.

He suffered through the guest skits; some of them were quite entertaining, while others were cringeworthy. Still, it was obvious that everyone was having fun.

When the pianist started playing after the awards were handed out, he found Elle behind the stage talking to a tall dark-haired man he'd seen serving food as well as walking around the grounds a few times.

"Hey," he said, getting her attention. Instantly, her smile fell, and she turned away from him as if ignoring him. What had he done to upset her? His mind whirled at their last conversation, but he couldn't think of anything that would have caused the disdain in her eyes now.

He moved closer and put his hand on her arm, breaking into the conversation.

"Can we talk?" he asked Elle, glancing briefly at the man. "In private?"

He felt her stiffen at his touch.

"Dean, we'll finish this later." She reached up and touched the man's arm. Liam gritted his back teeth.

He took her elbow lightly and started walking toward the exit as he tried to figure out what he'd done to piss her off. He was surprised when she didn't tug on him to stop from pulling her out one of the French doors that led to the pool area.

"What is this all about?" he asked when they were in the night air. She turned to him, and he could see the frustration behind her eyes. The pool lights made the water ripple, flickering stars over her face and dress.

"What?" She crossed her arms over her chest as she walked closer to the water. When she sat on one of the pool chairs and pulled off her shoes to dip her toes in the water, he watched her every move.

"Why the cold shoulder?" he asked, sitting next to her.

"I don't know what you're talking about." The tone in her voice tightened his jaw again.

"Elle." His voice softened. "I thought we had gotten to a place where we could talk to one another? I thought things left off pretty well between us."

She jerked her head up until her blue eyes bore into his.

"So did I," she said quickly. "Apparently, I was wrong." She turned back to the water.

"Okay, what the hell does . . ."

Just then her cell phone buzzed, and she pulled it out of a small clutch purse.

"Yes." She held up her finger toward him. She stood up, and if he hadn't pulled her a step away from the water's edge, she would have fallen in. "I'll be right there." She hung up, then bent to collect her shoes and rushed down the pathway.

He followed her. "What is it?"

"I'm needed inside," she replied over her shoulder as she continued toward the front doors.

"Elle." He took her arm, but this time she yanked it away.

"I have to go," she said, her eyes narrowing at him.

"Fine. But we will talk." Before she could reply, he turned and marched away.

It took a few moments for him to cool off. He decided a nice long walk was in order. He made his normal rounds, checking the outbuildings, the dock area, and the boathouse.

He noticed the lights of the big house across the water were all on and wondered if his father could be over there. This would be the next place on their search list. He headed back inside, feeling slightly better with this new possibility. How could the three of them sneak out of the camp and head across the water to visit the new owner and search for their father? Plans bubbled in his head.

But when he walked into the room that he shared with his brothers, he noticed Dylan's packed bag next to the door. But, seeing that his brother was fast asleep, he pulled off his own clothes and crawled into his bed. The visit across the water would have to wait. There was no way their father could know they were there yet.

The next morning, Dylan filled him in that Zoey and Scarlett's father had passed away and that he was going to fly Zoey to Vegas.

"He's falling for her," Liam said to Owen after Dylan had left.

"You think?" The sarcasm was obvious in his brother's tone.

"What do you plan on doing about it?" he asked, pulling on his shoes.

Owen's eyes narrowed. "Have you found out anything else about Elle?"

"No, she was pissed at me last night. I plan on finding out why this morning when I see her." He wished he could guarantee that he'd run into her today, but he knew he might have to go out of his way to bump into her. "I thought someone should go across the water and check out our old place—you know, in case Dad decided to go back there."

Owen frowned as he thought about it. "I'll check on it."

"Are you sure?"

"Yeah." Owen gave him a look. "If Dad is there, I'll find out."

Liam stood up but stopped before he left the room. "Have you thought about what Dylan said? Maybe if we can't be decent humans along the way, then we're no better than our father?"

Instead of answering him, Owen shrugged. "Let me know what you find," Liam said before leaving the room.

Liam found Elle in the main dining hall shortly after breakfast. She was leading a small group of guests in a game of bingo.

"Can we talk?" he asked.

She shook her head. "I have to fill in for Zoey and Scar. After this, I have to be at the volleyball courts." She called out a number. "Then I have to be at the stables to take a group out for a picnic lunch." She called out another number. "Then . . ."

"Okay, I get it." He held up his hands. "If you have a chance, find me—we need to talk."

He was turning to go just as an older woman yelled, "Bingo."

As he headed over to the woodshop, he glanced down at his watch and knew he had almost half an hour before he had a group of guests to lead through making wood bowls. So he worked on a few of his own projects before he got ready for the guests.

By the time he had everything set up, a headache twinged at the base of his skull.

The half-dozen guests in his carving class needed extra help starting the process of making a simple natural bowl. Most of the bowls were no bigger than his fist.

One of the guests, Dane, had some serious skills.

"You've done this before?" he joked.

"Shop classes back when they still had them in high schools," the man answered. "I've made a few ashtrays in my day."

Liam chuckled. "If you ever want to work on something more challenging while you're here, you're welcome to stop by again."

"Thanks," the older man said. "My wife was hoping that I'd learn how to carve one of those fancy vases you have there."

Liam had brought a few of his pieces to the camp to highlight his skills.

He walked over and picked up the vase. "This beauty I did when I was in India. Mango wood." He handed it over. Dane ran his hands over it with appreciation in his eyes. "They use this wood over there a lot when the trees stop producing fruit."

"Sarah would love something like this. You can't find this kind of craftsmanship in the stores."

"Thanks." He took the vase back when Dane handed it to him. "If you want it, it's yours. I have others like it."

"No." The man shook his head quickly. "I couldn't . . ."

Liam handed the vase back to him. "A gift. You can tell your wife you talked me down on the price." He winked at him, then went to help another student.

"Thanks," Dane called after him. "She's going to love it. It's her birthday next week."

His philosophy on his projects had always been to share them. Besides, to him they were art, and he always got more joy out of sharing his pieces than letting them collect dust on his shelves at home.

When the rest of the guests had left, he worked on a few projects he had going. He carved out a large bowl and finished staining it so it could cure overnight. Then he moved on to finish a small table-and-bench set he was building for the bar patio area. He figured on adding a few unique pieces to the purchased items. Something fun that would set the area apart.

He had already finished a mermaid bench and a palm tree tabletop, and the picnic table he was working on now had dolphins carved into the sides of both the table and benches.

He loved working with wood, using chisels and tools to create shapes where there were none.

As he worked, his mind wandered to Elle and how she'd looked in her swimsuit lying in the soft sand as the sun caused her skin to glisten. How wonderful she'd felt sliding against him as the waves caused their bodies to sway together. He couldn't help it: his imagination took over, and soon the visions were of them naked, moving together, until he was so hard and horny for her that his shorts were growing tighter.

By the time he was done with the last bench, he'd worked out all his sexual frustrations. His arms were almost numb, and his back ached as he put the finished pieces in the secured shed. It took him almost ten minutes to clean up all the wood shavings from the floor. Since Dylan was off for the next three days, he and Owen were filling in at the zip line area as well. Owen had picked the long straw and was filling in for Dylan that day, while Liam would have the next two days.

He was just finishing up and getting ready to head over to the pool area to fill in behind the bar when Ryan strolled up. He'd been so busy thinking about Elle and that kiss that his attention flagged, and he allowed Ryan to catch him off guard.

"Afternoon," Ryan purred, her eyes running over him.

He was hot and sweaty. His long hair had inched out of the little knot at the base of his head and now stuck to his neck and face while he cleaned.

"Hi." He figured he could play nice too. He had just put the broom away, only to discover she'd moved into the small space behind him and had shut the door.

"We need to talk," she said, moving closer. When her hands went to his shoulders, he blocked them, gripping her wrists and holding them away.

"So, talk, don't touch," he warned, wondering what she wanted now. Maybe this was her way of showing him that she held something over them?

She slipped her hands free and started tugging his shirt from his shorts.

"Why do the three of you always play"—she groaned and ran her hand over his shorts, her dark eyebrows lifting slightly—"hard?" She licked her lips and leaned closer.

"Ryan," he warned her, and he tried to take a step back but came up against the countertop. She'd blocked him in.

He glanced toward the door and thought about making a run for it. But then realized he was a grown man. He'd handled women like Ryan before.

He reached for her wrists again, but she was too quick for him. In one swift move, she ripped his T-shirt up the center and pushed the rest of the tattered material off his shoulders.

"Mmm," she said, leaning in.

"What the . . ." A voice from the doorway caused him to jump.

There, silhouetted in the doorway with the sunlight streaming behind her, stood a very angry Elle.

"I expect more from my employees," Elle said, stepping into the hut. "There's no handbook about relationships in our workplace. I didn't think we needed one. However, after seeing this display, I believe

I'll have to write out the rules." Her arms crossed over her chest. "Ryan, you're due on shift in ten minutes."

"I was just . . ." Ryan started, but when Elle's eyebrows rose, the woman shut her mouth and disappeared through the still-open doorway.

"It's not what you think . . ." He stopped when those arched eyebrows turned on him.

"I mean it, if you're going to run around . . ."

He didn't let her get any further. Closing the distance, he covered those soft lips of hers with his own.

He'd been heated up, it was true, because he'd been thinking about kissing Elle when Ryan had found him.

What he'd imagined had paled to the real feeling of Elle in his arms, pressed up against his bare chest. Her lips were softer and more delicious than he'd dreamed.

She fit him like no other woman had. Her hands were trapped between their bodies, her palms lying flat against his chest so that she could feel what she was doing to his heartbeat.

"There's nothing between us . . . Ryan and me." He rested his forehead against hers. "She pretty much just attacked me. Believe me."

Her eyes snapped into focus at his last words, and she took a giant step back from him.

"I'll expect better of my employees from here on . . ." She started to move past him, but he stopped her.

"What have I done?" he asked. She could have easily escaped if she wanted. He understood her past and wanted to respect the physical boundaries she had set.

The kiss was a moment of weakness. Seeing her eyes heated had done something to him, something he had instantly regretted. Not because of the kiss but because he'd crossed the lines she'd drawn.

Her eyes narrowed again. "You want me to believe you?" she said, walking toward the door, but instead of walking out, she leaned against the frame. "Yet, you're still hiding things from me."

"I am?" He moved over next to her, kicking his ruined shirt aside.

Her head tilted toward him. "Liam *Costa*?"

"How did you . . ." he started, but Elle's eyes tracked the path Ryan had just retreated down.

"Ryan told you?" he asked.

"She told Zoey, who told me," Elle answered. "Eventually."

Ryan is a bitch, he thought in his head. She'd betrayed them, even though they had promised . . . what? He realized they had strung her on for too long, and the woman had made her move. His shoulders sank slightly as he realized that he should have told Elle himself. "We have our reasons for . . ." Elle turned toward him, stopping his words. "I should have told you. Before I kissed you. I should have confessed."

"Yes, you should have." She stepped off the small porch and glanced over her shoulder, her eyes running over him. The fact that there was enough heat behind her gaze to give him a sunburn sparked his smile. "You'll need a new work shirt before you head to the pool bar."

"So, does that mean you forgive me?" he called out to her. When she didn't answer, he yelled, "I'm taking that as a yes."

She slowly raised her left arm, extended it all the way, and gave him the bird without looking back. He laughed even harder.

"You even do that gracefully, princess," he said between laughs.

After locking up the shop, he rushed back up to his room to collect another work shirt. By the time he finally stepped behind the pool bar, Britt glanced down at her watch.

"Noted," he said dryly. "I had to change shirts. Long story." He picked up the chain of outstanding orders.

"I'm all ears." Britt edged around him and filled her share as well.

"Later," he said and nodded to the guests waiting.

Almost two hours later, as guests trickled away one by one to get ready for dinner, he filled Britt in on what had happened with Ryan. Of course, he left out the kiss he'd planted on Elle.

"I knew there was something off about that one." Britt took a drink of her water, then waved the bottle at him. "Mark my words, she's got a few screws loose. I'd tell Elle about her myself, but so far Ryan doesn't even acknowledge I'm alive. Trust me, if she ever crossed me, she'd end up flat on that tiny little ass of hers."

He knew there was a reason he had instantly liked Britt when he had met her. She was leaning back against the bar now, listening to him.

"Who would end up on her ass?" Elle's voice broke in, and Liam watched Britt cringe visibly.

"Ryan," he answered. "I was just filling Britt in on what . . . caused me to be late to my shift."

Elle leaned on the bar and let out a huge sigh. "I need a shot of tequila."

"Sure thing, boss lady." Britt quickly disappeared to get the drink.

"Problems?" he asked. She was wearing the same outfit from before, but there was a dark grease stain on the front.

"Why do people think they can have sex anywhere?" She set her chin in her palms, then took the shot of tequila that Britt had set in front of her. "Another." Britt filled the shot glass quickly. She tossed it back, leaving the salt and lime untouched. She motioned for another as she swallowed.

"I think two is enough." He glanced back at Britt. "I'm going to clock out and walk our boss back to the main building."

"Sure thing." Britt smiled.

Liam took her arm and helped her stand up, making sure that once the effects of the tequila hit her, she wouldn't fall flat on her face.

CHAPTER EIGHT

Earlier that day, Elle couldn't help but smile and be in a good mood as she made her way down the path toward her next stop.

Before she could go any farther, Hannah messaged her that the alarm in the boathouse was going off.

Since she was on that side of the grounds, she texted that she'd check it out herself.

Less than five minutes later, once she had entered the dark, damp boathouse, she was about to reach for the light switch when she heard a grunt and a groan.

Praying it wasn't what she thought it was, she flipped on the lights to find the Youngs in full sexual congress on top of an old tarp near the inside dock.

She swiftly turned around with a shriek and bumped solidly into a large pulley hanging by the doorway. She reached over and switched off the lights. She didn't want to see any more than she had already.

She heard a chuckle behind her and retreated. "Please lock the door when you're . . . done," she called out before shutting the door behind her, with the image now burned into her retinas.

Pretty sure her face was bright red, she made her way to the volleyball courts. When the couple crossed paths with her a little later, she tried to avoid looking in their direction. She'd seen more of both of them than she'd ever wanted to.

She found it hard to concentrate on the volleyball game she was supposed to be refereeing and instead found her eyes flitting to where Liam was busy behind the bar. Remembering how he'd looked with his shirt off earlier that morning, she daydreamed about getting her hands on those muscles of his again.

After finishing up the last volleyball game of the day, and when the guests started disappearing back to their cabins to get ready for dinner, she was called once again. This time, an alarm was going off on one of the thermostats in the massage rooms.

Since she was nearby, she made her way to the area and noticed that the pool house was completely empty. She walked in and, just as she opened the door to the massage room, worried that the air conditioning unit was on the fritz, she once again heard grunts.

"Jesus!" she cried out upon seeing Mr. Young's naked ass up in the air as he pumped into his wife, who was bent over the massage table. Her one-piece swimsuit lay on the floor next to his own swim trunks.

Turning quickly away, she bumped solidly into the doorjamb with her chin. She rushed out the door and slammed it shut behind her.

Her mind now completely filled with a new image, she marched to the pool bar and decided she needed some help to get the multiple visions of the Youngs having sex out of her head.

Liam was his normal flirty self, charming her until he convinced her to allow him to walk her back to the main building.

The two shots of tequila she'd had hit her halfway back to the building.

"I'm tired of seeing old men's asses," she blurted.

"O . . . kay," he said.

She leaned in to him. "Why is it that old people have more sex than I do?"

He chuckled. "The Youngs?"

"Does everyone know about them? I swear, if I see his ass one more time . . ." She sighed and rested her head against his shoulder. "Not that it's terrible. I mean, for a man of what . . . sixty? Maybe it's all the pounding he does?" Liam stopped walking and laughed until he bent over, holding his sides. "What?" She frowned at him. "I mean, men do use more muscles during sex than most women, right?"

He shook his head and gathered her close. "You are a princess." He kissed the top of her head just before they walked in the front doors.

"Is she okay?" Hannah rushed toward them.

"She's had a few shots," he said. "I think it's best if she sits dinner out tonight."

"Thank you." Hannah took Elle's arm and started walking her toward the stairs. Elle turned to see Liam watching them. She waved at him, and he smiled and winked at her.

"It's the Youngs," she whispered to Hannah. "His ass. Always that ass."

Hannah chuckled as they made their way up the stairs. "I'll take over for you tonight. Rest." She let her into the apartment. "You've earned it, sweetie."

"I'm afraid if I close my eyes, all I'm going to see is . . ."

"Don't think about it." Hannah groaned. "Now that's all *I* can see."

"Liam kissed me." She sighed as Hannah pushed her back on the sofa and started removing her shoes for her.

"When? Just now?" Hannah asked, stopping her movement.

"Right here." She pointed to the top of her head, and Hannah's shoulders relaxed. "I should have had dinner. Shut down for a while."

She tucked a blanket over her. Hannah leaned in and kissed the same spot.

"Okay." She smiled up at her friend. "He kisses better than you."

Hannah laughed. "Good thing. Night."

Elle rolled over, pulling the blanket with her, and the moment she closed her eyes, she was fast asleep.

Over the next two days, she stumbled across the Youngs two more times.

It was beginning to cause her mental turmoil. Every time she found herself outside a closed door, she knocked loudly. Even if it was her own locked office door.

Since she'd given Scarlett a few days off, she made a point to text her and talk to her as often as she could. Scar was spending those days in the house in Pelican Point. When Elle had time the following evening, she stopped by to make sure she was doing okay.

Scar was dealing with their father's death differently from how Zoey was. It was almost as if she was in denial about the entire thing. Then again, Scar had had a different relationship with her father than Zoey had, since she'd been a lot younger when their parents had divorced.

Her mother, Kimberly, had been there, cooking dinner for Scar. She could only stay for half an hour, since she'd had to get ready for dinner herself. The conversation had been light, but Elle could tell that Scar was struggling with staying positive around Kimberly.

When she made it back to camp, she had just enough time to change and make it down to the dining hall.

She still wondered about the story behind the brothers being there. Liam hadn't opened up to her. The more she'd thought about it, though, the more it had started to make sense. After all, she knew all about how the media could twist things around.

If it had gotten out that the Costa men were working for a living, she was sure that there would have been some sort of scandal. After all, the family was one of the wealthiest in the Panhandle.

She knew that people who read articles about the wealthy could easily idolize people in high society. Even her grandfather had been treated as if he was famous and rich just because he'd started and run the summer camp here in town.

At one point, the council had come to him asking for money to build new signs for the town. They had figured that since he ran a large business, he would have plenty of cash to spare.

Of course, she knew that the Costas probably did have money to spare lying around, but that didn't mean they were willing to throw it around.

Was this a hideout from the media too?

She stepped out into the night and made her way toward the pool area, where a band was playing that evening.

She was happily surprised at the crowd of guests who had shown up there instead of at the dining hall.

She stepped up to the bar and waved at Liam.

"Evening." He smiled at her as he filled a beer pitcher. "Can I get you something"—he smiled at her—"other than tequila?"

She chuckled. "I think I'll stick to a Coke tonight." He nodded and disappeared down the bar.

When he returned, he bore a Coke and a basket of chips and salsa for her.

"I bet you didn't eat dinner," he said as he set them in front of her. "I put in an order for a grilled cheese sandwich too."

"Thanks." She sat down at the bar and started in on the chips. He was right: she'd skipped lunch and dinner that day. She'd been too busy running around checking on everyone else.

"It's busy tonight." She glanced around. "Looks like everyone's enjoying the band."

"Yeah." He wiped the counter off. "You may have to have them back, and often."

"I'll make a note of it." She pulled out her phone to do so, and he laughed at her before moving off to take more orders.

She watched as the music turned slow, and couples filled the dance floor.

As she sipped her soda and nibbled on the chips, she dreamed of a day when she would find someone to spend the rest of her life with.

She'd thought she'd found what she'd been wanting with Jeff. He'd filled all the requirements she'd come up with when she'd been thirteen.

Yet as an adult, Liam fit all her new requirements. Which, of course, scared her. She watched him move around the bar, interacting with the guests as if he'd been born to it. She'd talked over the weird Costa subterfuge briefly with the others, and they all had speculated, but so far, no one had any solid answers.

She looked over at him and figured that, after things died down for the night, she would corner him to find out more.

From what she could tell, he'd been telling her the truth about everything else. They had lived in the house across the way, and he and his brothers did live in Destin. What she couldn't figure out was why he'd kept up the lie.

"You're deep in thought," Liam said. It was then that she realized he was standing directly in front of her. She wondered how long he'd been there.

"Sorry," she said as he waved her grilled cheese in front of her.

Chef Isaac didn't do normal grilled cheese sandwiches. The bread was perfectly crispy, the cheese oozy, and the bacon crisp. And yet somehow the tomatoes, onions, and basil inside remained fresh enough to make her mouth water.

"I ordered us something." He held up another plate with a second sandwich. "How about we take these to a table? I'm due a break." He leaned in. "Right, boss?"

She smiled. "Sounds good."

"Great." He nodded. "Grab those chips."

She took her drink and the chips and salsa and followed him to a small table close to the pool deck, away from the loud, crowded dance floor.

"So," he began after they were settled. "What sort of deep thoughts were you having?"

"Why did you lie to us about your last name?" she asked after her first bite into the sandwich.

"It was my brother Owen's idea." He shrugged and bit into his own sandwich. "My god," he said. "Seriously? Who knows how to cook a grilled cheese this well?"

She chuckled, took another bite, and silently agreed with him. "You're stalling." She wanted more information from him. Needed it really badly. Why had he continued to lie to her?

"Like I said, it was Owen's idea."

"Why?" She set her sandwich down. "Why use a different name?"

"He thought . . . it would be best in order to not cause trouble." He closed his eyes, as if he was trying to come up with the words.

"Because you lived nearby before?" she asked.

He frowned. "That was part of it."

"What's the other part?" she asked.

"My family is sort of . . . known around places."

"Yeah, we now all know that," she said. "Why hide it from us?"

He shrugged and took another bite. "My father owns businesses. He has connections, and, well, we didn't want any favors."

"Yes, but that doesn't explain it. Not really."

"We wanted to hide. To be unknown was better than walking into this, flying our name as a large red flag."

The fact that she hadn't wanted to be associated with her father had pushed Joe to help her change her name from Bronson to Saunders all those years ago.

People all had different reasons for changing their names.

"Okay," she said after a minute. "Are there any more secrets you're keeping from me?"

He was silent for a while. "Our father's missing."

"He is?" She straightened; she already knew this from Zoey, but this was the first *he* was bringing it up. "For how long?"

"A few months," he said as he finished off his sandwich.

"You must be worried. Are the police—"

"No," he broke in, reaching over and taking her hand. "We have people looking for him, but it's not the first time he's taken a trip without letting us know all the details."

"Has Ryan bugged you since yesterday?" she asked.

"No." He smiled. "But I hear she ran into Owen a few times."

"Why does she have it in for you?"

He flexed his arm. "It has to be my muscles." She laughed. "I have to get back," he said after looking over her shoulder. "Britt looks like she needs a smoke break."

"Thanks for the sandwich." She leaned back as he stood up.

"Will you be around in an hour?"

She thought of the millions of things she could be doing. They had all put in extra hours since they'd decided to open River Camp back up. As if they had been holding their breaths to see if the camp would sink or swim, and choosing to do so instead of breathing and living. Still, knowing that the camp was off to a great start should have reassured her some.

After all, they were almost booked solid for the rest of the summer. Which should have allowed her at least a little time to relax. Especially with someone she enjoyed being around like Liam.

"Yes," she answered before she could talk herself out of it.

His smile broadened as he walked back to the bar.

She tried to avoid watching him walk away, but seeing him in the tight jeans was too much of a temptation.

When he glanced back and caught her watching him, he wiggled his eyebrows at her and smirked.

Damn, she thought and spun back around. She took another sip of her soda and figured she could use a dip in the pool to cool off.

She left her plate and drink and settled at the side of the pool, far from the view of the bar, and pulled off her shorts and camp shirt.

She slid into the water and relaxed back, letting the water cool her off.

"Long day?"

Lara Patterson, a guest who had been doing laps, approached her.

"Yes," she said with a smile. "How are you tonight, Mrs. Patterson?"

"Please, call me Lara." She smiled at her. The woman pulled off her water cap and let her long dark hair fall around her shoulders.

Elle nodded in agreement. "Did you enjoy your swim?"

"Yes, we have an indoor pool at our club in Oregon, but"—she glanced around—"nothing beats swimming under the stars."

Elle glanced up and noticed the sky was filled with the little lights.

"You're lucky to live here year round." Lara sighed.

"Yes," she agreed.

"I'm probably bothering you." Lara started to move away.

"No, not at all," Elle assured her. "I was just cooling off. It's been a long day. Please." She motioned the woman closer.

Lara returned. "The warmer weather has done wonders for my Ross." The woman's eyes turned sad.

"It always helped my grandpa's joint problems too," she said.

"Ross was diagnosed with Parkinson's," Lara said.

"I'm so sorry." Elle made a mental note to check and make sure they were getting everything they needed.

Lara sighed and leaned against the side of the pool. "The man took long enough to catch me." She smiled absently at the sky. The corner of her lip quivered. "Now, I hate the thought of losing him too early."

Elle was silent. She didn't know how to comfort someone who was grieving. Hell, she herself had refused her friends' help until they'd forced their love on her.

"Do you have family?" she asked.

"No." Lara shook her head. "No kids, if that's what you mean."

Elle nodded. "I lost my mother when I was ten."

"I'd heard." Lara turned slightly toward her. "Not that I'm a stalker, but I checked up on this place before booking a cabin. I read one of the articles about the five of you: you and your friends. How you built this place back up." Her smile was back. "Friendship like that comes around once in a millennium."

"Yes, it does."

"You're very lucky." Lara stood up. "I'd better get back to Ross."

"Lara, if you guys need anything to round out your stay here, don't hesitate to tell me." She stood up in the water and shook the woman's hand.

"I will. Thanks, Elle." She nodded and climbed out of the pool, leaving Elle to sink back under the dark water and stare up at the stars. Her thoughts turned to her friends and how far they had come in the last year.

A splash woke her from her daydream some time later.

Sputtering, she stood up and pushed her wet hair out of her eyes to see Liam smiling at her.

"Jerk," she said under her breath, causing him to laugh.

"Does your boss know you're taking the rest of the night off?" he asked, getting closer to her in the water.

"Does yours?" she asked, narrowing her eyes at him.

He took her free hand and moved it to his chest as their hips bumped together. Instantly, she felt him grow hard in his shorts.

"Sorry." He shrugged. "You look like a mermaid floating in the water."

"I thought I was a princess, no?" she teased as he shifted against her.

"Both." His eyes moved to her lips. "I've thought about kissing you again."

Her breath hitched, and her body vibrated with heat. "You have?" It came out as a whisper.

"Haven't you?" His eyes moved to her lips.

She could lie.

"Yes."

Damn, she thought. Should have lied, because his smile turned cocky.

His long dark hair was slicked away from his face. He'd shaved earlier that day, but now the dark stubble filled his face. Reaching up, she ran her hand over it.

"You need a shave before you kiss me again."

His smile fell away. "So, you'll let me?"

She swallowed hard and nodded.

"When?" he asked.

She glanced around and noticed that there were still some people around the pool, even though the band was packing up on the stage.

"Later," she said. "There are too many eyes."

He grinned. "That doesn't seem to bother the Youngs."

She groaned. "Don't remind me. I caught them again today."

He shook his head. "Old people are horny." She felt his chuckle against her hand on his chest.

"You're horny," she countered. "Or was that your cell phone in your pocket?" She laughed at the face he gave her.

"Too bad I have an early morning. We could take a long walk." His eyes met hers. "There's more things to do than kiss."

No man had ever made her on the verge of exploding with just words before. Her knees actually buckled, and if she hadn't been holding on to him, she would have slid under the water.

"What kinds of things?" She didn't know what made her ask, but she needed to know. Wanted the image in her head.

His fingers brushed against her back, the bare skin exposed by her swimsuit, and she shivered.

"I would start by touching you"—his hand moved to her hip as his voice lowered—"everywhere."

She had to swallow the desire to jump him right there with everyone watching. "Now I understand a little . . ." she murmured.

One side of his lips curved up. "You can keep touching me, if you want."

She realized that her fingers were already running over his biceps and stilled them.

"After that, I'm sure we can come up with something else to do." His breath caressed her lips.

A loud burst of laughter broke into her thoughts as several guests showed up. Two men jumped into the other end of the pool with big splashes while the ladies chuckled and slowly climbed in.

"I better . . . I've got"—she pulled away—"an early morning."

"Elle," Liam said, remaining where he was as she waded to the edge of the pool. She glanced back at him. "Maybe we could go for that walk tomorrow?"

Instead of answering, she dipped her chin slightly, then climbed out of the pool, wrapped a towel around her body, and collected her things.

As she lay in bed that night, her mind went over every word, every touch he'd given her. She couldn't help feeling like it was only a matter of time before she allowed herself to enjoy him fully. Either the hot summer nights or Liam would drive her slowly mad.

CHAPTER NINE

Liam tried not to smile too much the following morning as he helped get everything ready for the first group of guests at the zip line hut.

Spending an evening in the pool with Elle had put him in a permanent good mood, and he doubted anything could shake it from him.

His brother and Zoey were due back later today, so he could start having more free time with Elle instead of running around the campgrounds. He'd felt like he'd been sprinting between jobs in the past few days and was actually looking forward to a slower pace.

The first group had gone off without a hitch, and he enjoyed flying through the trees with everyone else. The second group was just getting ready when he noticed a man who looked vaguely familiar. It wasn't until they were on tower three that he placed the man, when someone addressed him as Reed.

"Reed Cooper?" he asked when he'd finally maneuvered him so they would be alone on the tower. The rest of the group had already moved on to the next one.

The older gentleman nodded. "Do I know you?"

"Not officially. I'm Liam Costa. My father is Leo. We used to own the house across the way." He nodded to where the massive place sat across the bay. Since he was done playing games and hiding who he was with Elle, he felt comfortable using his real name. Besides, maybe the guy knew something about his father? He'd heard Zoey and Scarlett talking about the man who lived in the house across the way and had looked for an opportunity to talk to him.

"Right." The man smiled and held out his hand. "I've talked to your brother Dylan."

"Yes." Liam relaxed slightly.

"You're looking for your father." It wasn't as much a question as a statement. "He's not at my place. I understand your frustration and concerns. Have you found out anything more?"

"No." Liam ran his hands through his hair. All the frustrations about not knowing where his father was had started to return to him as the high from being with Elle slowly faded.

"How long has he been missing?" Reed asked.

"A few months now. Almost six," he answered after thinking about it.

The man whistled. "Dylan mentioned that he'd done this before?"

"Yes." He leaned back on the railing of the tower. "But never this long without some contact."

"You know, I used to be special ops, I have a few buddies . . ."

"No, thanks." Liam stood up, shaking his head. "We've got this." He knew his father wouldn't be pleased at all if he had to be hunted down.

"You're sure?"

"Yes, thanks." They had already talked about keeping their father's disappearance as low key as they could.

"If you change your mind," Reed said, getting ready to head down to the next tower, "you know where to find me."

"Thanks," he said, making sure the man was secure and then giving him the thumbs-up before following him to the next tower.

His conversation with Reed had him reassessing things during lunchtime and all through his shift at the pool bar. Maybe they needed more help looking for their dad? Maybe this time, something else was going on. Could their father really be in trouble?

He didn't see Elle that day until just before Dylan and Zoey returned, and even then, it was only in the presence of everyone else, when they ran into each other in front of the main building for a brief moment.

"How are you doing?" he asked, stopping beside her.

She scanned him. "Good, I see you kept your shirt intact today."

"Yes." He chuckled softly. "I think you scared her off."

Her eyes narrowed. "One can hope."

"Why don't you fire her?" he asked.

"Brent hired her; technically, he's her boss." She shrugged. "Besides, it's hard enough to keep good labor around here with what we can pay."

"Maybe once you get a little more known . . ." He broke off as the car arrived.

Then he stood back and watched the women shuffle Zoey inside to catch up.

He turned to Dylan. "So? Did you find out anything new?"

"Let's go for a walk." He picked up his bag and ran his hands through his hair.

"Hell, you slept with her." Owen jumped in.

"Fuck off." Dylan's answer gave him away.

"Fuck." Liam started to leave.

"It's not like that," Dylan countered. "She's . . . different."

"She's the woman you're supposed to be spying on, not sleeping with," Owen hissed.

"As I said, fuck off." Dylan jerked his bag over his shoulder. "She has nothing to do with this. I know it." He strode toward the building, leaving them alone outside.

Owen turned to Liam, and he mentally recoiled. *Shit, here it comes.*

"Since our brother has decided that this plan is just a game to him, let's you and me talk." He lowered his voice and nodded to the pathway.

He followed Owen down the path until they stepped into a small clearing where they would be alone.

"Remember, Dad had an appointment set with Elle the day he disappeared. We need to find out if he kept that appointment, what it was about. Hell, break into her phone if you have to."

Liam kept his mouth shut, knowing it would be the only way to combat his brother at this point. He'd seen Owen on a mission before. He was a lot like their father in that area. Once his scope was set, there was no getting him off mark.

Owen turned to go. "I'm going to see if I can get into their office again. See what you can find out." His brother's eyes bore into his own.

"Sure," he mumbled as Owen walked away. He made his way back to their empty room and lay on his bed, closed his eyes, and tried to relax as he plotted. He was exhausted from the long day.

Of course, because his body was tired didn't mean his mind and his libido were . . .

For the next hour, he lay in bed thinking about Elle and dreaming of her. The way she'd smelled of something soft and floral, even in the chlorine-filled water.

When his alarm finally went off in the morning, he'd only managed a few hours of sleep, which put him in a grumpy mood.

He skipped breakfast and decided to hit the gym instead. Employees were allowed to use the equipment if the gym wasn't crowded.

Being the only one in there that early, he spent the next hour sweating out his sexual frustrations. Well, most of them anyway.

He was just leaving the gym when he heard Elle's voice in the next room. Checking his watch, he realized he wasn't due to the woodshop for almost two hours. As he stepped just inside the opened door, he had to pick his chin off the ground when he spotted her at the front of the workout room in a light-pink leotard and ballet shoes.

The fact that the outfit was sexy as hell on her didn't really register. What did was the pose she was currently in. It almost looked like a very low squat. Both feet were flat on the ground, her legs were bent, and her ass was almost touching the floor.

"Bend as far as you can," she was telling the small room of older women. "Make sure you hold on to . . ." Her eyes moved up to the mirror, and he could tell that she saw him in the reflection. When their eyes locked, she seemed to lose her concentration and rolled to the floor, landing solidly on that tight ass he'd been admiring a moment ago.

He would have rushed across the room to catch her, but there were too many people between them. Instead, he remained in the doorway, crossed his arms over his chest, and smiled wickedly at her.

"Smooth move," he mouthed to her when she recovered.

"Go away," she mouthed back.

He shook his head and chuckled when she waved him away.

"Keep the position as long as you can," she told the room and started walking around, checking on some of the women. "Good," she said occasionally.

Completing her circuit, she walked over to him, placed a hand on his chest, and pushed him out into the hall; then, with a large smile, she shut the door in his face.

He laughed. She had just wiped his foul mood away. Even bumping into Ryan along the pathway couldn't quash his new light mood.

He made a point to hunt Elle down during lunch and sit at her table. It was worth seeing her blush when he asked her how her back end was doing after the fall that morning. He worked the pool bar through the dinner hour, since the band was back.

That night as he lay in his bed, he noticed that Dylan hadn't returned. Owen had his days off and had returned to Destin to no doubt talk to the board of the family's business and try to convince them to give them more time.

He knew his older brother was more stressed about the entire situation than they were. After all, their father had been grooming Owen since childhood to take over the business when he retired.

He didn't know what would happen to Owen if he couldn't take over Paradise Investments. The family business had been his only goal for as long as Liam could remember.

Where Liam and Dylan had gone to college classes and had pretty much pissed those years and their father's money away, Owen had studied hard and attended all the classes needed to run a major corporation.

Something Liam had never really felt guilty about until recently.

Which was why he and Dylan were in the middle of this mess. Still, there were worse places to spend your summer. Besides, if he hadn't agreed to help out, he'd probably still be traveling around acting like the spoiled rich kid he was.

As he made his security rounds that evening, he was surprised to see Elle standing on the docks. When he approached, she turned as if she'd been waiting for him.

"Evening." He stopped beside her.

"It was such a nice night, I needed a walk," she explained as she leaned against the railing.

"Evening walks are one of my favorites." He nudged her shoulder. "As you know. Especially with company."

"Zoey filled us in on the search for your father."

"Oh," he said.

"Why didn't you tell me yourself?"

"I did." He turned slightly toward her. "Remember?"

"You made it seem like he does this all of the time."

"He does." He shrugged.

"But not with all that money." She turned and leaned back against the railing.

"No," he agreed. "Never with that much. Over the years, however, he's . . . shall we say, 'donated' a lot to several young women's businesses." Her eyes narrowed, and she shook her head slightly. "He tends to date younger women who all have business plans and spend a lot of his money, only for the businesses to fail."

"Oh." She nodded. "Is that what you think is going on now?"

It was true: Elle would have fit perfectly into the mold of women his father fell for.

With one exception. He glanced around the camp behind him. The lights strung between poles made the grounds glow. He could hear the band still playing up at the pool and people laughing and having a great time. River Camp would be successful, very successful. There was no doubt about it.

"You're worried about him?" she asked, her eyes searching his.

"Yes," he said. "It's why . . ." He bit his tongue when he realized what he was about to admit. Why they were at the camp, why he had gotten close to her. At least at first. Now, looking at her in the soft light, something else was drawing him to her. Shaking his head, he leaned in closer. "Owen's checking on things while he's gone. Hopefully, he's found something out."

Her hands moved to his arm as she edged closer to him. He reached over and took her hips as he moved closer to her.

"But I've been thinking of nothing but getting you back in my arms." It came out almost as a whisper.

"Me too." She grinned up at him, then gracefully reached up on her toes and placed her lips over his.

If he hadn't known he was standing on a dock, he would have thought he was floating. His arms tightened around her, and he sank into the feeling of her wrapped around him.

"I want to take you somewhere," he said against her skin. "God, I really . . ."

Something caught his peripheral vision, and he noticed a sailboat returning to the dock area. "Damn," he sighed. "We're about to have company."

She glanced over her shoulder and tensed. "Zoey and Damion took a group out for a sunset tour. That must be them." She took his hand and pulled him down a pathway.

"Where are we going?" he asked.

"Hush, they'll hear us." She giggled and continued to tug him through the dark woods.

"You're not taking me out here to tie me up and have your way with me, are you?"

"Maybe." She winked back at him. "But not likely, since where I'm taking you isn't very comfortable." She stopped at the base of a tree and frowned up at it.

"What is it?" He glanced up into the darkness but could only see black sky.

"The rope isn't here." She put her hands on her hips. "Damn. I could have . . . oh, here it is." She walked around the tree, and he followed her.

"Don't tell me we're going to climb that?" He frowned at the knotted rope she held in her hands.

"Don't be silly." She tugged on the rope.

He watched in amazement as a makeshift wooden staircase unfolded down to the ground.

"Wow," he said under his breath.

"Wait until you see the rest of it. It needs some updating, but . . ." She turned to him. "Welcome to my hideaway."

"Who else knows about this?" he asked as they climbed the narrow stairs.

"Joe started building this when I came to live with him full time at ten, so, of course, all of the Wildflowers, and Aiden, since I've asked him to make a few repairs on the place. He just finished adding the new staircase." She glanced over her shoulder at him. "We used to have to climb a rope ladder."

At the top of the stairs, she turned and pulled another rope that sent the ladder back up into the canopy of the trees. "This way, no one happens upon it." She turned to him and motioned toward the door. "Well, go on in."

He opened the door and stepped into the darkness.

She reached around him and flipped on a light.

"It was the first small cabin on site." She stepped around him. "I'm hoping that eventually we'll replace the old windows with tinted ones, so the lights can't be seen at night." Arms crossed, she glanced out a wall full of single-paned glass windows.

The cabin was one room, and probably just under twenty by twenty feet in size. A giant white bed sat on a wooden box frame on one wall; the opposite wall held a small kitchenette, including a small fridge. A half wall separated the bathroom area, which included a small shower.

The place looked like it could use some major updates, but it was solid enough.

"How long has this been here?" he asked, joining her.

From the windows, he could see across the top of the trees and just make out the lights from the main pool area.

Realization dawned on him. He must have passed this very spot more than a dozen times while searching the grounds. Two large tree trunks entered the space, with at least two more just outside the windows helping support the structure.

"Like I said, Joe built it for me when I was ten." She turned toward him. "Well, he had a contractor build it. It hangs partially over the stream. It was big enough for me when I needed to be by myself back then. To escape the life of camp and to have something of my own. There's a balcony." She waved at a glass door and plunked herself down on the bed. "Stairs lead up to the roof, but they need some repair still. You can see all the way to Destin from up there."

"Do you come here often?" he asked, sitting down beside her.

"When I need to be alone. I am sharing an apartment with four others, you know," she said. "Even if we're best friends, it's nice to have some time to myself."

He agreed with that. The camp was a busy place, but he usually had some quiet time when he locked himself in the woodshop.

"Do they come up here?" he asked, picking her hand up in his and enjoying the way her breath caught at the simple touch.

"No." She looked down at their joined fingers. "They knew it was off limits to them when we started working on reopening the camp. They call it Elle's Hiding Spot." She rested her head against his shoulder.

"Great friends." He leaned in and kissed her. "Who else have you brought up here?" He didn't know why he asked it, but he had to know.

"No one," she whispered, her breath floating over his face.

"Not even Jeff?" he asked between kisses. He felt her tense at the mention of her ex's name, so he slowly ran his hands up her arms and over her back until he felt her relax again.

"No," she sighed when he trailed kisses down her neck as she leaned back to give him more access.

"Good," he said before pulling her down to the bed. He covered her body with his, settling between her legs and letting her feel his hardness. She groaned and moved under him, making his cock even harder.

Her fingers dug into his shoulders as his hands lifted her shirt slowly up to expose the soft skin on her flat belly. He kissed her belly button and heard another soft moan reverberate from her.

"Liam." His name became nothing more than a moan, urging him on.

"I want you," he said to her.

"Yes, please." She pushed her hands into his hair, pulling him back down to her.

"Elle." He shook his head and decided then and there that he knew that, even though he wanted her, he couldn't cross the line his brother had.

But that didn't mean he couldn't blur some lines.

After all, he'd felt like there was more growing between them. He felt something more for her than his just trying to get knowledge from her about his father.

Nudging her shirt up and over her head, he took in her beauty. She was perfection.

"You don't have a ballerina body." He smiled down at her luscious tits.

"No," she chuckled. "I did before . . . these came in." She wiggled under him. Then closed her eyes as his hands moved gently over to cup her. "God . . . Liam, please."

"I'm right here," he said, gathering her closer and running his calloused hands over her soft skin. He needed to show her tenderness. She deserved it.

"I want." She nudged his shirt off and bit her bottom lip as her eyes ran over him. Then, slowly, she reached up and ran her fingertips over his chest.

"I like this." She traced the tattoo that he'd gotten on one of his first trips to Hawaii. The simple lines sat on his left pec. "Hawaiian?"

"Yes, supposedly it will ward off evil water spirits." He smiled. "Remember, I was a future marine biologist back then."

She chuckled before pulling him back down to press her lips against his.

"I have protection." She started to move.

"Elle." She stilled and tensed at her name. "I want to make love to you"—he rested his forehead against hers—"very bad, but . . ."

She shoved his shoulders until he rolled off her. "God, I'm such a fool." She got up, wrapped her arms around herself, and moved to the windows.

"No." He moved over and took her in his arms. "It's not . . . I want to make sure it's for the right reasons."

"What better reasons are there than pleasure?" she asked, avoiding his eyes.

CHAPTER TEN

She could see Liam struggle with his decision. God, was it so hard for a man to decide to sleep with her? She knew it was probably some of Jeff's old rejection surfacing, but when her eyes filled with tears, she had to turn away from Liam to hide the pain.

"Hey." He stopped her movement by putting a finger under her chin and lifting her face to his. "Don't." He gently brushed his lips across her forehead.

She was stronger than she had been in the past with Jeff. She'd grown so much and had thought she'd ditched all her past hang-ups.

Making a decision quickly, she shifted closer to him, more determined to show him what she wanted. To make him want her in return. It was now or never.

She watched his eyes close with pleasure when she began rubbing him through his jeans.

"Elle, if you keep doing that, I'm going to forget why I shouldn't touch you."

"Good." She moved closer to him, enjoying the primal lust she saw in his hazel eyes. "I want you to forget." She leaned up and, feeling surer of herself, brushed her lips over his jawline, then sunk her teeth into his chin lightly.

A low growl emanated from his chest just before he hoisted her up and carried her to the bed. She hit the mattress with a bounce before his body covered hers. Once again, he settled between her legs; this time, however, she wrapped her legs around him and promised that she wouldn't let go.

His hips thrust against hers, causing his cock to push against her pussy through her shorts. She was so wet, she wondered if her shorts were soaked at this point.

"Liam." She reached for his jeans, but his hands circled her wrists and hoisted them above her head. She tried to push against him, but he was so much stronger and more determined.

"No, we'll do this my way. Say it." His eyes bore into hers.

"Yes!" She arched, trying to get his body next to hers again.

In one quick move, he had her shorts down her legs, along with her silk panties. She thought she heard material rip but didn't care, since he shifted and covered her pussy with his mouth.

A scream was ripped from her lungs as she buried her fingers into his hair, holding him to her as he used his tongue to push her further than she'd ever gone before.

Her shoulders jerked from the bed as she cried his name and felt the sweetest release. When her back touched the cool sheets again, she closed her eyes as he slowly kissed the insides of her thighs, his fingers making small circles on her skin. The movement almost matching her rapid heartbeat, slowing it down until she drifted off into a dreamless sleep.

When she woke, it was to her cell phone chiming. As she reached for the dresser, or where her dresser normally was, she landed on the wood floor of the cabin with a bang and cursed.

"You okay down there?" Liam chuckled.

Pushing her hair out of her eyes, she glared up at him. "You let me . . ." She held up a finger and fumbled for her phone, then answered it in a calm voice. "Elle." Hearing Julie's calm voice on the other side had her questioning the time. She glanced around and realized there wasn't a clock in the place. "I'll be right there. Thanks," she said and hung up, then turned to Liam, who was lying on the bed, still in his jeans. "You let me fall asleep."

He chuckled. "I didn't let you do anything." He tilted his head. "Well, maybe I let you come on my tongue."

Her eyes narrowed as she started to move. Then she realized she was stark naked and gasped. Moving quickly, she tried to pull the blankets out from under him so she could wrap herself in them. However, with his full weight on them, she fell back on her butt, causing him to chuckle.

"You know, for a princess ballerina, you sure fall on your ass a lot." He laughed.

"Shut up and get up." She tried again, only for him to reach down, put his hands firmly under her armpits, and hoist her up.

"No, not until you come up here." He sat her on his chest and then scooted down. "Put those sweet pussy lips right here," he said against the inner side of her thighs. Causing her to moan and hold herself up. Her hair fell in knots around her face as she looked down at his eyes, which were watching her.

"Ride my tongue," he said and slid it up over her clit, then dipped it into her already-wet pussy.

"Oh god!" She held on to the wood bed frame and did what he asked, riding his tongue until she felt herself building. "Liam, I need . . ." She didn't get any further before he dipped a finger into her heat and sent her once more into an explosion.

"Damn you," she said, standing under the shower a few minutes later. She threw a glare across the room at him as he reclined back on the bed, still in his jeans, smugness emanating from him.

He chuckled. “Why? Because I can make you come?”

“No, because I wanted . . . you.” She tossed her hair out of her face.

“You had me.” He shifted until he could see her fully in the shower. She pivoted, trying to keep the solid half wall between them. “I’ve seen you naked, you know,” he added and tilted his head once more.

“Well”—she twisted the shower off—“now you’ve seen me naked and wet.” She yanked the towel off the hook and covered herself.

His smile grew. “And I’ll see all of it again. That’s a promise.”

“I have to go.” She hunted the small space for her clothes and, finding them in a pile on the floor, shook them off. After quickly pulling the wrinkled things on, she twisted her long hair into a knot and glanced at herself in the mirror. “It will have to do. Do you think you can find your way down from here?” she asked, tugging on her shoes.

“I’ll be fine. Go. I’m not due anywhere for a few hours.” He rested back on the bed. “I’ve never slept in a tree house before.”

She walked over and surprised him by kissing him on the lips. “Thank you,” she said and watched his eyes flood with tenderness.

“Anytime, princess,” he said before she turned and left.

When she walked into the lobby, Julie was talking with Aiden.

“Morning,” she said, trying to avoid the curiosity as to why she’d entered through the front door and hadn’t come down the staircase. “What’s all this about a problem with plumbing?”

“There’s a shortage of new pipes going out to the new cabin,” Aiden said. He’d started to follow her to her office when the front phone rang.

“What?” They heard Julie’s gasp behind them. “Yes, I understand.” She hung up and screamed, “Bear!”

Elle had somewhat prepared for this. After all, it hadn’t been the first time a predator had been on the grounds. “Put us in lockdown. Call everyone and send out the notices to the cabins.” She started to rush toward her office to make some calls herself.

“No, I mean, yes, but Zoey!” Julie cried out.

"Oh god." Elle must have turned white, because Aiden gripped her arms tightly.

"She outran it," Julie added quickly.

Elle could barely breathe. "Is she . . ."

"She's okay. She's with Carter. They're going to head over to the new cabin—the one that's almost done. That's where it was spotted. Dylan is locked in the cabin. The bear's just outside it."

Carter was one of the veterinarians on staff at the Alaqua Animal Refuge, which sat just on the other side of town. She'd convinced him to stop by a few times each day and act as part-time caregiver to the horses they kept in the stables.

She glanced at Aiden, who confirmed her unspoken thoughts. "Aiden and I are going there," she said to Julie. "Just handle the lockdown."

As Aiden drove, she thought about Zoey. Her heart beat faster as they got closer to the new cabin. Cabin. Liam! She fumbled for her phone and punched his number.

"Miss me so soon?" he answered.

"Don't go outside," she said. "There's a bear. Your brother—"

"Where?" he broke in.

"The new cabin . . ."

"The one that's almost built?"

"Yes, but . . . damn it!" she said after he'd hung up. The truck came to a dusty stop, and before it settled, she jumped out and rushed to Carter's truck, where Zoey was sitting in the passenger seat, hugging Dylan.

Elle hugged Zoey tight. "Are you two all right? Julie said you outran a bear."

"I didn't—I just snuck past her. Dylan was the one she chased," she answered.

"It's a good thing you two walked by this morning," Aiden said as he came up behind her; then he walked over and looked at the tranquilized bear from a few feet away. "I'd hate to think of what would have happened if a guest had stumbled upon this."

The way that Zoey was avoiding Elle's gaze made her realize she was hiding something. Then she noticed the flush on her cheeks and smiled. "It's a good thing the place had a door and windows," Zoey added. "Otherwise Mama here would have joined us in the cabin."

"Mama?" Aiden asked, turning back toward the bear.

Carter walked over to them. "Her two cubs are stuck in the dumpster. They look okay, but we'll want to check them out to make sure. Which is probably why she made such a big mess last night."

"Damn it," Aiden said and headed to the dumpster. "I told my men not to throw food trash in here. The smell of leftovers probably drew the bears in the first place." He glanced over to Elle in frustration. "I'll make sure this doesn't happen again."

"Thanks." She grinned at him, knowing he'd take care of it.

Just then another golf cart skidded to a halt in the dirt. Owen and Liam leaped out and rushed to their brother's side.

"You okay?" they asked at the same time.

"Yeah." Dylan suddenly looked uncomfortable.

Elle broke in. "If it's okay, I'll take these two back up to the main building in your truck."

"We can . . ." Liam started but stopped when she gave him a look.

On the trip back to the main building, Zoey filled her in a little more on what had happened. How she had slipped out of the small bathroom window in the back of the cabin and run through the woods toward the stables to tell Carter. Due to running through the thick woods, Zoey was covered in scratches that needed to be cleaned and looked at. Elle convinced her to allow Dr. Val to examine her when they returned.

"I didn't know you had prepared for cases like this." Zoey reached over and squeezed her hand. "You thought of everything."

"It's a good thing I did." She wrapped her arm around her friend.

When they pulled up, she convinced Zoey to head into Dr. Val's office to look over the scratches on her legs.

"I'll help you inside." Elle held on to Zoey's arm.

"I can . . ." Dylan started, but Elle raised her eyebrows at him, and he backed off. "Let me know how it goes," he added before he retreated.

"So," Elle said when they were a few feet away from the brothers, who were by now all standing in the parking lot together. "Sounds like you two were very lucky you were there this morning. Together."

"Shut up," Zoey hissed as she hobbled toward the doors.

As Zoey was getting looked at by the doctor, Elle sneaked out to talk to Julie, who had been informed that mama bear along with the babies had been relocated, and she'd given the all clear already.

"Thanks." She took a deep breath. "Exciting morning."

"Elle, there've been a few messages for you. I've left them on your desk."

"Who from?" she asked.

"He wouldn't leave his name, just a number," Julie answered.

"Thanks." She frowned and wondered why someone wouldn't leave their name in a message. But then she turned back down the hall in time to see Zoey hobbling from the doctor's office and dismissed the missed calls to rush to her side.

"I'm okay, no stitches," she said and was quickly hugged.

"You're taking the rest of the day off," Elle insisted, "and heading upstairs right now. I'll have breakfast delivered." She motioned for Scar to help Zoey up to the apartment.

"Really, I'm fine. I can . . ." Zoey started, but she stopped when Elle turned and looked at her.

"Okay, seriously, you have to show me how to do that look," Zoey said with a slight frown.

"Go." She nodded to the stairs and nudged Scar along.

"Okay, but get me some cookies. I want chocolate!" Zoey called back as she was being pulled up the stairs.

"Julie, can you order Zoey and Scar some lunch? Just have it delivered upstairs," she said, checking her calendar on her phone and moving around a few things of hers so she could fill in for Zoey.

"With cookies," Julie agreed. "Need anything else?"

"No." She turned and, instead of heading to her office, jogged down to the changing room to take over Zoey's morning yoga class before she taught her own class.

She enjoyed yoga, but not as much as ballet. Fortunately the yoga class was almost full and even included several men. Afterward, she changed and went about her day, filling in for Zoey where she could. It worked out smoothly, since there were four of them to help out.

When dinner rolled around, she rushed back up to the room and changed into her best 1950s outfit.

Hannah had come up with a fun idea of having a themed dinner once a week for the guests. Everyone could dress up in costume if they wanted to.

She was happily surprised to see how many ladies had poodle skirts. Even the men had gotten into the swing of things. Some were dressed as greasers, while others wore old sports outfits.

Fifties music played loudly from the speakers, and during the meal, tables were moved aside so everyone could dance.

She even started relaxing and danced with a few guests when asked. It was good form to let people see her.

She'd just been swung around when she bumped solidly into Liam's chest.

He grinned down at her. "Having fun?"

"Yes." She laughed.

"Looks like you've done this a time or two before." He nodded to the busy dance floor.

"I took several different dance classes. Shall we?"

"I've never taken classes." But he took her hand as "Chances Are" started playing.

Just swaying with him in a crowded dance floor had her heartbeat speeding up. Their bodies swayed together as the lights were dimmed.

"You look amazing tonight." His smile grew. "I really like leather pants. I don't think girls really wore that stuff in the fifties, though. Did they?"

She glanced down at her outfit. "I'm not completely sure, but they did in *Grease*." She shrugged. "That should count for something."

He chuckled. "It does, believe me."

"Thanks." She rested her head against his shoulder.

"I want to hold you again, to be with you."

She felt her knees go weak. "Me too."

"Soon," he said when she looked back into his eyes.

"Yes," she whispered. "Soon."

"I'd better get off the dance floor before your fan club decide to kick me out of here." He glanced over to where the other men she'd been dancing with were watching them. "Good night."

"Night." She stood in the middle of the dance floor, feeling her body vibrate with want as she watched him leave.

It took a few days for the bear talk to die down. Elle found herself so preoccupied that she hadn't found any more free time to be with Liam again.

Every night as she crawled into her own bed, her body ached for his touch as she fell asleep. She dreamed of him making love to her, kissing her everywhere, so much so that she woke soaking wet with her desire building until she thought she'd jump him the next time she saw him.

The guest parties had died down, and she had only heard of a few rumbles of further private parties from Zoey or Hannah.

The Youngs seemed to have settled down. She counted herself lucky.

She was in her office, going over their latest financial reports, when Zoey walked in. Stormed in was more like it.

She slammed the door and plopped down on the chair opposite her desk.

Elle shut the accounting program down, since she knew she wouldn't get anything else done for the day. "What's up?"

"I've fired Ryan."

"O . . . kay," she said, crossing her hands on her lap. "What happened?"

Just then there was a knock on her door.

"Yes?"

Julie poked her head in. "Dr. Val was called to the pool area."

Elle stood up. "Is a guest hurt?" Their occasional medical help had so far focused mostly on bad sunburns or hangovers.

"No, Dylan—" Julie started, but at this point, Zoey jumped up.

"Wait, what? Is he okay?"

"Ryan hit him over the head with a tequila bottle."

Quickly, they both rushed out the door and ran down the hallway.

"He's in Dr. Val's office already," Julie called back, and the two of them quickly switched directions.

"Looks like we had plenty of reason to fire her," Elle said. "Julie, have the police—"

"The guys said no police." Julie's words stopped her in her tracks. "Dylan didn't want the bad publicity for the camp."

"Right." She hadn't thought of that. "Okay, then . . . have Aiden and a few of his men help remove Ryan from the premises."

Julie nodded and rushed back to her desk. Zoey had disappeared through the doctor's office doors. No doubt she was already by Dylan's side.

When she stepped in, Dr. Val was already done assessing Dylan.

"He has a nasty bump, but other than that, he's fine. He'll need someone to look out for him for the evening."

"I'll take care of it," Zoey said, holding an ice pack to his head, then turned to speak to him.

Elle stood back as Liam and Owen rushed into the room. No matter what she thought of the brothers, the bond there was obvious.

Which had her heart doing little flips even more when she was around Liam.

Jeff had been an only child, like her. He didn't even have a best friend, which should have been a huge warning sign.

As she watched Liam with his brothers and with guests of the camp, she could tell that he was as far from being like Jeff as anyone could be.

CHAPTER ELEVEN

A few nights later, Liam was asked to help set up several campfires along the beach area for the guests. He had an idea to drag some of the heavy logs over to the pit areas for people to sit on. What he wanted to do was build some benches and chairs for people to use instead, but he figured he could add that to the growing list of items he wanted to get done around the place.

He felt like the investigation into his dad's whereabouts had stalled. Dylan was off on his own adventures with Zoey, while Owen was more withdrawn than before while he focused on nothing but trying to find their father. It really felt like they were all going in different directions, when they were supposed to be working on their common goal.

After Liam had set things up, Aiden walked over to him.

"Hey, did you get that sign done for the new cabin?"

"Yeah, I finished it up just today. Want to head out and hang it up?"

"If you have the time," Aiden said. "I've got a cart." He nodded to a golf cart.

They swung by the woodshop and picked up the new sign he'd carved, then headed toward the new cabin. They were going to hang his hand-carved sign over the cabin, which had technically saved his brother's life.

"So, you and Elle?" Aiden asked as they pulled up to the cabin.

"Who told you?" he asked.

Aiden chuckled. "Everyone's talking about it. Dylan and Zoey and you and Elle—it's the only thing everyone can seem to talk about lately."

"Yeah, well . . ."

"What's up with Hannah and Owen?" He pulled out a ladder from the back of the cart.

He thought about their tactics to get information out of the women and felt dirty. So, instead of answering, he just shrugged.

"I've known Elle a long time," Aiden said, motioning for Liam to climb the ladder and hang the sign himself. "That last guy—"

"I'm nothing like him," Liam broke in, his eyes on Aiden's.

"No." Aiden smiled. "Even a blind man could see that. And, I and a few other people are thankful for it, but the fact remains, she's been hurt once." His voice lowered. "I'd hate for it to happen a second time."

Aiden's warning was clear.

"I have no plans to hurt anyone." He rolled his eyes at the thought. Whatever was building between them had nothing to do with his father or the money he'd taken with him.

"Thanks also—good to know." Aiden held the ladder as Liam hung the sign.

He stood back and looked up at his handiwork. He had spent a day etching the words "Bear-Foot Bungalow" into a piece of pine and had even taken the time to carve out a black bear and her two cubs in the corner. He had stained the whole thing for good measure. He had rather enjoyed making the sign and thought about doing others for the rest of the cabins. He'd always liked working with his hands, ever since finding an old chunk of driftwood one summer and turning it into a stork that still sat on his mantel.

"Perfect." He dusted his hands off.

"Yeah." Aiden slapped him on his back. "Now all we need is to let Elle know it's ready."

"I'll do that. I've got to stop by the bonfire again before making my rounds." He helped Aiden clean up the mess they had made hanging the sign.

Aiden held out his hand, and Liam took it easily. "Thanks for everything. Want a ride?"

"No, I'll walk. I could use the fresh air. Good night," Liam called back as he headed toward the main part of the camp.

As he made his way down the lit pathway toward the bonfires, he thought about convincing Elle to stay with him again in Elle's Hiding Spot. He'd even carved her a sign for the outside of the place—one that he intended to give her soon.

"Hey." He glanced up when he heard someone approaching and smiled when he saw Elle walking toward him.

She stopped directly in front of him. "Why didn't you tell me your father is *Leo* Costa?"

"Um, okay." He felt his throat close. "I thought you knew. You said that Zoey told you—"

"That your name was Costa, not that Leo was your father." Her eyes were searching his. He could see something close to hurt behind them and wondered why she'd be upset.

His eyes narrowed as all the reasons they were at the camp surfaced. Suddenly, the thoughts that Elle was more to his father than he knew surfaced again. Could she really have been his mistress at one time? "How do you know my father?" he asked, his hands moving to her shoulders, but she jerked away from him.

"It doesn't matter, what matters is . . ." She threw up her hands. "Hell, I don't know what matters anymore." She started pacing in front of him. "Zoey's going with your brother to spend a few days at his place . . ."

She started rambling, and he allowed her to chatter as she moved back and forth in front of him. His eyes tracked the sway of her hips as she went. Hell, his mind had been on getting her in bed before she'd stormed up to him, and he wanted her even more now that he'd seen her angry.

"It's all lies, everything," she was saying when he focused again.

"What is?" he asked.

"You haven't been paying attention," she accused him and moved closer.

"No," he said. "I get that you're pissed that I didn't come out and tell you my father was Leo Costa, but you've known our real last name for a while now. As I said before, Owen didn't . . ."

She moved closer, and his eyes moved over her skin and fell onto her lips and stayed there. "Didn't . . ."

He couldn't think anymore. He'd lost track of what he'd been saying. What she'd been saying. "God, I really want to kiss you right now."

When she frowned, he knew he'd missed the mark.

He shook his head clear and tried to focus. "Sorry, I've told you all this before. I honestly thought you knew who our father was when you found out my real last name. I didn't think it mattered." For some reason he felt the need to apologize. Not everyone knew who Leo Costa was. Did this mean she had known more about his father than she'd first intimated?

"I didn't." She had her arms crossed over her chest again. "It doesn't . . . not really."

"I'm sorry." He moved closer to her, his hands going to her shoulders. "Really I am. I thought when we talked . . . I thought you knew. That you understood everything." He was having a hard time coming up with the right words.

"I didn't," she said softly.

"My mistake. I'm so sorry. I should have made sure"—he rested his head against hers—"that you knew everything. Including my father's name."

"Yes." She nodded. "You should have."

"My brothers . . . think that you're my father's mistress." His heart skipped as he waited for her response. Instantly she tensed; then she shocked him by laughing.

"That is the best joke I've heard." She wiped a tear from her eye and then focused on him and stilled. "You're serious?"

He nodded. "It's one of the reasons we kept our last name from you."

She stepped back and crossed her arms over her chest defiantly. "What do you think?"

"I think it's bull," he said quickly, earning a nod from her.

"At least we have that."

He walked over to her and took her arms again. "I stopped thinking that before I kissed you. I would have never done so if I believed—"

"My relationship with your father is anything but sexual." She looked away from him.

He could tell she was closing up again and knew that he didn't want her to make some excuse to disappear on him again tonight. So, instead, he changed the subject.

"How was the bonfire?"

Her eyes returned to his, and he could see the internal struggle she had.

"Fine," she finally said and rolled her shoulders. "I guess I overreacted."

"It's probably the wine," he suggested, earning him a look. "I stopped by earlier and saw you and your . . . Wildflowers enjoying the fire and the s'mores. I really am sorry. I thought you knew everything when . . ." He shook his head. "Well, you know."

"I suppose we should have talked about it more." She closed her eyes. "So much has happened in the past few months. I feel like I haven't even had time to breathe."

"We have a few days off coming up." A thought rushed into his mind. "Let's get away together? That way we can have time to catch up on . . . things."

"Get away?" she asked, her voice sounding unsure.

"Sure." He nodded. "I'll take care of everything. You've been so busy; I bet you can't tell me the last day you really took off, and not just sitting on the beach doing work. I mean, really getting away."

She bit her bottom lip, and he could tell she was thinking about it. "Okay," she finally said. "After Zoey and Dylan return."

He nodded and felt like jumping into action. "Now, how about we head back to the campfire?"

"I . . . can't." She took a step back. "There's a few things I have to take care of tonight."

His eyebrows shot up. "It can't wait?"

She shook her head.

"Elle . . ."

"Liam." She stopped him. "I need to get a few things done tonight."

He nodded and took a step back as she started walking away. "By the way, Bear-Foot Bungalow is all set to go." He caught up with her quickly as they made their way toward the main building. "Aiden and I just put on the finishing touch."

"Thanks." She glanced over at him. "I'll let Julie know."

He held the door of the main building open for her and waited until she stepped through before saying, "Aiden was telling me you have a few more cabins going up soon?"

"Yes, one is in the framing stages, and we just cleared the areas for two more," she answered, heading toward her office. He followed her, not wanting their time together that evening to end.

"You must be confident that there's going to be a need for them."

She stopped outside her office door and turned toward him. "We're booked solid for the next six months."

This was news to him. He'd chatted with Julie at the front desk, trying to get information from her about how well the business was doing, but she hadn't really talked about business. Instead, she'd flirted with him, which had made him feel bad, since he hadn't meant to lead her on.

"That's good news," he said.

"You sound surprised?" Her eyes narrowed.

"No, not surprised, just . . . I'd wondered about the financial aspects of this place. I mean . . ."

"Don't be." Her chin rose slightly. "You'll get your paychecks on time." She turned and stormed into the office. It took him a few seconds to catch on to her genuine anger before he followed her inside.

"Hey." He took her hand and stopped her from sitting behind the desk. "I'm happy that this place is making it. Really, it's just I've never taken part in the business side of things before."

She was silent for a while. "But Paradise Investments is your family's business."

He nodded, feeling even more ashamed. "My father's business, which he's made sure that Owen is ready to take over." Again, she was silent.

"Your dad must have shared some part of it with you." She searched his eyes.

Hell, why not be honest with her about this part of his life? He already felt like shit whenever he looked back at it now. It was funny—until he'd come here, he hadn't felt bad about any part of his past. Now, however, he wished he'd worked harder in those areas.

"If he did, I was too busy being a spoiled kid to pay attention." He leaned against her desk and crossed his arms over his chest while she sank into her chair. "Part of me wonders if his disappearance isn't his way of teaching us how to sink or swim."

Her head tilted. "You mean, you think he's disappeared so the three of you will step up and run the business?" When he nodded, she continued, "Then what are you doing here?"

He sighed, heavily. "Again, following a hunch."

"You mean, checking to see if I had something to do with his disappearance?" she asked. When he remained silent, she stood up slowly. "I have a ton of work to do still, if you don't mind . . ." She nodded toward the door.

"Elle." He stood up and rested his hands on her shoulders. "For what it's worth, I know you had nothing to do with my father's disappearance. Like I said, I'm sure it's just him . . . being his old self."

She nodded, but he could tell she was done talking. Surprising her and himself, he leaned in and laid a gentle kiss over her lips.

"Think about going away with me after Dylan and Zoey return. Regardless, I'll set everything up. All you'd have to do is pack and show up." He kissed her again, this time letting his words sink in a little as he touched her softly. He felt her relax into his touch. "Night," he said softly, then slipped out of the room, shutting her office door behind him.

He made his way to the back door and stood outside in the warmth. He realized his body was still vibrating from that kiss. Maybe he should have realized he'd be just as affected as she would. He shoved his hands into his pockets and started his rounds by walking by the firepits.

Seeing that everyone was gone and the fires already put out, he moved on to his normal rounds. Which included the pathway that led to Zoey and Scarlett's mother's place. Seeing a dark figure leaving from the narrow pathway and heading toward the boathouse, he stilled, then quickly followed the shadow.

It wasn't until the man crossed under a light that he realized it was Reed Cooper. He must have heard the gravel crunch under Liam's feet, because suddenly the man tensed. Liam could easily see why most people in camp thought he was a spy. The man looked ready to defend himself, to the death if necessary.

"Burning the midnight oil?" Liam said.

Chuckling, Reed relaxed.

"Just out for an evening walk." He tucked his hands in his pockets, like Liam.

"And a sail, apparently." Liam nodded to the man's small sailboat, bobbing in the water at the end of the dock.

"True." Reed smiled. "Still playing security guard?"

"It has its benefits, like knowing who's up to what." Liam smiled back. "So, do Zoey and Scarlett know you're seeing their mother?"

Reed was silent for a while, and Liam could tell the man was about to deny having something going on with Kimberly, but then he shook his head and looked off toward the dock.

"No, Kimberly wants to tell them." He ran his hands through his hair. "It's just been a few dinners, a couple rounds of Frisbee golf, and the zip line." He smiled. "I never thought at my age I'd find the one."

"The one?" Liam asked.

"Sure." Reed chuckled. "I was a skeptic too." He walked over to the edge of the dock, and Liam followed. "Hell, I've been married and divorced. I have a son about your age." He glanced over at him. "Still, I've never felt the way I do around Kimberly."

"Does she know?" Liam didn't quite understand why he asked.

"You're smarter than your brothers," Reed joked and slapped him on the shoulder. "You remind me of your father."

Liam's eyebrows shot up. "You knew our dad?"

"In passing. We met when I purchased the place from him years ago." He nodded to the dark waters. "I remember the three of you boys running around the yard when I looked at it. It was one of the draws, seeing you three enjoying it. I thought my boy, Ben, would like the place."

"Did he?" he asked, leaning on the railing.

"A few summers. Until he decided to settle in school and live with his mother full time."

"Ouch," he said under his breath.

"Not his fault; I wasn't always the best dad." Reed glanced his way. "I was selfish back then. I thought I'd have all the time in the world to raise him, to mold him into the boy I wanted. I never thought about what he would want or what kind of role model I was to him. They don't make you take a course to become a father." He sighed. "Or how to be a good husband."

"Yeah." Liam stood back up and shifted. "Well, I'll let you get back home." He started to go.

"Liam," Reed called out to him. "Dylan's refused my services, but if you need help looking, just say the word."

"Thanks." He waved at him before he turned and continued down the pathway.

That night, he thought about his talk with Reed more than the kiss with Elle.

It was strange, but most of his memories of his father were good ones. Sure, they'd had fights between the four of them. Mostly with Owen and their father, but still, those memories had fallen to the side.

The times he remembered most were the family trips, them playing ball in the backyard, and the dinners they used to cook together.

Then, all of that stopped one day, and Liam had to admit that he didn't understand why. It had been shortly after he'd graduated high school, just before Joel had started working for their dad.

Joel wasn't a Costa, officially. Even though he could easily pass as one of the brothers, there was no blood between them, as far as any of them knew.

Joel claimed he'd been an orphan, raised by a nice couple from upstate New York. Their father had left for a trip and returned with a new factotum. Basically, Joel did everything and anything their dad needed. He often ran around fetching lunch or making travel arrangements, but after a few years, the three of them just started looking at Joel like part of the family, even if their father couldn't own up to it.

It was shortly after Liam's high school graduation that their father started acting off. His travels became longer, less planned. Even Joel didn't always know where he would end up.

When Liam finally did fall asleep, he dreamed of Elle and him swaying in a bed on top of the trees.

The next few days were busy ones—so busy, he hadn't even seen Elle. When he tried to connect with her at lunch, he was surprised when Zoey mentioned she'd gone off campus to pick up some supplies. He didn't see her at dinner that evening either.

It was as if she was avoiding everyone. He had even heard Zoey complain about not seeing Elle around.

When Dylan and Zoey drove away for their two days off together, he knew at that point that his brother was gone on Zoey. Just the way his brother looked at her told him that there was no turning back. He'd never seen Dylan act that way before.

Owen, on the other hand, had at one point had a girl he'd been crazy over, until she'd gone on vacation with some girlfriends and come back pregnant with someone else's baby. His brother had been a broken man ever since, never trusting women too much and never getting close enough to be burned again.

Liam hadn't even gotten close enough to a woman to make the big jump into the love realm. Sure, he'd had plenty of girlfriends and even once had thought about moving in with one of them. But, common sense sank in quickly when Shelly'd confessed to him one night while she'd been too drunk to care that she was still in love with her ex-boyfriend. He'd quickly moved on, and less than a year later, she'd married the guy.

He ran into Elle finally just after Zoey and Dylan had pulled out of the parking lot.

"Hiding?"

He stopped next to her and bumped shoulders with her, lightly. She glanced up at him as if she hadn't heard him approaching.

"No." She shook her head and hugged her notepad to her chest. "I've been super busy." She turned and started walking toward the doors.

"Too busy to eat?" He fell into step with her. "Like now, I bet you haven't had breakfast yet."

"I had an apple after class."

"An apple?" He frowned. "That's not breakfast, that's a midmorning snack." When she broke into a laugh, he took her arm and turned their direction toward the dining hall instead. "If you're not hungry, you can at least sit and watch me eat."

She sighed but followed him into the building. "I suppose I could have a bagel."

"Again, that's a snack, not a meal," he said, handing her a tray and taking one for himself. They walked through the buffet line. He piled up mounds of food, while she scooped onto her plate a small spoonful of egg whites, a bagel, and some fruit.

When they sat down at a small table, one that he picked for the purpose of being left alone, he nodded to her food. "At least it's more than an apple."

"Lunch is my big meal," she admitted before nibbling on the eggs.

"Every meal is mine. Where have you been hiding yourself?" he asked after a moment of silence.

"I told you . . . I've been . . ."

"Hiding," he finished for her, causing her eyes to narrow. "What I want to know is why?"

She finally relented. "I've had some . . . things to look into."

"Like?" he asked between bites.

"Just things." She shrugged, and he could tell she was hiding something from him. It wasn't something generic but something to do with him specifically.

"Does it have to do with my father?" He felt his stomach roll. When her eyes avoided his, he shoved his plate aside. "What?"

He'd come to the conclusion that Elle and his father would never have been lovers, as they had suspected. But just knowing that she had some information on his father that she wasn't comfortable telling him sent his stomach into flips.

"I did get a call from him. He left a message that he wanted to meet. I didn't get the message until late, by that time . . ." She shook her head. "He never showed."

"Okay," he said. "When was this?"

"Early spring," she admitted with a shrug. "March sometime."

"You haven't heard from him since?" he asked, his stomach settling some.

"No, but there is something else." When her blue eyes met his, he felt his heart skip a beat.

CHAPTER TWELVE

"Liam, your father is . . . my godfather," Elle finally admitted. "It wasn't a well-known fact. Only my grandfather and . . . well, your father knew about it."

"What?" He shook his head. "I . . . don't understand." His hands were resting on the table, but she watched them slowly curl into fists.

"Leo Costa and my mother were . . . had . . . a history together. Or so Joe said." Her eyes moved back to the table as tears started to burn them. "According to my grandfather, Leo was the man my mother should have married instead of . . . my father."

"Did your mother have an affair with my father?" His words came out almost as a whisper, but she felt them as if he'd slapped her across the face.

Is that what he'd thought all along? First he accused her of sleeping with his father; now he was accusing her mother? Is that why he'd gotten close to her? To use her as he believed his father had?

"There was something in one of the news articles . . ." he started.

"As you said, you shouldn't always believe everything in print." She jerked her words out as if they stung.

She stood up slowly and braced herself on the table. As her eyes met his, she knew she projected anger, but damn it, he'd just accused her and her mother of . . . of . . .

"No, Liam. Neither my mother nor I, to the best of my or my grandfather's knowledge, ever had an affair with your father." She turned to go, but he was there, holding her in place.

"I told you, I never thought . . ." He dropped his hands when she glared at them. Then he ran his hands through his hair and tugged on the long locks. "I know your father was and is a . . . killer. There's no excuse for what he did to your mother, but after finding out . . . there has to be a reason . . ." He groaned. "God, I'm fucking this up. Big time. Take a walk with me."

"I can't." She raised her chin. "I have work." She picked up her tablet, which she would have forgotten on the table, and turned to go.

"Elle." The tone in his voice stopped her. "Meet me somewhere for lunch. We need to finish this."

She dipped her chin slightly. "I can't. I have work."

"Then, meet me in your office. We need to be alone," he suggested.

"Fine. Noon," she said and then left.

She held it together until a breeze that was warm and filled with salt air hit her face. Glancing around, she realized she'd walked to the small beach area without noticing. Seeing that the beach wasn't deserted, she found the shade of a tree and sat down underneath it.

She pulled up her iPad and tried to focus on the numbers on the screen, but when everything turned wavy, she gave up and tucked her head to her knees and cried. Had her mother been in love with Leo Costa? Probably so at one time. She would have been far better off with any man other than her father. Maybe if she'd chosen Leo, would she still be alive today? But wouldn't that mean that she herself never would have been born? It would be a small price to pay, if she could turn back time.

Her mind turned to Jeff and how her friends had tried to warn her away from the domineering man. Did her mother have friends who had warned her about her father? Had anyone known that she'd been in trouble? Or had she been alone until the end?

Elle could only remember a few things from before her death. They were more like feelings than true memories. She remembered her mother reading her a book before bed or helping her with homework. One memory she had was of baking with her mother and enjoying the hot cookies once they were out of the oven. Still, her eyes stung every time she thought of her.

"Everything all right, sweetie?"

The voice shook her from her self-pity.

Glancing up, she smiled at Kimberly as she moved over and sat next to her. Zoey and Scarlett's mother was a beautiful woman inside and out. Her natural silver hair was something that most women, young and old, envied. Her skin had a warm tan glow to it, and when the woman smiled, her dark-hazel eyes almost glowed like her daughters'.

"Yes." She sniffled. "I'm just . . . wallowing in self-pity."

Kimberly chuckled and wrapped an arm around her shoulders. "Elle, I've known you for a very long time. I've never seen you wallow in self-pity before."

Elle relaxed into the embrace. Over the years she'd known Zoey and Scarlett, their mother had been nothing but kind to Elle and the other Wildflowers. On several occasions, Elle had visited the girls at their place in Jacksonville and had gotten very close to their mother in the process. It was one of the reasons Elle had agreed to (and had even suggested) moving Kimberly onto the campgrounds.

"I've never had any cause to before," she answered.

"What has you doing so now?" Kimberly asked, giving Elle's shoulder a squeeze. "A boy?"

Elle sighed. "Ugh, I'm that predictable?"

Kimberly chuckled. "Men will always push a strong woman to her knees. Whether it's by physical force or just a good old-fashioned mental breakdown."

Elle chuckled and wiped her eyes. "He thought I was sleeping with . . ." She couldn't even say it. The thought of someone accusing her of being with the man she'd always thought of as Uncle Leo hurt her beyond anything. Leo Costa had never been anything but kind to Elle. Whenever he'd visited her, before or after her mother's death, he'd showered her with small gifts. "Never mind."

"Someone else?" Kimberly suggested.

"Yes." She nodded, not liking the sour taste in her mouth the thought gave her.

"Men." Kimberly sighed and rested back against the tree.

Elle glanced over at her. "How are you liking living here?"

She knew she was changing the subject, but talking about something else could help get her mind off the hurt.

Kimberly glanced at her and nodded, as if she understood. "I love it here." She smiled and patted her knee. "Thank you so much for all that you've done for me and my girls."

Elle placed her hand over Kimberly's. "You deserve happiness."

"So do you," Kimberly said. "Men can be jerks—trust me, I was married to one of the biggest of them. But . . ." She smiled, and Elle noticed a light in the woman's eyes that she'd never seen before. "Some other men make up for it. You just need to be patient and find the right one."

"Have you?" Elle asked, turning slightly toward the older woman.

Kimberly laughed. "Time will tell." She stood up and dusted off her shorts. "Which reminds me: I'm going to be late for my next meeting." She winked. "Don't be too quick to judge Liam. His brothers can put their feet in their mouths sometimes, but if you give them a chance, they'll pull it out sooner or later."

She winked again and then disappeared down the pathway.

After that, Elle picked up her stuff and made her way back to her office. It wasn't as beautiful a spot to get some work done as the beach was, but she found it easier to focus on the numbers on her screen.

Just before noon, she was still sitting at her computer when her accounting program crashed, which then left her on hold with the company for more than an hour.

After balancing her budget and shooting off several payments, she smiled at the positive number left over. She had enough extra that the next cabin could move into the framing phase. She picked up her phone and sent a text to Aiden and told him to order the materials.

When Hannah walked in a few minutes later, Elle held up her hand for a high five.

"What's that for?" Hannah asked after slapping it.

"We just ordered, and could pay for, the material to frame the next cabin."

"Seriously?" Hannah did a little booty dance.

"I'll join in that." She stood and shook herself. She was stiff and realized she must have been sitting at the desk for more than an hour without moving.

"At this rate, we're going to run out of names for cabins soon," Hannah joked and sat down in the chair across from her desk.

Elle sat back down. "Not if we keep having animal interventions."

Hannah sighed. "We got lucky with that one. Someone could have been seriously hurt."

"Yes, we did."

"Which is kind of why I'm here to talk to you."

Elle shifted and closed her computer screen. "Okay, what?"

"I was thinking. I know that with Dylan and Zoey being . . . close . . . well, our living arrangements aren't necessarily accommodating for them."

Elle thought about it. "When we moved in together, men weren't on the radar."

"No, they weren't," Hannah agreed.

"We could always . . ." she started but then stopped. "We don't have any extra rooms on the second floor open, do we?"

"No," Hannah said. "We don't. As it is, people are doubled up already."

"We planned on building a larger place for worker housing eventually." She sank back in her chair. "I don't foresee us setting that kind of money aside for at least another year."

"Yeah," Hannah sighed. "So, what do we do?"

"Let me think about it." She stood up. "I need to go chat with Isaac. When I come back, I'll see about moving something around." She bit her lip. "What? I don't know."

"I didn't mean to lay a heavier burden on you. I know you have a lot on your plate just managing the place." Hannah stood up to go but stopped. "Have you found out anything more on the Costas?"

"No, other than . . ." She thought about the messy web and remembered Liam's words and how they stung. She didn't want her friends to know what the brothers had thought about her or her mother. If they found out that the brothers had assumed that she had been their father's mistress, it could jeopardize the happiness that Zoey and Dylan had together. "No," she finished.

"Let me know when you do. Owen is . . . determined." Hannah sighed.

"Has he made any more moves on you?" Elle asked.

"Tons." Hannah chuckled. "But I can handle myself. Besides, when I stop liking the moves, I'll let him know."

Elle chuckled. "Does he know that you know who he is?"

Hannah shrugged. "I'm sure the brothers talk like we do. But he hasn't said anything so far."

"Has he asked you any strange questions?" Elle remembered that Liam had said he hadn't believed she was his father's mistress. Did that mean that his brothers did?

"Not outright, but he does ask a lot of questions about how we got Isaac on board and how I have connections."

"Have you told him anything?" she asked. Not even she knew how Hannah had been able to pull that off.

"No. He has his . . . talents." She wiggled her eyebrows at her. "And I'll keep my secrets."

Elle chuckled. "They are good at their talents."

"Tell me about it," Hannah said as she opened the door.

Elle was surprised to see Ryan standing just outside her office door. She noticed that Hannah instantly went on guard and reached for her phone. "Can I help you?"

"Yes." Ryan's eyes moved over to Hannah, then back to Elle. "I was hoping to have a little chat with you, in private."

"I'm sorry, Ryan, but your employment has already been terminated."

"I feel that if you heard the facts and not the lies that were spread about me—" Ryan started.

"I've reviewed what several witnesses said happened, and I stand by Zoey's decision." Elle moved toward the door and held it open for the woman to walk through.

Yet Ryan grabbed her arm and tugged.

"Hey!" Hannah stepped in front of Elle. "I'd back off if I were you."

Elle almost laughed at her friend. Here she was, five nine to Hannah's five six. Elle probably had ten pounds on Hannah as well. But still Hannah jumped in to protect her.

"Thanks." She placed her hands on Hannah's shoulders, feeling her friend vibrate with anger. Elle turned to Ryan. "I think it's best for all of us if you leave. We've already filled your position. You'll have better luck looking for a job elsewhere."

"You think I care about a job in this dump?" Ryan's voice rose slightly. "That's a joke." She chuckled, and both Hannah and Elle saw her for what she was. A troublemaker. "I thought I'd share some information I have on those three brothers you hired. Do you know, really know, who you've hired on?"

"Yes," Elle said, holding her ground. "We know everything there is to know about—"

"The Costas?" Ryan interjected.

By the fire in her eyes, Elle could tell that Ryan was expecting them to be shocked. When they weren't, her eyes narrowed.

"You know who the Costas are? What kind of power, and how much money, they have?"

"Yes," Elle said again in the same tone.

Ryan glanced around as if she was expecting an audience. "What are they doing working here? They have enough money to buy this place ten times over. Why would they need to work here?"

"I'm sure they have their reasons," Elle said. She'd asked herself the same question a dozen times since finding out who they were. But, with her past experience, she knew looks could be deceiving. If the brothers were here, they had their reasons, and Ryan had nothing to do with any of it.

Elle was done with playing her games. "If you need help finding the door?"

"You knew?" Ryan's voice rose to a high-pitched squeal. "You *knew*. This was your plan all along?" She pointed at Elle's chest. "They'll find out about you."

Ryan drew closer—so close Elle could see the red lines in her eyes—but then was suddenly jerked away. The woman instantly started fighting off whoever held her, until she glanced around and realized it was Liam. Then she laughed.

"You fell right into her trap," Ryan yelled as Liam frog-marched her toward the front door. "She planned this, everything. It's a trap."

"What the hell was that about?" Hannah asked, wrapping her arms around Elle.

"I have no freaking clue." Elle felt herself shiver. "That woman scares me."

"Ditto," Hannah said. "I need a drink. Secret stash time."

Elle agreed and opened the cabinet door in her office.

When Liam and Aiden walked in a few minutes later, Hannah and Elle each had a glass of white wine.

"Are you two okay?" Aiden asked, worry filling his eyes. "When Julie called us, she sounded shaken."

"Yes." Hannah waved him off. "Elle handled her like a pro."

"Did she find her way off the premises?" Elle asked, avoiding Liam's eyes.

"Yes, I've informed the staff to keep an eye out for her and let us know immediately if she shows up again," Aiden said. "I think at this point, however, it would be a good idea to let the local police know what's happened."

Elle made a note on her calendar to call Brett Jewel at the local PD and file a police report on Ryan. She had her notes from the witnesses when Ryan had attacked Dylan and Zoey earlier, and she'd make sure to copy them and send them to Brett as well.

"Well, as long as you two are okay . . ." Aiden said and turned to go.

"Head on up there; I need a minute alone with Elle," Liam said, holding the office door wide. His eyes moved to Hannah.

"Oh." She jumped up and set her glass down, but not before swallowing the rest of the wine. "That's my cue. See ya." She disappeared quickly out the door with Aiden.

"Deserter," Elle said under her breath and swallowed the rest of her wine as Liam shut them in her office alone.

CHAPTER THIRTEEN

Liam took a couple of deep breaths before he spoke.

"Are you sure you're okay?" he asked, not moving away from the door.

Instead of answering, Elle just nodded.

He waited a few more beats before he moved closer. "Want to fill me in on what she meant when she said we'd find out about you?"

Elle surprised him by laughing. "I'd love to know it myself. I'm beginning to think the woman is off." Elle stood quickly, and he noticed her reach for the back of her chair to steady herself.

"Drinking during business hours?" He walked over and tapped her glass.

"Sometimes it's necessary. I suppose I should have had more of a breakfast." Her smile fell away as her chin rose.

"What did she mean?" He was a breath away from her, his hazel eyes searching hers.

"I don't know," she said between clenched teeth.

"What trap? What did she mean by 'you planned this all along'?" He knew he was pushing her, but the possibility that Ryan knew something that they didn't stirred in his mind. Was this a trap? Had she called his father out there for a meeting to bait him and his brothers? As his mind instantly answered with a quick no, the seed of doubt Ryan had planted started to take root.

"Get out," Elle said, moving to get around him. But he blocked her. She surprised him by pushing on his chest. He didn't budge.

"Elle, this isn't a game," he said.

"Do you see me laughing?" She pushed again. "You're in my way." He could hear the frustration in her voice.

"I'm not moving until we have that talk," he said, crossing his arms over his chest.

"Fine," she said and quickly sat down, then motioned to the chair across the room. "Sit. Let's have that talk."

He knew it was her way of controlling the situation, putting space between them, but he figured he could give in to her small demands. He moved around the desk, sat on the chair, and smiled over at her.

"When was the last time you spoke with or saw my father?" he asked.

She glanced down at her computer screen and clicked a few times.

"Tuesday, May tenth," she answered as if she'd been setting a date for the dentist.

"This year?" he asked.

"No."

"Last year?" He frowned.

"Yes."

"Where?"

"Here, it was shortly after"—she took a breath—"after my grandfather's death."

He thought about it and nodded. His father had still been in town and still acting somewhat normal. "Have you spoken to him since?"

"No." She frowned. "I did get a message, as I told you earlier, but by the time I returned and got it, it was too late to return his call.

Then, well, the next day he never responded. And I never heard from him again."

"Did you try calling him again?" he asked, trying to place the timeline.

"No, I was busy," she answered, crossing her arms over her chest.

"What did Ryan mean by 'it's a trap'?" he asked.

Elle chuckled. "If you figure that one out, let me in on the secret." She stood up. "Now, if we're done . . ."

He stood as well and placed his hands on her desk. "I didn't mean to hurt your feelings." His eyes locked with hers. "If roles were reversed and it was your grandfather missing, wouldn't you do everything you could to find out more?"

His words seemed to rock her, and she closed her eyes. "Yes," she finally said. "I would." She met his gaze.

"If you think of anything else . . ." he started.

"All I have is the number he left for me to call him back at," she said.

"You mean his cell number?" he asked.

"No." She shook her head. "It was a different number, a Canadian area code."

"Canada?" He frowned. "Do you have it?"

She nodded, then pulled up her computer screen again and wrote it down on a piece of paper and handed it to him.

"Liam, I really do hope you find him. Uncle Leo has always been nice to me."

"Uncle?" he asked, taking the paper from her hands and letting his fingers brush against hers.

She nodded slowly. "He . . . asked me to call him that a long time ago. I've always thought of him as such." He could see the sadness in her eyes, and for the first time, he realized it was the love of family that he saw there. Not the love of a mistress, as his brothers and he had once believed.

"Elle." He took her hand in his, but just then, there was a knock on the door.

"Come in." Elle pulled her hand away as Aubrey and Scarlett walked in.

"We heard . . ." Aubrey started, but she stopped when she noticed Liam standing there.

"I was just leaving," he said, tucking the paper into his pocket. "Still on for lunch?"

"I have some catching up to do now," Elle answered, sitting back down behind her desk and avoiding his eyes. He wasn't about to argue with her in front of her friends, so he turned away.

"Make sure she eats something," he said to Aubrey, then left.

Since he'd been helping Aiden out with another project when he had gotten the call from Julie, he knew he had to meet the guy back at the woodshop and finish their discussion. Aiden had been talking to him about building some bench swings with the wood from the trees they had cleared.

He'd been pretty excited about the idea. He enjoyed seeing something beautiful and useful come from his time.

As he walked back to the shop, he thought about how to turn Elle back around. He knew she was upset with him. He should have kept his mouth shut about what he and his brothers had assumed before he'd gotten to know her. There was, in his mind, no doubt that Elle and his father had never been anything other than family to one another. He knew that, even now, Owen still believed that Elle and their father were more than that.

It was strange to hear Elle talk about his father and her mother. He itched to ask his father questions about his past that he'd never asked before. Why hadn't he? He supposed it was because he'd been just as selfish as his old man.

He knew the one thing he could do now was to clear Elle's name in the eyes of his brothers, and he'd start with Owen after his meeting with Aiden.

Liam knew that Dylan had lost part of himself in Zoey. The man was in love, and it showed clearly on his face. Especially after the bear incident. Which meant Dylan was probably in agreement with Liam that the girls had had nothing to do with their father's disappearance or the missing money. Owen, however, probably still needed some persuading.

When he made it back to the woodshop, he found Aiden talking with a couple of guests who were waiting for him outside the shop area.

Several people still had projects they were working on. One woman, Denise, was making her husband a vase like the ones he had done himself. She was pretty good at the lathe and didn't need a lot of his instruction. A few of the others ate up a lot of his time, though. Seeing the crowd standing in front of the closed shop made him realize he might not get to his brother before dinner.

"Sorry," he said as he unlocked the shop. "Aiden, how about we meet later today to finish talking?"

"Sure." Aiden stepped aside as two new people walked into the shop. "I can see you're busy."

"We heard you could help us make these cute little bowls?" one of the women asked him; the other held up a small decorative bowl he'd carved one day when he'd been bored.

"Yes." He turned to them, and for the next two hours, people came and went in the woodshop. He was beginning to really enjoy his job. When he had time to work on his own projects, he lost himself completely in working with the wood and let everything else drift away.

He took some time to draw up the plans for the swing idea he and Aiden had briefly talked about. Then he snapped a picture and shot it off to the man in a text message.

He sent a text to his brother as well and asked to see if he could meet him for a quick dinner somewhere. They decided to meet on the beach. He would have just enough time to swing by the cafeteria and grab a bagged sandwich and make his way there. When he stepped onto the soft sand, Owen was already sitting under a tree eating.

"Hey." He sat next to Owen and took a drink of the water bottle he'd grabbed.

"How's it going?" Owen asked, finishing off his own sandwich.

"Busy." He pulled out his food and dug in. With all the excitement, he hadn't really had time to eat lunch and was starving.

"Have you gotten into Elle's phone yet?" Owen asked.

"About that." He turned to him and filled his brother in quickly on what he and Elle had talked about.

"Dad's Elle's godfather?" Owen shook his head. "Why didn't he ever tell us?" His brother looked as shaken by the news as Liam had felt when he'd heard it.

"I guess we never asked." He shrugged and tucked his trash into the paper bag. He was still hungry and figured he'd swing by the cafeteria once more for some dessert before making his way over to the pool bar to help out for the evening rush.

The sun was going down, and he knew another band was playing that evening, which meant he'd be busy.

"This changes things," Owen finally admitted.

"Yeah." He nodded. "She said he left this number for her to call him back." He pulled out the paper with the number on it. He'd had a moment to try calling it and had reached a hotel in Charlottetown, on Prince Edward Island. As far as Liam knew, his father had never visited the place before.

"I'll call—"

"I already did. It's the Holman Grand Hotel on Prince Edward Island."

"Canada?" Owen balked. "Dad hates Canada."

"Well," Liam sighed. "That's more information than I knew about him." He stood up and shook his shorts off. "I'm needed at the bar."

"When Dylan gets back, we need to discuss our plan. If what you said is true, I don't think we need to stick around much longer."

Liam's heart skipped a beat. He hadn't thought about leaving, though of course they'd have to.

He was thankful Owen was too busy dusting off his own shorts to see the flicker of disappointment on his face.

"I'm trying to convince Elle to spend her time off with me again, maybe get more information from her."

"Sounds like you got all we needed." Owen ran his hands through his hair. "It's been a total bust with Hannah and the others." He glanced around as the sky turned a brighter shade of orange, pink, and purple with the sunset. There were dark clouds in the distance, but they didn't hinder the bright sky. "They've got a great place here, but I doubt Dad's money had anything to do with it. From the new rumors I'm hearing, it sounds like this place is one hundred percent paying for itself already. After the five friends' initial investment . . ." His brother trailed off. "It was a smart one."

"You would know better than I." Liam felt himself being drawn deeper into the hole of depression. "I've got to go."

"I'll text Dylan," Owen called after him.

Liam couldn't shake his shitty mood the rest of the night. He didn't want to leave River Camp. He didn't want to leave Elle. Not when he still had feelings that he hadn't explored with her yet.

To top his evening off, rain started halfway through the band's set, and he had to scramble to help them save their equipment.

As he was rushing around, he quickly thought of adding decking or a covered pergola above the stage area, which would protect the equipment from adverse weather. His mind had completely designed it all out before the realization set in that he and his brothers would probably leave long before he could build it. Would Owen urge him to leave the camp when he took off? What about Dylan? Would he have the right to stick around after they'd found their father? Would Elle want him to stay, or, for that matter, to even come back if he did leave?

Sinking into the sadness again, he helped Britt shut up shop, since everyone had dashed back to their cabins. It appeared the rain was going to continue for the rest of the evening, and as he walked back to the main building, the wind kicked up, spitting the water into his face and making his mood even darker.

When lightning filled the sky, he glanced up and saw movement in the trees and realized he was standing directly under Elle's tree house.

He reached around for the rope and tugged the ladder down.

He didn't bother knocking, since he could see light under the door.

As he stepped into the small room, Elle turned away from the window. Her hair was wet and pushed away from her face. The thin material of her soaked blouse clung to her body like a second skin. Her face was cleaned of makeup, and when she saw him, he watched her take that full bottom lip of hers between her teeth.

His mood changed quickly, like someone had flipped a switch. Without a word, he crossed the small space and took her into his arms, his mouth covering hers as his desire for her, for the future he wanted, poured out of him and into her.

Her body melted against his. He felt her tremble with want, or was that his own body vibrating?

He moved quickly, too quickly, as his hands pushed the soaked material off her skin, exposing the softness as he devoured her.

Her own nails scraped his skin as she yanked, then ripped, his shirt off his shoulders. He laughed until she pulled his shorts away. Then it was all speed as wet clothes fell discarded to the wood flooring.

When they hit the dry sheets on the bed, laughter burst deep from his chest.

"This, I needed . . ." he said between kisses down her neck. "You," he finished as he peeled off the last layer of silk that covered her. She arched into his touch and moaned when he found her soft folds.

When he dipped his head lower and covered her breast with his mouth, she cried out and yanked on his hair.

"This time," she warned, her eyes locking with his, "don't stop."

"No," he agreed with a smile. "Tonight, you're mine." Her answering smile made him move slower, more purposefully.

As his skin slid over hers, his fingers moving to please her, to get the soft sounds of pleasure from her, he thought about making the night last forever.

When he slowed his movements, she made noises of disappointment, causing him to chuckle softly.

"I want to enjoy this. I've waited long enough."

"Liam"—she gripped his shoulders—"we can enjoy it later."

He laughed. "We can have both. Speed and pleasure." He continued to kiss her as she arched into his hands.

She wrapped her legs around his hips, trying to hold him to her, but he moved down and trailed kisses over her, causing bumps to rise on her perfect skin.

He reached for a condom, only to have her take it and slip it slowly onto him. He would have given her anything at that moment, would have promised her the world.

"Liam." His name on her lips was the sweetest thing he'd ever tasted. "Please."

She gripped his hips, and when he slid into her, he realized, just like his brother, he'd lost part of himself at River Camp.

CHAPTER FOURTEEN

Elle was floating. She'd never felt like this before. Never. Not with Jeff and not with Corey, her first high school boyfriend/first lover. No man had ever made her body shake this much before or after sex.

She knew it had nothing really to do with the physical things he'd done to her. It was the heat in his eyes as he looked at her, as he touched her.

Her body had cooled already, even with his body still covering her. She tried to reach down and pull the blankets over them but couldn't tug them free.

"Here." He rolled, taking her with him and shifting the blankets over their bodies. "Better?"

"Mmm." She snuggled against his warm chest. "I didn't realize how chilly it got up here."

"This place needs some good insulation," he mumbled; then she felt his stomach growl. "You don't happen to have any food in that fridge, do you?"

She leaned up and looked down at him. He was eyeing the fridge as if willing it to float over to him, which caused her to smile.

"Work up an appetite?" she asked, resting her chin on her fist atop his chest.

"Starved." His hand was running over her backside under the blankets, warming her further.

"There might be some leftover chicken salad in there from yesterday's lunch break. Sometimes I need a quiet place to work." She shrugged. "I can get it if you want."

His arms tightened around her. "In a while. For now, this is nice." He pulled her down until she placed her lips over his. "Really nice."

She felt him grow hard again next to her hip and smiled. "I hope you brought more than one condom." She slid over him and heard him groan with appreciation.

"Of course I did." He flipped them quickly until he was looking down at her. His hair fell in his eyes, and she reached up and pushed it out of his face. "I need a haircut."

"I like it," she said as he leaned in and started running his lips over her collarbone, causing her nipples to peak. Her fingers closed around his hair as she wrapped her legs around his.

Reaching down, she took him in her hand and felt him stiffen even further.

"I think I owe you," she said into his chest.

"Hmm." He had stilled above her, allowing her to explore him more fully.

"From before," she clarified, watching his face change as enjoyment overtook him. She smiled when he closed his eyes and leaned his head back. It took only a little nudge to have him rolling so that she could settle on top of him. Her eyes ran over him, all of him, for what seemed like the first time.

His tattoo and his chest had been the only thing she'd really paid attention to before. Now, however, she scanned all of him and appreciated every inch.

With her eyes locked on his, she leaned forward and placed her lips over his flat nipples. When her tongue darted out and licked the same spot, she felt him jerk underneath her and smiled.

"Witch," he groaned as his hands moved to her hair.

"I thought I was a princess?" she teased, and she moved her mouth lower, enjoying the play of each muscle as she ran her mouth over them slowly, following a light dusting of dark hair downward.

When she reached his hardness, she gripped him softly and felt him jerk once more. His hands tangled in her hair as she closed her mouth over him. Using her tongue as he had used it on her, she enjoyed the taste and feel of him until she heard him growl and grip her elbows to hoist her up so she was sitting on his chest.

"You've done it," he said, his voice sounding strained as he twisted and had her once more underneath him.

She didn't know when he'd gotten the other condom, but she watched him put it on himself quickly before putting his hands on her inner thighs and settling himself between them.

She smiled as he slipped into her again, feeling him stretch her inner muscles as he settled fully into her.

She arched and moved with him, enjoying the soft kisses he gave her, marveling in the smell and feel of him surrounding her, consuming her.

His eyes locked with hers as she felt herself sinking deeper; her nails scraped his back, holding him where she wanted, where she needed him.

When she felt her body convulse around him, she heard his shout of triumph and knew she wanted to feel this way over and over as much as she could. Possibly even for the rest of her life.

This time, by the time her body had cooled, Liam was across the room digging into the fridge. Still stark naked.

"Want anything? There's more than the chicken salad in here," he asked, glancing over his shoulder at her.

She peeled her eyes from his tight ass and said, "Just water."

"There's brownies, beer, and are these cookies?" he exclaimed. He dug his head farther into the fridge, causing her to laugh. He cracked open a beer.

"You're like a kid in a candy store." She flung her arms wide on the bed. Hell, she felt like a schoolgirl after kissing her first love interest. Thinking back on it, she realized *this* was the better moment in her life.

Rolling over, she tucked the sheet around her and glanced at the windows. It was too dark to see, but she could tell the rain was still falling down, since the windows were dripping rain on the outside.

"I think we're going to be stuck here all night," she said absently.

"Stuck?" He frowned at her, then shoved a full cookie in his mouth.

"Well, not *stuck*, stuck." She shifted and felt like that schoolgirl again. Awkward and unsure what to say next. He handed her a bottled water, and she drank from it, then set it on the table next to the bed.

He moved over and sat next to her, then dipped a cookie in what she assumed was the chicken salad and shoved it into his mouth.

"Gross." She shivered.

"Don't knock it until you try it," he said, then took a sip of his beer.

"I'll pass," she said when he held up a cookie for her.

"Are you sure?" He smiled. "You'll need your energy, since you're . . . stuck with me here, all night." He wiggled his eyebrows, and she laughed and took the cookie from him.

"I had a talk with Owen," he said. He shifted to get fully on the bed and leaned against the headboard. She moved next to him and tucked the blankets around them both.

"What about?" she asked. She finished off the cookie and reached for another. She'd forgotten Isaac had given her a bag of them with her lunch yesterday and was thankful.

"You," he answered. "I told him what you said about our dad. How you two know each other."

She nodded and reached for her water. "What did he say?"

Liam was silent for a while, and when she glanced over at him, he was frowning.

"He said we'll probably leave when Dylan and Zoey return."

She stilled. Liam was leaving? Her throat dried.

Is that why he'd been with her tonight? She didn't know what had drawn her to the tree house, or that he'd even show up. But the moment he'd stepped in the door, lightning had flashed behind him, and she'd seen his eyes and known that he was the one she wanted more than anyone else.

"Elle?" His voice brought her back to the moment.

"What did you say?" she asked, taking another sip of her water, then setting it aside since it hadn't helped.

"I didn't say anything." He shifted, set the empty plate down, and finished off his beer.

"When will you leave?" she asked, trying to hide her disappointment.

He pulled her close and kissed the top of her head. "Not tonight. Let's worry about it later." He pulled her down and tucked the blankets around them. "Even if I do leave, I live less than half an hour from here. If you want, I could always come back." His tone told her that he was unsure in some way.

Maybe he was waiting for her to ask him to stay?

"You do?" she asked, feeling better instantly.

"Yeah." He yawned. "Besides, I promised Aiden I'd finish those benches, so I can't leave right away." He tucked her tighter into his chest, and she closed her eyes to the sound of his soft breathing.

When she woke, it was to soft kisses being rained down all over her breasts and neck.

"Liam." She sighed and held on to his hair, enjoying the softness of it on her skin.

"Elle!"

The voice sounded wrong. She peeled open her eyes and looked over at Jeff, hovering above her. "Who the hell is Liam?" His fist rose, and she screamed just as it connected with her cheek.

"Hey." Liam shook her slightly. "It's me."

"Liam?" she cried and held on to him. The spot on her cheek where Jeff's fist had connected in the dream still stung.

"I'm here, baby," he said into her hair.

"It was a dream," she said, more for her own benefit.

"A doozy, by the sound of it." He shifted slightly, and she held on tighter, thinking he was getting up. "I'm just turning on a light." He flipped on the small light, and she realized it was still dark out as the light filled the small space.

"I'm sorry, I didn't mean to wake you." She shifted. She wiped the tears from her face, checked her cheek, and felt that it was unbruised.

"Want to talk about it?" He held out her water bottle for her. She took a sip and then closed her eyes on a deep breath.

"Jeff."

"Your ex?" he broke in. She nodded.

"He . . . had a temper."

"I knew there was a reason I wanted to kill the SOB," Liam said between clenched teeth.

"He didn't hit me often."

"Once is too many times." Liam took her water bottle from her and set it back down. He pulled her back into his arms. "I've never raised a finger to a woman, and I never will." He kissed the top of her head again.

"I know." She sighed and relaxed into his embrace.

"What happened?" he asked after a moment.

She shook her head. "It was just a dream."

"No, I mean, what caused you to finally leave him?"

"Joe got sick." She remembered the phone call. "He'd gotten a bad report from the doctor. He tried to play it off as if it was just a small thing, but I could tell." She closed her eyes as more tears formed behind them. "I lost him five months later. I kick myself all the time for not coming home sooner. The last time Jeff hit me, he had warned me not to come back here, that it was probably just a trick of Joe's to get me away from him."

"Have you heard from him since?" he asked.

"No," she sighed and ran her fingers over his chest, feeling the stirring of desire for him spread through her once again. She sat up and straddled him, her hips pressing against him as her arms wrapped around his shoulders. "Enough *then*. I want to focus on the now."

"I can do that." He smiled up at her.

She'd never made love until the sun came up, not until now. She'd never thought it was possible with anyone. Liam made everything new again.

Even as they showered together, she laughed and cried out his name. He lathered her up with soap and used his hands on her until her knees grew weak; then he leaned her against the shower wall and pleased her until she felt like she could slip into a sex-induced coma for the rest of the year.

A little over an hour after sunrise, she walked into the gym and started getting ready to teach Zoey's yoga class. She felt limber and sore at the same time and enjoyed getting her body a little more centered before starting her day.

"You're glowing," Hannah said at their breakfast meeting later.

"I am?" She sipped her coffee to hide her smile. "Must be the yoga class."

"Whatever it is, you should do it more often," Aubrey suggested.

"So, I was thinking," Hannah said, "about Zoey and Dylan. We all know they've been banging."

Elle choked on her coffee and had to focus on not having the hot liquid fly out her nostrils.

"What's your point?" she asked when she had recovered.

"Well, I don't think Scar wants to join in the fun." This time coffee did come out of Elle's nose, causing her eyes to burn.

"Jesus." Elle coughed to clear her sinuses.

"Sorry." Hannah chuckled. "Warning: I'm not done, so maybe hold off on the coffee."

"Thanks for the warning." She set the mug down and picked up her napkin to wipe her eyes.

"Anyway, I'm sure Dylan's brothers feel the same." She tilted her head. "Well, maybe. But I'm not willing to let Zoey have all three brothers."

Elle was thankful she'd had the warning and had kept her coffee in the cup for that statement.

"Your point?" Aubrey asked.

"I was thinking, so far, we've only had one booking on the schedule for Bear-Foot Bungalow. Why not let them have it, at least for a while?"

Scar jumped in. "That's a great idea."

She'd been thinking about their predicament since talking to Hannah about it earlier. Not once had she thought about the new cabin, though. It was a great idea.

"We can move the booking to another cabin. I checked with Julie before I came in here; she's tentatively moved it," Hannah told Scar, then turned to her. "What do you think?"

"I think it's a great idea." She should have thought of it herself.

"I think he's the one," Scar added.

"I second that," Aubrey said.

"Ditto," Hannah said with a smile.

"Jesus," she said again. "You mean, the one, the one? As in . . ." They all looked around the table.

Hadn't she been thinking the same thing about Liam earlier that morning? Hell, what did it mean when two of the Wildflowers fell for brothers? Then she remembered the way Zoey looked at Dylan and nodded. "Agreed. I'll get it from its hiding spot." She smiled, remembering the small ring they had all purchased together that first summer.

"Do you think it's still there?" Aubrey asked.

"I'll find out soon enough." She added the hunt to her mental list.

"You have a lot on your plate. Every day, actually. It's been a stress on you, running this place—a stress on all of us," Hannah said.

Scar reached for her cup of coffee and added, "Hey, speak for yourself—I'm having a blast."

"Having two days off every now and then really helps, but I was thinking about a longer-term schedule for us," Aubrey said. "Like a real vacation-type thing."

"Who needs a vacation when we live in paradise?" Elle smiled. "Besides, what would I do on a vacation without you guys?"

"Aww," the three of them said at the same time.

"Get laid," Aubrey added after.

Hannah chuckled. "We could all use getting laid."

"Ladies." Owen walked up to the table and set a large plate of food down next to Hannah, who was turning a bright shade of pink. "Morning," he said as if he hadn't just heard Hannah's last comment, which Elle was positive he had.

"Morning," Elle replied, trying not to give into the silent giggles consuming Scar and Aubrey. She glanced around to see if Liam was nearby.

"He's helping Aiden with something," Owen said to her. "But he'll be along shortly."

"Um, who will?" She picked up her cup and tried to act like Owen hadn't been talking to her, but the entire table.

"Liam. What were the four of you talking about?" He started eating, since the table had grown quiet.

Scar answered, "Your brother and our sister."

"Oh?" Owen shifted to look across the table at her.

"Yes, we think they should have their own cabin," Aubrey said, her chin raised as if ready to be challenged.

"Cool," Owen said between bites.

"That's it?" Hannah asked.

"What did you expect?" He chuckled. "Dylan is his own man. He's been on his own since he was eighteen. He may be my little brother, but I'm not his keeper."

"Then it's settled." Aubrey slapped her palm on the table.

"I'll go make sure Julie changes the schedule." Scar jumped up from the table and cleared her tray just as Liam arrived and took her spot next to Elle.

"Morning." He smiled at everyone. "What's everyone so happy about?"

CHAPTER FIFTEEN

He listened over breakfast as the ladies came up with a plan to tell Dylan and Zoey about the cabin that afternoon, together.

Then Elle surprised him by asking him to go on a hike through the woods. She claimed she was retrieving something of importance but wouldn't tell him what. As they made their way off the trails, he realized that he hadn't been to that part of the woods before. Most of what they were walking through was swampland, and he had just stuck to the clearings and dry land, thinking his father would be in one of the cabins, not out in the middle of the wetlands. The rains last night had left almost an inch of standing water in most places around them.

"Now I know why you brought me along," he said as his shoes sank into the mud. "Just in case you get stuck out here, you didn't want to die alone."

"Ha, ha." She rolled her eyes at him. "I need you to hoist me up." She stopped at the base of a giant magnolia tree.

"It must be two hundred years old." He looked up with an admiring glance at the massive tree.

"Close." She waved him over. "I'll need you to help me up to that branch." She motioned to a limb almost ten feet up.

"No way." He shook his head "You're not going up there."

"I've done it before." She put her hands on her hips.

"When?" he asked, not believing her.

"When I was eleven. I stood on Zoey's shoulders, since we were the tallest, so I could put what I needed up there. There's a small hole, from a dead limb . . ." She craned her neck. "There, I can still see it. Come on."

"Why in hell would you put anything in a hole in a tree?" he asked, moving over to her, since she was trying to jump up and grab the bottom limb herself. He figured if he didn't help her, she'd find another way to scurry up the thick trunk.

He placed his hands on her waist and lifted her easily enough. She surprised him by putting her foot on his knee, then climbing his body like a spider monkey until her feet stood on his shoulders. He held still as she moved above him, holding on to her ankles to steady her. When her feet suddenly disappeared from his shoulders, he jerked around, expecting to catch her falling body. Instead, he looked up and witnessed her expertly hanging from a thick limb as if she was a gymnast. He watched her swing several times back and forth until she lay across the limb, then rotate her body until she sat on it.

"Good job, princess. Just one question. How do you expect to get down from there?" He stepped back with a grin.

She frowned and looked around. "You can catch me." To his horror, she started climbing the tree.

When she disappeared through the thick green leaves, he called out to her.

"How high did you need to go?"

"I've got it," she called out. "I'm coming down."

"Go slow." His heart stilled until he could see her making her way back carefully to the lowest branch.

She sat once again on the limb, her feet swinging, and flipped around until she was hanging from the branch again.

"I'm going to drop like a cheerleader would. Open your arms wide, and I should fall right into them."

"Got it." He stood under her and held his arms out, and she dropped easily into them.

When she was there in his arms, smiling up at him, he laid a soft kiss on her nose.

"Ballet, gymnastics, tree climbing, and a princess." He chuckled. "Is there anything you can't do?"

"You do not want to hear me sing." She laughed, then tugged free a small ring box and held it out.

"This is what you risked your life for?" he asked as she opened the box.

A small unicorn ring sat inside. Its bright silver shone in the light, and its multicolored mane wrapped around its body.

"We all bought this together. That first year," she murmured. "We fought over it and decided to hide it here." She glanced up at him. "Whichever one of us was lucky enough to fall in love—real love—first won the ring."

His heart skipped as he looked into her blue eyes, and for a heartbeat, he wondered what life would be like with Elle. *Perfect* was the word that instantly popped into his mind.

"It's for Zoey," Elle said and smiled up at him, and he swallowed hard. "We took a vote. We'll give it to her tonight."

He remained silent as they trudged back through the swamp to the main part of the camp. His mind raced with the possibilities of a future with Elle and, worse, a future without her.

Zoey and Dylan returned to camp shortly after they returned from their hike. Liam made his way to the workshop and started on the swings. He tried to keep his mind and body busy so he wouldn't be focused on Elle.

His phone buzzed less than an hour later.

"Yo," he answered on the second ring.

"Dylan's been shot," Owen almost screamed.

"What?" He nearly dropped the phone in shock.

"Well, not shot. Attacked somehow. I don't know what the hell is going on, but I'm almost there to pick you up. I guess they're up at the main building already. Hell, I don't know what happened, only that someone tried to kill him."

The golf cart stopped just outside the shop; he heard Owen honk the horn.

Liam didn't even lock up the building; instead he rushed outside and jumped on the cart. Owen took off for the main building, the tires on the cart spitting up gravel and dirt as they went.

"Why are we always the last to find out this shit?" Owen grumbled as he drove as fast as the golf cart would go.

"Shit," Liam responded. "Do you think it was Ryan?"

"Hell," Owen said after a moment, and Liam could see that his brother hadn't thought of it. "Shit."

"Yeah." This time his heartbeat was going as fast as the golf cart's wheels.

The cart came to a skidding stop at the front door of the main building, and they both jumped out.

When they rushed in the front doors, their brother was coming down the stairs with a silly smile on his face.

They met him on the second-floor landing.

"What the hell?" Owen jerked to a stop, almost causing Liam to plow into him. "You're not shot. Not even a scratch." Owen's eyes ran over Dylan.

"Thanks to Zoey," Dylan replied, his smile slipping slightly.

"Ryan?" Liam asked. Dylan nodded. "How is Zoey?"

"Okay. She's resting. A few scratches from knocking Ryan into the bushes. But she's okay." Dylan ran his hand through his hair, and Liam could see the concern. "I love her," he blurted out.

"Duh." Owen slapped Dylan on the back. "Congrats, bro."

"What happened?" Liam asked.

"I'll tell you as I pack." Dylan walked toward their door.

"You're leaving?" Liam asked, suddenly concerned.

"No, I'm moving in with Zoey," Dylan said, a large smile on his face as his eyes sparkled with happiness. "Besides, I was tired of your snoring."

"Right." He laughed.

"What happened?" Owen asked once they were in their room as Dylan tossed his things into his duffel bag.

Dylan quickly filled him in on how Ryan had shown up at the zip line hut with a gun and had told him that their father had promised her things, things such as money and fame, then disappeared on her, so she had hunted the brothers down to get what she deserved.

"So, Ryan and Dad?" Owen asked.

Thinking about it, it totally made sense. Ryan was their father's type in every way. Young, manipulative, and desperate for attention and money. Everything Elle wasn't. "From the sounds of it, Dad was pretty intimate with her," Dylan said, packing the last of his things.

"Yeah, I can see that. She's more Dad's type than Elle ever was," Liam said, wondering if their dad and her mother had ever hooked up. Then he realized he didn't want to know and shook the thought from his mind.

"The gun was pointed at my chest, and then . . ." Dylan stilled and sat on the edge of the bed as he ran his hands over his face as if everything had just hit him. "Zoey, she just flew at her. Why would she put herself in danger for me? She, she, knocked the both of them into the bushes." He looked up and smiled slightly. "It was the most amazing thing I'd ever seen, and the scariest."

"Hellcat." Owen slapped Dylan on the shoulders. "Are you sure this is the one?"

Dylan chuckled. "Hell, yeah." He zipped his bag. "I'm going to sell my condo. We're going to build a place here. Well, somewhere near here. Close enough that we can continue working here, but far enough away that . . . you know."

"In Bear-Foot Bungalow?" Liam asked.

"Yes." Dylan smiled. "Until our place is done, we'll be staying there." He glanced around the room. "At least now the two of you will have more room."

"I'm heading home soon," Owen surprised them by saying.

"What?" Dylan frowned. "Why?"

"Dad's not here," Owen said. "Nor is his money. I'll stick around until I'm one hundred percent sure of it, but . . . there's no reason for me to stick around longer than that."

"But . . ." Dylan glanced around once more.

"This isn't a joke. I have a business to run. If the board will let me in, that is. Until we find Dad, or he waltzes back in from wherever the hell he has been, I may be our family's only hope."

"I'm staying," Liam said. "Elle may not know where he is, but I still think Dad contacted her for a reason. Until we know what that reason is, I'm staying put. Besides, this place beats sitting around my condo, waiting for something to happen."

"Suit yourself." Owen shifted. "I may stick around for another week or so, until the board of directors' deadline; then I'm heading back to do damage control."

"Thanks for that." Dylan nodded to Owen. "We've never really told you how much we appreciate you being there for us and in the forefront of the business."

"You two had other things. I've only ever had Paradise Investments in my future." Owen sighed. "Besides, it's what I'm good at."

"Whatever you decide, you don't have to fall into line with Dad's wishes," Dylan observed.

Owen fell silent for a moment. "I'm going to head back out. I left a bunch of people stranded on the beach when I heard what happened." He stopped. "Next time it would be great to hear *from you* that you'd had a gun pointed at you. Instead of hearing a rumor that you'd been shot."

Dylan's face turned a little pale. "Shit, that's what you were told?"

"Yeah, scared the hell out of us," Liam agreed.

"Sorry," Dylan said to them both.

Liam watched as Dylan loaded his stuff onto a cart and headed out to his new place. Standing on the lawn and looking around the camp, he thought about returning home himself.

He was thankful he'd decided to stick around. A warm breeze blew past him from the beach, and the salt air hit him just as the sounds of people happily enjoying themselves did. He loved the dynamics of the camp, and he enjoyed working with his hands and helping others create things they would treasure, and he realized he not only didn't want to leave, but he never wanted to leave. For the first time in his life, he felt like he'd found somewhere he belonged.

He walked back to the woodshop. He finished working on the first bench and cleaned up for the night. He had blisters and a few slivers of wood lodged in his hands, not to mention that his back ached from being hunched over the equipment, but he was probably the happiest he'd been in years.

He could feel the night cooling as he made his way toward the pool area. They'd probably have more rain in the middle of the night. He figured it was one of the perks of living by the ocean.

He wasn't on duty at the bar that evening, so instead he pulled out a cool beer, peeled off his shirt, toed off his shoes, and slipped into the water to cool off.

"Does your boss know you're taking a break?"

The female voice had him glancing over. He couldn't remember the woman's name, but he remembered she'd been there with her same-sex partner. He must have imagined the flirting tone he'd heard, since he knew that most women who swung one way didn't usually swing both.

He smiled. "What my boss doesn't know . . ." He tipped the beer and took a deep sip.

The woman moved closer, her hands going to his shoulders, and he tensed instantly.

"I'm sure there's more you do that your boss doesn't need to know about."

"Sorry," he said. "I'm spoken for."

"And, on the job," Elle said from directly behind him.

"Busted," he said with a smile as the woman sighed and moved away.

Turning around, he glanced up at Elle. "Thanks for that."

Elle moved to sit on the edge of the pool, then slipped off her shoes and dunked her feet into the water. "Ahh." She sighed and rolled her shoulders.

"Hard day?" he asked, taking her feet in his hands and rubbing them. She groaned again, and visions of her underneath him flashed quickly, and he felt himself growing hard by just hearing those sexy sounds of hers.

"Not as hard as yours." Her glance darted to where the woman was putting her moves on someone else.

"It's not easy being this hot," he joked, enjoying the way Elle chuckled. "We lucked out today." His hands continued to move over her arches, releasing the knots he felt there.

Her smile fell. "Yes, we did. What a mess."

"What will happen to Ryan?" he asked.

"I'm not sure, but she'll spend some time in jail. At least until her bail is set. After that . . ." She shrugged. "Your brother and Zoey will press charges. Besides whatever else the police throw at her." She closed her eyes for a moment. "Zoey told us that she was trying to blackmail you three."

He stopped rubbing her feet and reached to grab his beer. "I thought she was off, but not the 'whip a gun out' kind of off."

Her phone chimed, and she glanced down at it. "Well, that's my break." She started to get up, but he held on to her ankles.

"Are we meeting later?" he asked her softly.

Her eyes almost shined as she looked down at him. "I was hoping to, yes."

"I'll see you then." He let her go and watched her slip her shoes back on and walk away.

"Lucky lady." The woman was back, but this time she kept her distance.

"I'm the lucky one." He hoisted himself up out of the water.

"If you two ever decide you want to play . . ." the woman called after him, and he chuckled.

"We have each other," he said. He tossed his empty beer into the trash and strolled toward the kitchen to grab some dinner.

He figured while he was there, he could stock up the little tree house with some supplies. There was no use starving in the place while he and Elle stayed there.

After stashing the supplies, he took his time hanging the new sign outside the front door and then climbed down the steps to make his rounds.

Even though the parties had completely gone away since that first night, the brothers had agreed to continue making their presence known. Besides, he enjoyed his evening strolls. Even if halfway through this one, a light rain started to fall.

By the time he'd made it back to the tree house, Elle was there. She had set up candles around the room. He instantly wished he'd thought of the idea himself.

"What's all this?" he asked, pulling off his muddy shoes before stepping into the small place. She walked over and greeted him with a kiss.

"I wanted to do that earlier." She glanced up at him as his hands ran over her hips. "Thanks for the sign." She motioned to the front door. "I love it."

"You're welcome."

"I'll be honest: I would have hated to gouge out Donni's eyes, but I totally would have." She chuckled.

"Who's Donni?" he asked, enjoying the feeling of her in his arms.

"The lady at the pool." She sighed and relaxed into his embrace.

"Oh, that's right. I thought she was here with her partner?"

"Trilla," she said and nodded. "She is, but apparently, Donni swings both ways, and Trilla knows about it." She pulled back. "Don't ask me how I found out about that."

He rubbed his hands up and down her arms. "Have you been here long?"

"Long enough to see the massive stash of your food." She walked over and pulled out two beers. "We'll need a bigger fridge if you plan on keeping anything more here."

"This one will do for now." He took a sip. "Owen's probably leaving soon."

She stilled, the beer halfway to her lips, then sighed. "I suppose I knew this would happen soon. Especially after things seemed to be resolving."

"Dylan's staying," he added.

"Yeah, Zoey told us that they're going to build a place together."

"Is that something you okayed? I mean, building a home on the campgrounds?"

"It's not up to me. We all own this land and place together," she answered.

"All?" he asked.

"Joe left it to us that way. Split in fifths," she said. "In his way, he knew I'd need them to make a run of it."

"I told my brothers I'm staying," he blurted out.

She was silent for a moment. "What did they say?"

He shrugged, not wanting to go into what his brothers had said; besides, he didn't want her to worry. "Not much." He moved over and, taking her beer, set it aside. "If we could, I'd like to spend as much time as possible up here, in the trees, making love to you."

She wrapped her arms around his shoulders. "I'd like that."

When he kissed her, he poured everything he'd been feeling since he'd held her last into it.

"Does this mean you'll go away with me this week on our days off?" he asked.

She tilted her head. "I suppose I could arrange it. Just two nights."

"That's all we need," he agreed with a grin.

CHAPTER SIXTEEN

Elle stood at the water's edge a few days later looking at the colossal yacht sitting at the end of the dock.

"When you said going away, I thought"—she arched her brow—"something else."

Liam nudged her shoulder. "If you have to go, go in style." He swung her bag over his shoulder and held out a hand to help her board the boat.

"Welcome aboard." A crew member took the bags from Liam.

"How are we ever going to maneuver this thing out of the shallow river?" she asked, stepping onto the yacht.

"We"—his eyebrows shot up—"won't. Captain Eddie will." He nodded to the blond man standing in front of them. "With a small crew, we should be comfortable on our trip to the Keys."

"Welcome, miss," the captain said and nodded to her.

"We're all set," Liam told the man.

"Very well." He turned to go.

"The Keys? There is no way I'm going all the way to the Keys and back in this. It'll take longer than two nights."

"Easy." He pulled her into his arms. "We're taking a nice slow trip down there. We'll spend our last night in the Keys, then fly back the next morning. It's all set." He kissed her softly.

"What the . . ."

Zoey's voice caused her to jump and look toward the dock. There she was, standing at the end, dressed for a morning horseback ride. "Whose boat is this?"

"Relax." Liam chuckled. "It's not mine." He dropped his hands from Elle.

"He kissed you." Zoey's eyes narrowed as she moved to step aboard.

"And, you're not invited to join in," Liam joked, blocking her from getting into the boat. "We're under a time constraint here, and as you can see, we're almost ready to depart."

"You must have time for me to look around . . ." Zoey started, then sighed as the crew members unhooked the last line. "Go have fun." Her shoulders sagged slightly. "When you get back, I want all the details. All of them."

"I promise nothing." Elle laughed at the gesture Zoey made back to her. "She loves boats." Elle sighed, then turned to him. "What if I was the kind of girl who got seasick?"

The dock grew smaller behind them as they made their way out to the bay, then the gulf.

"Then, I guess this wouldn't be such a fun trip for you." He leaned on the railing and watched her instead of the shrinking horizon.

"Okay." She turned to him; they had been standing on the back deck watching the camp disappear. "Whose boat is this? Is it your father's?" She knew that they could afford something this amazing but hadn't heard Leo ever mention a boat.

"It's a friend's." He shrugged. "I know a guy who . . . well, I know a guy. We've got it for the trip to the Keys, where we'll get off, and he'll jump on to take it down to Brazil for the next few months."

"This is all ours for now?" She turned and really looked at the sheer size of the ship.

"All five staterooms, but more importantly, ten crew members, including our own chef, to make sure we're comfortable on the trip. Come on." He took her hand and pulled her toward a set of double stairs up to the next deck. The next level held a swimming pool, which they walked around, and then they continued past deck chairs to another set of stairs. This level had a deck area with tables, chairs, and sofas. One more set of stairs and they reached the top deck, where a circular hot tub sat toward the front of the boat, with a great vantage point over where they were heading.

"It will take us a little over twenty hours to get to the Keys, so we'll stop just outside of Saint Pete to refuel tonight, then continue on and make it to the Keys early tomorrow."

"All of this." She sighed and rested against the railing. "Your friend must have owed you big time."

"He did. I introduced him to his wife."

Her eyebrows shot up. "That's a story I'd like to hear."

He motioned to the circular sofa, and she sat; then he walked over to a small black fridge and pulled out a bottle of champagne and poured her a mimosa. "Fruit?"

When she nodded, he brought the bowl with him and set it down. "Carl is your average nerd."

"What does Carl do to afford all this?" she asked, motioning with her champagne glass.

"He started a small DNA-testing business."

"Small?" She glanced around. "Right."

He chuckled. "He loves what he does."

"How do you know Carl?"

"School." He reached for a blueberry. After popping it in his mouth, he continued. "Carl had been on exactly two dates in his life before he met me. Needless to say, by the time he met Candace, he'd racked that number up a little."

"How did you know Candace?" She pulled off her flip-flops and tucked her legs under her.

"We dated," he answered, causing her to giggle.

"Of course you did. What happened? She traded you for Carl?"

He laughed. "I caught them together one night. I wasn't pissed, because I had already decided they had more chemistry, no pun intended, than we did. They were meant to be. You can tell each time you're around them. You'll meet them in the Keys."

"I'm looking forward to it." She put a raspberry into her mouth and reflected on the trip ahead of them. She could imagine herself letting go, trusting Liam, and that scared her. After all, she'd trusted Jeff. Was this relationship destined to be doomed? She didn't believe every man was like Jeff or her father, but the amount of secrets Liam and she had was a major roadblock. Would there ever be a time when she could feel completely relaxed and open with him? What would such a relationship look like? Could she trust someone like Liam with her heart?

She gazed out at the water, almost unseeing. "I've never been on a boat trip before."

"Not even a cruise?" he asked.

She glanced at him. "No, we—the Wildflowers—planned to go on one, until Joe got sick."

"You must miss him a lot," he said, wrapping an arm around her shoulders.

She relaxed into him and sighed. "He was my everything."

She talked to Liam about Joe and how her life had changed drastically after her mother's death.

"I'd gone from head of the class to the girl everyone was whispering about." She shifted, looking up at him. They had already made it to the gulf and were heading into open waters.

She finished off her drink, and he poured her another one, as she told him about her school days prior to meeting the Wildflowers.

"They changed you," he murmured against her hair.

"I changed me. But they helped me believe in myself again." She glanced over as a younger man walked onto the deck.

"I'm Ricky. I'll be taking care of you during this trip. I wanted you to know that lunch will be served on the main deck in fifteen minutes," he said, then disappeared.

"Would you like to go see our cabin first?" He stood up and took her hand.

"Show me everything."

He hadn't been joking when he said there were five staterooms. Their bags were already sitting in the biggest one, which she deemed the master stateroom. The king-size bed sat facing a wall of windows overlooking the horizon. The shower in the bathroom was bigger than her own in the apartment and in the house in Pelican Point.

He informed her that the crew members were housed in the bottom two decks, while the upper three were reserved for the owner and guests. Seventeen employees were housed in the quarters below, where the kitchens and other facilities were located. The bridge was the only part of the third floor where the crew had to be, and even then, Elle and Liam had a private staircase to get back and forth. Unless they were needed, staff members went unseen.

There was even a theater room of sorts, with a massive television screen and lounge chairs with a sofa. But her favorite spot so far was the pool area. Even though it was a small jet pool, the deck around it and the open sitting area just inside were where she imagined spending most of her time aboard. Just inside glass doors sat a circular dining room. When they walked in, three staff members, including Ricky, jumped into motion.

She'd been wined and dined by Jeff before but nothing to this extent. With Jeff, however, it had all been for show, to win her over.

He'd shown his true colors shortly after she'd committed to the relationship.

With Liam, she could tell this trip, this boat, and all its wonders were just a means to enjoy his time with her. He wasn't trying to impress her, not really, since he'd made it clear that none of it belonged to him. Even though she knew he could probably afford it, he wasn't trying to impress her or sway her in any way. Instead, he was just trying to relax and have a good time with her.

But still, part of her questioned if, in the end, she could trust him completely.

She had to admit it was an amazing lunch. Almost equal to Isaac's meals. They had shrimp and scallops, followed by lemon cake.

"How about we lay out by the pool?" he suggested when they were finished and the table had been cleared.

"Sounds perfect. I brought some books."

He leaned in and kissed her. "What if I promise to keep you too busy for reading?"

She melted against him and wondered how she was going to stay grounded for the next two days.

She used the bathroom to change into her new striped blue swimsuit and pulled her cream wrap around her hips, then braided her hair to the side and tugged on her hat and sunglasses. She picked up her bag with her sunscreen and books in it and met him at the pool. He was already in the water, floating on his back. The fact that he was almost as long as the pool made her chuckle.

"Come on in."

"I thought you were supposed to wait an hour after eating," she teased.

"I doubt either of us could drown in this thing," he said, leaning against the edge of the pool and watching her carefully. "Then again . . . I guess it depends on what we're doing at the time."

She felt her knees buckle and slid down to sit on the edge of the chair to remove her sandals. She was thankful she had dark sunglasses on to hide the heat that had flooded her expression.

"Is that a challenge?" she asked, recovering quickly.

She watched him swallow as she stood and pulled her wrap off, his Adam's apple bobbing up and down on his neck.

"Get in here," he said, his voice making her inner muscles ache for him.

"What about the crew?" she asked, glancing around.

"They're nowhere near us. This isn't their first rodeo." He held out his hand so she could step into the water.

She took his hand and let him help her into the water. He nudged her hat off and set it on the side of the pool, then removed her sunglasses. When his hands moved over her, she could almost forget everything. She tried to keep her eyes from glancing around for fear that they would be interrupted.

"There, now I can watch your eyes change as I touch you." His hands moved over her shoulders, slowly playing with the thin strap that held her suit over her breasts. With his hot mouth roaming over her skin, she relaxed into his hands as she forgot all about being watched.

She moaned and leaned back against the side of the pool as her nails sank into his shoulders.

"Hold on to me," he said, running his lips down her neck, causing a trail of bumps to rise on her skin. Her fingers almost dug into his muscles as his hands moved slowly over the material of her suit, causing her nipples to peak. He circled each one with a fingertip before nudging the straps off her shoulders and exposing her to the sun and to him.

When he ducked his head down and lapped at her breasts, she arched toward him and found herself slipping. She must have tensed.

"Easy, I've got you." He shifted his hold and circled her waist with one of his arms, holding her better in place. Then, he moved them both to the corner, where he set her on an underwater bench. "Better?"

She nodded, feeling totally exposed, since her swimsuit was now on the deck by the pool. She wanted to cover her breasts, but she enjoyed the heat from his gaze and the sun. With him touching her, holding her, talking softly to her, she would have allowed him to do anything to her. She no longer cared that he'd lied or that he was keeping secrets from her and her friends. All that mattered now was being with him, getting him to make her feel the way she wanted, knew, that he could.

"Lovely," he said, moving back slightly to get a better look. "But you still have more for me to remove." He smiled and leaned in to kiss her until she was fully relaxed again.

When his finger dipped below her swimsuit, she moaned out his name and felt her body respond to his touch.

"God, I want you. Here, now, like this." He shifted, and she felt his cock rub against her through his shorts.

"You still have some clothing to remove." She reached for his shorts.

"Soon," he promised her. "I'm not done touching you." He nudged her suit down her legs, running his hands over her thighs, her knees, and her calves. Then he tossed the wet bottoms next to her top.

His fingers slowly circled her body, and she felt her breath quicken as he edged a finger into her, spreading her, filling her.

"Liam," she begged after a moment. "Please." She reached for him once more, only to have him sidestep.

"I'm in charge—not until I feel you come first," he said. "Come for me."

"I . . ." She shook her head and closed her eyes. "Liam, I want you . . ." She bit her bottom lip.

"Soon." He moved his fingers again and had her almost there. "Let go."

He moved over and over and soon had her tossing her head back and losing the last hold she had.

"I told you," he whispered, shaking her from the fog of aftershock.

Her eyes opened, and she met his hazel eyes. "We didn't drown."

"Not yet," he said as he slid slowly into her.

CHAPTER SEVENTEEN

That evening, Liam held Elle in his arms as they watched the sun set from the top deck. They had enjoyed a candlelit dinner that had been expertly set out as soft music played from the speakers around them. He couldn't have asked for a more romantic setting, nor would he have wanted to share it with anyone other than Elle.

She'd changed into a soft, flowing blue sundress for dinner, and he'd pulled on a pair of tan shorts and a button-up shirt, but he wished he'd packed something a little more special for her.

She'd tied her hair in a low knot and had freshened up her makeup after the shower they had shared. They had both gotten a little too much sun that day, which had her cheeks and shoulders a little pink.

She claimed he'd distracted her, and she'd forgotten to put sunblock on. He'd made it up to her by rubbing lotion onto every part of her. Which had made them work up an appetite.

Dinner was even better than lunch. His steak melted in his mouth.

"I could get spoiled eating like this," she said between bites. "At camp, I don't really get to enjoy Isaac's food as much as I want."

"You've accomplished a lot. The camp is an amazing place."

"Hopefully, it won't always be like that. If all goes well . . ."

"Nope," he interrupted her. Already, he could see her work wheels turning. "Change gears. No work talk. You're on vacation, remember?"

She laughed. "Okay." She reached for her champagne glass and finished off her second glass, only for it to be filled again by one of the staff members. "Tell me what our plans are for the Keys?"

"Okay." He slid easily onto the topic. "I have us booked at a bungalow."

"You booked us a private bungalow?" she asked.

"Sure, we'll have the place for the night with our own private pool and beach. We'll have lunch with Carl and Candace here on the boat before heading out and spending the rest of the day enjoying Key West. We can take in the culture and local life there, then have some dinner before heading to the bungalow."

"I've always wanted to eat at Sloppy Joe's. Last time I was there, we ran out of time," she admitted.

"We?" he asked.

She chuckled. "Zoey, Scar, and I went down there two summers ago." She rested her elbows on the table. "Something tells me you've been down to the Keys a lot."

He nodded. "They have one of the best marine-biology labs for that there: KML."

"You lived there?" she asked, and he nodded in agreement. "How long?"

"Almost a year. That's where I met Carl." He remembered the first time he'd seen the man struggling to unload some heavy equipment.

"And Candace?" she asked.

"Yes." He smiled, remembering meeting the pretty brunette at a party the night he'd arrived in Key West for the first time. It was strange, but even now, Liam could only ever imagine Carl and Candace together back then. It was as if they had been fated to meet and fall for one another.

"They mean a lot to you." It was a statement, not a question.

"They're like family," he answered easily. "When I was going through a rough patch, they're the ones who helped me out—showed me what it's like to be around people who get you and who care for you."

"You and your brothers seem to get along fine enough."

"We do." He nodded in agreement. "But it hasn't always been the case. Besides, since we've all moved out and gone our own ways, we're more like polite strangers." It saddened him to say it, but it was the truth. Their time at the camp was the most time they'd spent together in years.

She was watching him closely, and he guessed she'd seen his mood darken.

He didn't trust people that often. The fact that he was still cautious toward her in a few areas played heavily on him. He didn't think that she had anything to do with his father's disappearance, but he did wonder if she knew more than she was letting on. It wasn't as if she'd come directly out and said she hadn't slept with his father or had even known him. Then again, he hadn't asked, for fear of the answers.

"Why was this boat in Destin?" she asked, interrupting his memories.

"Carl was getting some repairs and upgrades there," he answered. "I knew about it and was hoping it would be ready for this trip. I called Carl and asked if we could hitch a ride. We lucked out."

She held up her glass, and he did the same, clinking them together. "Yes, we did."

That night, holding Elle in his arms while they were docked in Saint Pete, he couldn't explain why he was nervous for her to meet his friends.

Carl and Candace were more than his friends; they were friends who knew him better than any others. Living together in a small boat while they worked on fixing the reefs off the coast of Florida, Liam and Carl had gotten to know one another better than even he and his brothers had.

Carl's opinion mattered more to him than most people's. He knew Carl would love Elle, but he wanted Elle to see past all of Carl's little . . . issues.

The man was a recluse at best. Candace had helped him come out of his shell a little, but still, Carl tended to fall into bouts of seclusion and depression. Hence the trip to Brazil he and Candace were taking.

He felt Elle stir next to him and pulled her tighter against his chest. He knew that she'd had a few bad dreams about her ex. If he ever met the guy, he was sure nothing could hold him back from punching the man instantly.

When she settled back down, he closed his eyes and drifted off to sleep with the smell of her hair floating around him.

The next morning, by the time he woke, they were already back out to sea.

Breakfast was served on the deck, and they ate watching as they slipped past the rest of Florida. They watched a pod of dolphins play off the side of the boat, and Elle snapped a ton of pictures on her phone: some of them together, several selfies, and a lot of the boat.

"For Zoey." She smiled. "She really was jealous."

"Next time Carl has it up near us, I'll make sure she gets a tour and a trip."

"Really?" She bit her bottom lip. "She'd love that."

"What's that look for?" he asked after seeing worry flash in her eyes. He knew this look of hers signaled that she was concerned about something.

"Nothing." She started to shake her head, but he stopped her by placing a finger under her chin and nudging it until her eyes met his.

"I've seen that look before," he teased. "Tell me what the worry is."

She sighed. "Okay, it's just . . . well, your brother and my . . . sister are, well . . ."

"What? Engaged?" he said.

"What?" She jerked in his arms. "No, they're . . ."

"For all practical purposes, yes. I'm sure it's just a matter of time before Dylan asks."

"Really?" Elle's eyes got huge. "You think?"

"If he hasn't already." He smiled. "He told us that Zoey is the one. Which means . . ."

"Marriage." She sighed. "Okay, yes, I suppose I knew it was coming, but . . ."

"Why the concern?" he asked, shifting her closer to him as they glanced out over the water.

Her head rested against his shoulder, and for a moment she was quiet, and he didn't think she'd tell him.

"What if things don't work out for us? I mean, I've never been friendly with . . . someone I've dated after a breakup."

He thought about it for a moment. Hadn't he been thinking the same thing moments ago? But, looking at her, he couldn't imagine feeling anything but kindness and desire toward her. At least at the moment. If he found out she'd had anything to do with his father and the missing money, then those thoughts might change.

"We're friends, right?" he asked finally.

"Yes," she agreed.

"Then, no matter what happens, we'll remain so. We both love Dylan and Zoey, so as long as we focus on them and not us, we should be okay." He turned her toward him again. "Trying to break it off with me already?"

She reached up and wrapped her arms around him. "I'm just getting started with you." She leaned up and kissed him. Heating his body instantly.

"We have time," he said between kisses, "to sneak down into the bedroom one last—"

Just then, the horn honked, signaling they were coming into port. He sighed. "Tonight." He laid his forehead against hers.

They stood on the top deck and watched as they pulled into port.

"There are Carl and Candace." He waved and pointed to the couple standing on the dock.

Elle turned and smiled, then waved. "They look just like you said."

"Really?" He glanced down at her.

"Yes, she's beautiful, and he's . . . well, a nerd." She chuckled.

He shifted his glance over at the couple. Carl was a skinny, freakishly tall man with thick black glasses and a mop of black hair that was blowing in the wind every which way. Candace's long hair was tied in a braid laying over her shoulder. She wore a white sundress, and a large brimmed hat covered her face.

"Carl can be . . . well, he's a hypochondriac, among other things."

Elle poked a finger at him. "I'm sure I'm going to like him. Stop worrying." She leaned up and kissed him.

"I'm . . ." He was about to deny it but realized it was the truth. "Okay, why does this feel like I'm introducing you to my parents?"

She chuckled and hugged him before stepping away. "Remember, I've known your father most of my life. Maybe you just haven't come to the realization that these two"—she nodded to the couple, who were now a lot closer—"mean more to you than you care to say."

He wrapped his arm around her shoulder. "Hell, just don't let *them* know that."

He watched the trio carefully—so carefully that shortly after sitting down for lunch, Candace reached across the table and took his hand in hers.

"Relax." She smiled at him. "We're not going to devour her. I think both of us have made up our minds about Elle already." She smiled across the table. "We like her." She dropped his hand and reached for Carl's. "Don't we?"

He relaxed instantly. It was strange; his friends hadn't even met his brothers. He'd kept these two sides of his life separate. Maybe it was because he felt like he could be himself around Carl and Candace, more so than he ever had been around his family.

"Any woman that Liam feels is strong enough to meet us, we love." Carl winked at Elle.

"The feeling is mutual." Elle toasted him with her glass. "Eat." She nodded to his food, which he had barely touched at this point.

The conversation turned to his time on the island.

"He really dove down and positioned a mannequin dressed as Aquaman where you'd be diving the next day?" Elle asked.

"The vintage Aquaman, not the new one. Green tights, yellow shirt. Yeah." Carl laughed. "Scared the shit out of me. He even had a pitchfork."

"Trident," Liam corrected him.

Candace jumped in. "*That's* who Liam reminds me of. We saw the new movie a few months ago and both agreed, Liam is a younger version of the star." She turned to Elle and practically purred. "I do love me some Jason Momoa."

Elle quickly nodded in agreement, then turned to him and tilted her head. He watched her run her tongue over her lips.

"I can't really see it." She chuckled. "Maybe if he had some green tights . . ."

He laughed. "No way in hell." He kissed her hand.

They finished lunch, and he hugged the couple goodbye.

"Safe travels." He kissed Candace's cheek. "Keep me posted on the trip."

"Will do." She leaned in. "If all goes well, when we come back, we might have some . . . news."

He stopped. "What kind?"

"The 'expanding the family' kind," she whispered.

"Really?" He hugged her again.

"It's funny, I have to kidnap my husband and take him away on a monthlong boat trip to get enough time with him." Candace wrapped her arm around Carl.

"I can work anywhere," Carl added with a chuckle.

"Not if I throw your computer overboard," Candace warned.

"You wouldn't dare . . ." Carl leaned down and kissed her. Then he turned to Elle. "It was really nice meeting you."

"The same, safe travels," Elle said as Liam set their bags on the dock. They were whisked away to the car that had been waiting to take them to the bungalow so Elle and Liam wouldn't have to drag their bags around for the day.

They stood on the dock and watched the boat disappear into the horizon.

"Part of me envies them," Elle said as they turned to head down the dock, hand in hand.

"You want to be stuck on a boat with me for a month?" he joked.

"It might be fun." She shrugged. "But no, I mean, the way they are together. You built up this . . . vision of them. They're some of the nicest and richest people I've met."

"If it was up to Carl, he'd still live in his parents' basement." They started to stroll down Front Street. "Where to? Shopping?"

She thought about it. "I suppose I could do some shopping." She glanced at a shop window. "After some gelato." She pulled him in.

For the next few hours, they walked around Front Street. He carried a few small bags after she'd bought some trinkets for her friends. He was surprised when she pulled him into a hot sauce store and purchased a bottle of Fighting Cock Barbeque Sauce.

"Zoey's favorite." She smiled when she bought it. "It might make up for not giving her a tour of the boat."

They walked a few blocks and had dinner at Sloppy Joe's, where they ate burgers and sipped cold beer as a band played on the stage.

When they stepped outside, the sun was sinking lower, and they made their way toward Mallory Square to watch the sunset and enjoy the street performers. Elle took more than a dozen pictures of the chickens roaming the streets along the way.

"What time is our flight tomorrow?" she asked, resting her head against his shoulder as their cab drove them across the island toward their bungalow.

"Noon," he answered. "We have plenty of time to sleep in." He wished they could spend more time away from the camp and the worries of his family. Not that he didn't want to find his father, but being with her away from it all was addictive.

He hated the thought of going back to their problems and the idea that they were each keeping secrets from one another.

"Good." She covered her mouth as she yawned. "I can barely keep my eyes open. Thank you for today." She shifted and looked up at him. "It was one of the best vacations I've had."

"Thank you for coming with me." He kissed the top of her head.

The car pulled up in front of the place, and when they stood out on the sidewalk in front of the two-story house, Elle glared at him.

"We seriously need to discuss the definition of a *bungalow*."

She followed him onto the front patio and waited as he used the code to unlock the place.

"This is all ours for the night?" she asked, walking around the entryway.

"Yup." He picked up the bags that had been set right inside the door. "Lead the way."

"Not yet. I want to look around." She motioned for him to set the bags down.

He followed her around the place, remembering how it had felt living there years ago. He'd felt as if he'd been in control of his own life. Something he hadn't felt since, until he'd stepped foot on the camp and had seen Elle.

"Look at this . . ." she said over and over again.

"I've seen it," he finally said. "I've rented the place a few times before." She stopped.

"You're just now telling me this?" She turned toward him.

"I thought I had," he said. "This is where Carl and I lived while . . ." He stopped when her eyes narrowed at him. "Oh, I thought I told you."

She huffed, then turned toward the stairs. "I'm going to want a swim in the pool," she added as he followed her up the stairs.

"God, I was hoping you'd say that," he said, his eyes locked on her backside. Images of what he wanted to do to her under the water flooded his mind.

He wondered if he'd always want her this bad. He didn't think he'd get used to the desire that shot through him every time she looked at him. Nor would he want to.

He tossed the bags on the bed and waited as she looked around the upstairs, then changed into her suit.

"You won't need that." He walked across the room toward her and touched the straps of her suit.

"You won't be needing those"—she nodded to his shorts—"but yet, you're still wearing them."

"So let's head downstairs before we get naked." He grabbed two towels. "The backyard is pretty private, but some of the windows up here face the neighbors."

"Good to know." She wrapped a towel around her. "Lead the way."

When they stepped out on the back patio, he flipped on the pool lights and dropped the towels on a chair. Then he followed her into the water and instantly took her into his arms.

CHAPTER EIGHTEEN

Elle was dreaming about lying in the warm white sand on her beach, Liam lying beside her, slowly stroking his hands over her heated skin, when she heard her cell phone ring.

"Don't answer that," he murmured in her ear.

She had already tensed, since it was the first time her phone had rung during their trip.

"They wouldn't be calling if it wasn't important," she said, slipping out of his hold. She wrapped a towel around herself, hunted for her phone, and found it under his towel.

"Hello?" she answered without looking at the number.

"Elle."

Hearing Jeff's voice on the line had her back stiffening.

"I thought you would want to hear it directly from me," he continued when she didn't speak. "My firm has been hired by a client recently, one suing you and your new company, River Camp. She's claiming there was a hostile work environment and that it was work-related stress that caused her to lash out. She's also claiming employment discrimination."

"You're in Colorado," she said, unable to process any of what he'd just said to her. Liam came to her side. She turned and tried to avoid his eyes but could see the anger there when he guessed who she was on the phone with. "My business is in Florida."

"I took a position and was made partner at a firm in Pensacola a few months ago," he answered. Elle closed her eyes and held her breath. "I thought I'd give you a heads up. You should be getting notice soon. I just wanted . . . to tell you personally." The fact that there was zero remorse or concern in his voice somehow stung even more.

"Is it Ryan?" she asked, though it was obvious.

"My client? Yes, Ryan Kinsley."

Her stomach roiled, and she sat on the edge of the bench. "She tried to kill someone."

"I can't discuss the case with you," Jeff said. "I'm already breaking so many rules by calling you personally. I just . . . thought you should know."

"I've been informed," she said, then reached down and hung up.

"Tell me that wasn't—" Liam started.

"Ryan is suing River Camp." She closed her eyes.

"What? The hell . . ." He took her phone and punched in a number. "Hey. Yeah, I know."

She listened to his one-sided conversation. "Elle just got a call from a lawyer who claims that Ryan is suing River Camp. How the hell should I know. Find out if it's true. Yeah, then have . . . yeah, okay. Thanks." He hung up and took her in his arms. "Owen's on it. He's going to have Joel contact our team of lawyers and countersue, if it's true."

"She really does have long claws." Elle leaned into him. "I thought . . . she'd go away."

"Women like her—people like her—don't let go easily." He drew her closer.

"I have to call—"

Her phone rang again. She glanced down and saw Hannah's number on her screen. "That will be them."

"Tell me there's some sort of chocolate in the fridge," she said before answering the phone.

While she filled Hannah and the others in over the speakerphone, Liam disappeared inside and returned with a bottle of champagne and some chocolate-covered strawberries. She'd had half a dozen of them with two whole glasses of champagne by the time she got off the phone with her friends.

"I agree with Hannah," Liam said, pulling her into a hug again. They had moved inside, since she had suddenly felt chilled in the warm night air. He'd even wrapped a throw blanket around her shoulders. Now, he ran his hands up and down her arms. "Get some rest. You can't do anything more tonight."

She felt drained. Even the sugar from the chocolate couldn't help her perk up. "You're right." She finished off the rest of her drink.

"I often am," he said, then surprised her by lifting her into his arms. She held on to him and enjoyed the play of the muscles in his shoulders as he started walking up the stairs.

"So, the question now is"—he bent his head down and ran his lips over hers—"who gets to be on top?"

She burst out laughing. Somehow, when things were darkest, he made the sun come out.

She somehow found sleep that night. Her mind just shut off after they lay together, their bodies cooling in the night air, tangled together. She didn't even dream, that she knew of.

When she woke, the sun was already streaming into the room. She must have groaned, because Liam tightened his hold on her.

"Morning," he said.

"What time is it?" She tried to glance around and realized there wasn't an alarm clock anywhere.

"Probably around eight."

"Probably?" She reached for her phone and was surprised that he was about right. "Ten after."

"See, we still have plenty of time." He tried to pull her back into the bed, but she had to use the bathroom and slipped from his hold.

"Bathroom first," she said and disappeared. She had sneaked her cell phone in with her and sent a text off to Hannah to see if she'd heard anything else yet.

She got an almost-instant reply.

—Paperwork showed up today.

—So, it's official?

—Owen is looking over it all right now. I'll keep you posted. When will you be back?

—Should be there around one.

—Enjoy the rest of your trip. We've got this covered.

She thought about sending a text to Zoey and asking the same but knew that Hannah had probably already talked to everyone that morning.

When she stepped back out to the bedroom, Liam was missing. She pulled on a fresh shirt and shorts and then found him downstairs in the kitchen, making breakfast.

She sat at the bar top and smiled over at him. "What are you doing?"

He chuckled. "Haven't you seen a man cook before?"

"Sure, I watch Isaac every now and then, and Joe could make several great meals." She leaned over and glanced at the stove, where he had an omelet heating up. "I didn't know you could do it, though."

He shrugged and continued moving around the place. "I'm probably the best cook out of the three of us—four if you count my dad.

And he doesn't really count, since he burns coffee if he makes it himself." He set a mimosa in front of her. "What did your friends say?"

"Nothing new." She sighed as she sipped. "I'm going to want mimosas every morning now."

"You can, if you want." He continued working. "I talked to Owen. He says the lawyers will contact you later today, after we get back."

"Thanks." She shifted in the seat. "I never thought it would come to something like this. I mean, sure, I have insurance that covers being sued as a business, in case someone fell or was injured, but . . ." She sipped again. "Not injuries from an employee who tried to kill your brother and my best friend."

"I knew there was something off about her from the start." He turned and looked at her. "She ripped off my shirt."

"I've ripped off your shirt," she reminded him.

"Yeah, but with you, I wanted it." He smiled. "Let's eat this outside." He grabbed the two plates of food.

She held open the door and then took the glasses and pitcher of mimosas out to the patio. He set a plate down in front of her, and she had to admit, it looked good.

"Try it," he suggested, sitting next to her. "I swear it's not poisoned." He took a bite. "See."

"It's pretty enough to take a picture." She pulled out her phone from her shorts and snapped a few shots; then she pushed her drink in the frame and snapped a few more.

"It's going to get cold," he warned. "I've never understood the fascination of taking food pictures."

She set her phone aside. "To remember how good it was, or . . ." She laughed. "As evidence of my last meal." He laughed with her. She took a bite and groaned at the richness and the tang of sweetness she tasted. "It's as good as it looks. Is that—"

"Lime juice," he said. "It gives it a little zing."

"Wow," she said, taking another bite. "You should cook like this back home," she said, shoveling more into her mouth. When he remained silent, she glanced up and realized what she'd said.

"I mean . . . at the camp." She felt her stomach roll.

"Yeah." He shifted and pushed his plate aside. "I was thinking about that."

Oh god, here it comes, she thought. He was going to tell her he was leaving, like his brother had. Sure, he'd said that he'd told them he was staying, but that didn't mean he'd be there for long or that he wouldn't change his mind.

"I have a small condo, in Destin, and I have a few things there . . ."

He sipped his drink, and she wondered if her heart would burst from not beating.

"I was thinking of clearing my stuff from it and bringing it to the camp. I might need a storage shed—the room I'm in is small, but I could make it work."

Her heart started again. "You want to move to the camp? Full time?" she asked, finally finding her voice.

"Yes, I was thinking . . . yes." He nodded. "If it's okay with you and your friends?"

"Yes." She reached for his hand. "I'm sure we can find a place for your stuff."

"Great, because if not, I was going to have to dump it all at the donation box."

She laughed and then finished the first meal any man other than her grandfather had ever cooked just for her.

After breakfast, they took a dip in the pool and walked on the small plot of sandy beach that sat behind the house before packing up and jumping into a car to head to the airport.

The airport was as small as the one she was used to, and it took less than ten minutes to get through security and find their gate.

Once they were loaded on the plane, she wasn't surprised to find that he had booked them in first class.

"I've never ridden in first class," she admitted, getting comfortable on the small plane.

"Seriously?" he asked.

"Yeah." She nodded.

"You've never traded up your points or miles to ride in style?"

"Nope, never." She snapped on her seat belt.

"Well, then, sit back and enjoy it." He waved a stewardess over and asked for mimosas.

"More?" She thought she'd explode.

He chuckled. "One last one. To toast the end of a wonderful two days."

"Thank you," she said, "for everything."

"Anytime." He took her free hand and brought it up to his lips again.

She leaned back in her seat and sipped her drink as they prepared to take off.

She had to admit: there was a lot more legroom up in the front. She always struggled with her long legs. Being five nine had its perks, but cramming into a small airplane seat wasn't one of them.

"Doing okay?" he asked once they were in the air.

"Yes." She smiled. "You probably heard about Zoey's phobia for air travel. I enjoy flying."

"Good." He relaxed slightly. "So, do you have any phobias?"

She thought about it. "I guess spiders." She shrugged. "Although, I don't kill them, since they eat mosquitos, which I hate even more."

"What about yellow flies?" he asked.

"Okay, those can just be wiped off the face of the earth, and I wouldn't blink an eye," she joked.

"Agreed—do you think god created them after Adam bit into the fruit of knowledge? You know . . ." His voice grew deeper. "I'm pissed at man, so I'm going to create little flying bugs that will wreak havoc and annoy the shit out of man for the rest of his days."

She laughed again. "Hey, men lucked out on that whole thing. Women get cursed once a month and have to deal with childbirth."

"I don't know; if it was up to dealing with that or wiping out all of the biting bugs in the world, I'd gladly trade."

"So would most women. I think."

He took her hand in his again. "I'm glad we have this in common."

"What? Our hatred for biting insects?" She finished off her drink.

"Yes, you know, a lot of couples don't agree on things like this." He leaned closer. "It's the number-one cause of separations."

She reached up and kissed him. "You're lucky you found me, then."

His eyes met hers, and she felt like she could drown in the hazel pools.

"Yes." His voice grew softer. "I am."

Liam kept her laughing until the plane landed. She felt completely relaxed until they stepped outside and the realization of what she would have to face back at the camp hit her.

"Hey," he said, taking her hand in his. "Don't let it affect you just yet."

"It's hard to keep it at bay." She sighed and fell into step with him.

"Do you really think Ryan could win anything? I mean, there's a history of her workplace problems. You said yourself you have written accounts from several other employees. Most likely a judge is going to toss out everything she and her lawyers throw your way."

She knew he was right, but still, the nagging feeling was causing her stomach to sink.

"You're right," she agreed. "Even if my mind tells me you're right, the rest of me has butterflies."

"Then you'll just have to listen to your head," he said, opening the car door for her.

"Whose car is this?" She frowned when she realized they'd stopped at a parked car in the airport parking lot.

"My brother's. It's a Tesla." Liam smiled. "He dropped it off earlier this morning and gave me his log-in information so I can drive it."

"You have his keys?" She frowned when he got in beside her after putting their luggage into the trunk.

"No, my phone is the key." He waved his cell phone.

"Zoey was telling me about this car." She sat back. "Fully electric?"

He nodded and started backing out. It was strange not hearing an engine humming as he drove them back toward the camp.

When he finally parked the car in the employee parking lot, she turned to him.

"What do you like better, this or my Jeep?" she asked.

"They're different animals." He shifted and looked at her. "The Tesla is nice for highway driving, while your Jeep is kick ass for hitting the beach or cruising around town and enjoying a breeze. But we do have tinted windows in this car." He kissed her.

Then her phone rang, and she pulled it out. Frowning at the blocked number, she took a deep breath, then answered, thinking it would be the lawyers. "Hello?"

"Elle."

Hearing Leo's voice, she reached for Liam's hand. "Leo?" She felt Liam's hand jerk.

He reached over and took her phone from her.

"Dad?" Liam said into her phone.

CHAPTER NINETEEN

"Liam?" Leo Costa's voice was nothing short of a whisper. "You there?"

Liam tried to control his temper. "Dad? Where the hell are you?"

"Liam, what are you doing with my Elle?" Leo asked instead of answering. His father always did things on his own terms.

"We came here to look for you. Where are you?"

"Came where?"

"Dad." Liam felt his control slip, and his tone changed. "Where are you?"

"I'm standing in the lobby of my damn building. Why are you with my Elle?"

"She's not *yours*." Liam didn't know why he'd said it, but his father was pissing him off. "So you're home?"

"Put Elle back on the phone," his father said.

"Where were you?" he asked instead of handing the phone over.

"Fine, I'll just call her—"

"Dad, you had the three of us worried sick . . ."

"No, I had the board calling you and complaining to you three that I was gone, and then you boys jumped like three little puppies through a goddamned hoop." His father's voice rose slightly.

Liam took a deep breath to calm down. "You've been gone for six months."

"It's not the first time," his father replied.

"Fine." Liam jerked the phone away and handed it to Elle. "He wants to talk to you."

He stormed out of the car when she answered the phone. Pulling out their luggage, he felt like throwing it across the parking lot. Instead, he took out his cell phone and called Owen.

"Guess who I just got off the phone with?"

"Who?" Owen asked.

"Dad."

"What?" He heard Owen fumble with the phone. "Where is he?"

"Home, apparently."

"Son of a . . ."

"Yeah." Liam ran his hands through his hair. "He didn't even call me. He called Elle." He glanced back at the car and could see Elle listening to his father on the phone. She had a worried look in her eyes as she watched him pace in front of the car. "He's talking to her right now, instead of filling me in on where he was."

"Where are you?" Owen asked.

"We just got back. I'm in the parking lot," he answered.

"Shit, I'll be there—"

Something crashed, and he thought he heard a female voice, but then Owen was back.

"Meet me at the pool bar in half an hour. I'll talk to Dylan. We all need to talk."

He agreed and hung up, but he turned when Elle got out of the car. "Well?"

"He . . . needed a favor." She straightened her back.

"Are you going to tell me?" he asked after a moment.

"He made me promise . . ." She took a deep breath. "Liam, I can't." She shook her head. "Not . . . yet."

"Fine." He picked up his bag and started to storm away. She grabbed her bag and followed him quickly.

"If I could . . ." she began.

"Yeah," he said over his shoulder. "I get it." He was feeling more than pissed now. When he opened the front doors, he didn't wait for Elle and quickly climbed the stairs to dump his bag in the room he shared with Owen.

When he stepped out a few minutes later, Elle was standing outside the door, her luggage still sitting by her feet.

"Liam," she started.

"I need some time. I'm not pissed at you, but . . ." He closed his eyes. "I'm just pissed."

"I get it." She wrapped her arms around him. "I'm sorry. If it was my choice, I'd tell you. But it's not."

"Is he sick?" he asked, unable to avoid voicing the worst thought.

When she didn't answer right away, he jerked back as if he'd been hit.

"Shit." He ran his hands through his hair. "What is it? Cancer?"

"Liam, I . . ." She shook her head.

"Fine." He turned and started walking down the hallway.

"Are you coming to the tree house tonight?" she called after him.

"I need to be with my brothers," he said without turning around.

When he found Owen and Dylan, they were sitting at a table by the pool. He sat down and wondered what he should tell them. Then he figured that since he didn't officially know anything, he should keep his mouth shut instead of throwing his speculations around.

"He called Elle?" Dylan asked first.

"Yeah, I only found out because we had just pulled into the parking lot."

"What did he say to you?" Owen asked.

"He said he was standing in the lobby of his building," Liam answered.

"Which one?" Owen asked. "We own more than a thousand."

"Shit." Liam leaned back. "I . . . assumed the main one."

"Yeah, that's the thing with Dad. Never assume. I called Joel. Dad's not in Destin. He's calling around to all the other locations and seeing if he's there."

"Shit." Liam tugged on his hair. "Shit."

"What did he want with Elle?" Dylan asked.

"She won't tell me." He shifted. "She said that Dad made her promise not to tell us, yet."

"Do you think that he's getting married?" Dylan asked.

Why hadn't Liam thought of it? Instead, he'd jumped to the idea of his father dying. Hell, is that why Elle hadn't answered him? Maybe his guess had been so far off the mark that she hadn't wanted to answer him?

"Who would Dad even marry?" Owen asked.

"With our luck, it would be Ryan," Dylan said.

"Don't even joke about that." Liam cringed.

"He hasn't contacted the board yet," Owen threw in, "but that doesn't mean he won't."

"Okay, now what?" Liam asked.

"Now, I go back into town," Owen answered.

"What about us?" Dylan pointed out. "I'm staying put, no matter what."

"Me too," Liam said. Even if he was slightly irritated that Elle wouldn't tell him his father's secret, he still wanted to be with her.

Owen turned on him. "You're just as gone as he is. I can see it—both of you have *sucker* written on your foreheads."

"It's better than *fucker*," Dylan joked.

"Still." Owen stood up. "I was going to hold off, but I see no reason not to return today."

"What about your work?" Liam asked, glancing around.

Owen stopped. "My work is in Destin." His eyes moved around the pool area. "This was play." He turned and walked away, almost bumping into Hannah, who stood two feet away, looking at Owen as if she wished to shoot daggers into his back.

Dylan jumped up. "Have you heard anything more?"

Hannah turned her eyes to him. "No, not yet." She started to move past them.

"Hannah." Dylan stopped her by taking her hand. "I'm sure he didn't mean—"

She jerked her hand free. "He meant it."

She stormed off.

"What was that about?" Liam asked.

Dylan sat back down. "Our brother is an ass."

"I've known that a lot longer than you . . ." His eyes moved to where Hannah was following Owen down a trail, and suddenly, the light bulb went off. "Oh."

"Yeah," Dylan sighed.

"Oh, shit." He leaned back in the chair and desperately wished for a beer, but he was needed behind the bar soon. "Owen and Hannah?"

"Yeah, I caught them . . . fighting yesterday," Dylan said.

"Shit," he said again under his breath. "What a mess."

"I don't know what's between you and Elle, but whatever it is, it better not fuck up what I have with Zoey," Dylan warned him. "I asked her to marry me."

Liam was silent for a while. "You've only known her for a little over a month."

"Who the hell cares. She's the one." Dylan stood. "You know it when it's real." He stormed off, leaving Liam to brood by himself until he stepped behind the bar and had to get to work.

He didn't return to the tree house that night. He felt bad halfway through the night, when he realized Owen hadn't even returned to their room.

Thinking he must have returned to Destin, he tossed the rest of his brother's things in his bag the next morning and shoved it in the back of the closet—pissed that he'd leave without saying goodbye. Hell, before coming to the camp, the brothers had only really seen one another a couple of times each year.

It wasn't as if his brother owed him anything. He didn't even really know him anymore. It had been seven years since they'd lived together.

"Is someone sitting here?"

He glanced up to the pretty blonde who had taken Ryan's place in the dining room.

"No." He motioned. "Lindsey, right?"

"Yes." She beamed. "I'm still trying to remember everyone's names. You're Liam—Dylan and Owen's brother, right?"

"Yes." He glanced around. He'd sat in the corner booth, hoping to be left alone, but since the girl was young and obviously inexperienced, he gave her a break instead of pushing her off. Besides, maybe it would cheer him up? She looked like a ray of sunshine.

"Is this your first job?" he asked.

"Does it show that bad?" She frowned into her food.

He chuckled. "No, it's just . . . you're young."

"I just turned seventeen." She shrugged. "Not that young."

"No," he agreed, feeling stupid. He'd hated people calling him young when he'd been that age. "How do you like it here?"

"Oh, it's fine. Better than where I was."

"Where were you?" he asked.

"Home, with my stepmother." She rolled her eyes. "My dad's military and stationed overseas for the next year."

"That must be hard."

"It is with Robin." She sighed. "You and . . . Elle, are you two . . ."

"Yeah . . . rumors going around?"

She nodded. "Elle is so pretty"—she sighed—"and nice. I've never run into someone who was both at the same time."

"I know what you mean," he said, then stood up when he realized his plate was empty. "I better get going. I have a class this morning."

"Oh." She glanced around. "Okay, thanks for sitting with me."

"Anytime," he said and then dumped his tray in the wash area and made his way across the camp to the woodshop.

His mood stayed improved for the rest of the day. Even when he didn't see Elle for lunch. He stopped by her office after to see if she was hiding out in there, but the door was locked, and she didn't answer his text.

He thought about texting her again but tucked his phone into his pocket and went for a walk instead.

He wasn't due to work the pool bar that evening and, to be honest, hadn't thought of what to do with his free time.

Maybe he'd stop back by the shop and finish the rest of the benches for Aiden.

Instead he ended up at the base of the tree house. He didn't know if she was up there or not, but his mind started in on his decision to move his stuff. From there, he thought about how to store some of his favorite things in the tiny place.

Two hours later, Elle found him hunched over the small kitchen table with drawings spread out all over the place.

"What's all this?" She set a box of food down on the countertop. She looked tired and a little paler than normal.

"What?" He glanced down where she was pointing at the table and came back to reality. He thought about quickly stacking the papers, but she'd already picked one up from the floor and was looking at it.

"These are great," she said, sitting across from him. "You drew these?"

"Yeah." He stacked a bunch of the other ones, but she took them from his hands.

"These are really good," she said, looking over each of his drawings. "What are these for?"

He shrugged. "I was just thinking . . . about how to make some more room."

"For this place?" She glanced around. "Like a second building?"

He shrugged. "I don't know. I thought we could attach them all, kind of like a fort."

"They're small tree houses. Like the cabins, only, in the trees," she said, looking through each page. "Some of them are . . . are these stilts?"

"It's how you have to build places over by the beach. I'm not an architect, but . . ."

"I love them. Can I have these?"

"Um, sure." He felt foolish. "They're just scribbles. Are you sure?"

"Yes." She collected them all, even the ones he'd wadded up and tossed in the trash can.

Once she put them aside, she walked over and took the box from the countertop and set it in front of him.

"What's this?"

"A peace offering." She sat back down across from him.

He opened the box slowly, giving her a look as if he expected the thing to blow up, which had her chuckling.

"It's not a bomb," she joked.

"No, it's a cake." He smiled down at the massive chocolate-covered thing.

"I stole it," she admitted. "I hope Isaac doesn't quit because of this." She sighed, looking even more tired than before.

"I thought you'd be with Hannah tonight," he said after she'd handed him a fork and had gotten one for herself.

"Why?" she asked.

"Because Owen left," he said, taking a bite of the cake.

"He did?" She frowned, then shrugged and dug into the cake. "He did tell me he was thinking about leaving."

"You're not mad?" he asked between bites.

"No, why would I be?" she asked.

"Because." He set his fork down. "Hannah and Owen . . ." He waited until her eyes grew big.

"I mean, they kissed, but . . ." She closed her eyes. "I'm such an idiot." She stood up and started toward the door.

He gathered the cake, then quickly cut off a large piece and set it on a plate for himself. "I think she'll need this more than I do." He leaned in and kissed her. "Go, save your friend from my stupid brother."

She took the cake, then leaned up and kissed him again. "Be here when I get back."

He nodded and watched her leave the place he was starting to think of as his home.

CHAPTER TWENTY

Elle didn't realize what had just happened until she stepped inside the main building. Liam had just selflessly given up their time together so she could be with Hannah.

As she climbed the stairs, her body ached as if she'd just run a marathon. She was probably coming down with a cold, but she couldn't afford any more days off. Especially since Liam had just confirmed that Owen was gone. She felt her heart melting at the thought that Liam cared for her friends so much. Even knowing it was his brother that had caused Hannah's pain.

When she opened the door to the apartment, Scar and Hannah were watching a scary movie on the television.

"What's this?" Elle said, frowning at them.

"*Alien*," Hannah said, waving Elle off. "The original one."

"Shh," Scar said, not even glancing in her direction.

"Fine." Elle shrugged. "I'll take my chocolate cake and . . ."

The movie was quickly paused as both of her friends surrounded her. The box was lifted out of her hands, and she was nudged into a chair.

"Wine," Scar said and moved into the kitchen.

"I'll get the plates and glasses," Hannah said, retrieving as she talked.

They all sat down. "What's up?"

"What do you mean, what's up?" She frowned as a piece of cake was set in front of her, along with a glass of wine. Her head had started pounding, and she thought the sugar would help, so she dug in.

"You don't bring chocolate unless you're upset," Scar said between bites.

"I'm not . . ." She thought about the reasons she'd stopped by the kitchen to begin with and sighed. She'd gone looking for chocolate because she'd felt terrible and had been upset at Liam. After seeing the cake sitting by itself and then stealing it, she'd forgotten her reasons for taking it once she'd spied Liam's drawings. "Okay, I was, but . . ." Her eyes turned to Hannah. "How are you feeling?"

Hannah's eyebrows shot up. "Me? I'm fine." She motioned with her fork. "I didn't bring cake."

"Right," Elle said, drawing the word out. "But Owen went home."

Hannah chuckled. "Right." She took another bite of cake. "I know."

"We've been through this," Scar said with a sigh.

"You're not upset?" Elle asked, taking another bite of cake. The sugar was helping a little with her aches.

"No." Hannah sipped her wine. "Should I be?"

"Liam thinks . . . you and Owen . . ." Her frustration had her setting her fork down. "Are you two sleeping together or not?"

Scar gasped for show, causing Elle to roll her eyes at her.

"We had some pretty hot and heavy make-out sessions, but no . . . we didn't, like, totally do it," she said in a Valley girl tone.

"Will you be serious for a moment?" Elle reached across the table. "Are you okay?"

"Yes." Hannah smiled over at her, but Elle could see pain behind her friend's blue eyes. "But the cake makes any hurt go away. Thanks for that."

"I tried to get her to talk earlier," Scar said.

"Is that why you were watching a scary movie?" Elle asked. "You know Hannah hates them."

"I thought I could scare it out of her." Scar chuckled.

"Hey, I'm the one who thought of watching the movie. Besides, it's a classic, and I figured it was about time I watched it."

"Seriously?" Elle sighed. "You two are hopeless." She started to get up, wishing to walk down the hallway and soak in a hot bath instead of making her way across campus again. Then she remembered Liam was waiting for her and smiled.

"Elle." Hannah gripped her hand. "Thank you." She squeezed it before letting it go.

Elle hugged her. "If you need to talk, you know where to find me."

"Thanks. Go, be with your man."

"Right." She started reaching for the cake.

"Utt un," Scar said with her mouth full. "Collateral damage. The cake stays."

Elle's chin rose slightly. "Fine, I wanted ice cream anyway."

"Bring some back here . . ." Scar called after her as she was leaving.

"Nope." Elle turned and stuck her tongue out at them.

As she jogged down the stairs, she bumped into Aubrey, who was rushing up the stairs, looking a little haggard.

"You okay?" she asked.

"Yes." Aubrey shook her hair, and Elle could have sworn a tree branch fell out of the red strands.

"Did you fall?" Elle reached up and took a leaf out of the mess.

"No." Aubrey's eyes narrowed.

"Okay, keep your secrets." Elle tried to smooth a few more twigs out of her hair. "I left you chocolate cake . . ."

Aubrey swatted her arm away. "You wouldn't be lying to me," she said. "Would you?"

Elle laughed. "No, unless Hansel and Gretel have eaten it all, there's half of it left up there."

Aubrey hugged Elle, hard. "Thank you, you are the best." She rushed up the stairs and called back, "Night."

Elle made her way back to the kitchen and bumped solidly into Isaac as she was trying to sneak into the freezer. Guilt hit her full force.

"I . . . umm."

"Coming back for more?" Isaac asked, and for a split second she feared he was angry, but she noticed a slight smile on his lips.

"I needed . . ."

"Ice cream." He pointed at the chocolate container in her arms.

"Yes." She nodded. "For . . . um . . ."

"Elle." Isaac surprised her. "If you wanted cake and ice cream, all you had to do was ask."

"Can I . . ." she started.

He chuckled. "Take it; there's more. The cake was an extra, which is why it was sitting out, in case someone wanted a piece."

"Oh, thank god." She took a couple of deep breaths, causing Isaac to laugh.

"What did you think, I'd leave because someone stole a cake?"

"I don't know." She shrugged. "I've never worked with a famous chef before."

Isaac leaned closer and whispered. "I'm not like the guys on TV."

"Thank god for that. I mean, you cook like them, but don't . . ." She felt her face heat.

"I know what you mean. Go, enjoy. Before that melts." He nodded toward the gallon.

"Thanks," she said again. "Night." She rushed out of the kitchen, unwilling to give the man time to change his mind.

"What did you do? Raid the kitchen?" Liam asked when she returned with the ice cream.

"I . . . wanted more chocolate." She sat down and handed him a spoon. "Besides, I didn't finish my piece of cake. Most likely someone else will, but . . ."

He pushed what was left of the large chunk he'd taken earlier toward her. Smiling, she put a huge scoop of ice cream on top of it and dug in.

"How's Hannah?" Liam asked after a moment.

"She seemed unfazed. But something's up. I can tell. Chocolate wasn't powerful enough to get it out of her." She motioned with her fork. "Yet."

"Okay." He chuckled. "What is more powerful than chocolate?"

"Wine," she said between bites. "But I have an early class and can't drink tonight." And wasn't feeling quite herself to handle it. "Besides, I'm letting Scar work on her tonight. Hopefully, in a day or two, I'll get my friend drunk, and she'll spill everything."

He laughed. "Remind me to never try and keep a secret from you again."

She met his eyes. "Liam, you know I would tell you what your dad told me, really. But . . . I promised him I wouldn't . . . yet."

He held up his hands, stopping her. "I get it. I mean, in the past, when Dad wanted us to know where he was, what he was doing, he would contact us, but this time . . . it's different. Elle, we need to know something. Please."

She frowned, and since she wanted time to think about things, she got up and put her dish in the sink and tried to shove the ice cream into the small freezer.

"We really do need a bigger one of these," she said after she managed to make it all fit. She knew what she'd promised Leo, but even though she had loyalties to him, she also had new ones to Liam. Finally, deciding that she could give him and his brothers a small clue, she closed her eyes and prayed that what she gave him wouldn't put Liam into the danger Leo feared. "He's in Europe," she said without turning to him.

Liam rushed over to her and spun her around. His hands on her shoulders.

"I promised I wouldn't tell the three of you anything that was going on," she added quickly, "but I never promised not to say where he was. Besides, Europe is big."

"I'm going to call Owen." He pulled out his phone, and she could see the anger behind his eyes.

"Liam." She stopped him. "He just needs some time. You'll understand soon." She felt even more tired than before the sugar.

Without another word, he left out the front door. To call Owen, she suspected.

Elle peeled off her clothes and stood under a warm shower. Her skin ached as the water pelted her, and she wished it was a hot bath instead. She stood under the water until she felt a little more stable. The long day had hit her hard, or maybe it was the traveling. Was she coming down with the flu? She couldn't afford the time off.

Liam hadn't returned by the time she crawled into bed, and she drifted off immediately.

The next morning, her alarm woke her early. She realized Liam hadn't returned to her bed at all, and she felt even worse than she had the evening before.

Suddenly, a sinking sensation filled her. She'd believed they'd made it past all the troubles, all the lies, but now she had to keep something important from him. Something she'd promised his father she wouldn't share with him or his brothers. It wasn't as if it had been her choice.

Was he that upset at her now? Why? He'd been the one who had lied first: about his name, about why he was there at the camp. She'd just kept something from him. Something she'd promised to keep to herself.

Just remembering the fear that had laced Leo's voice had her shivering and holding on to herself. She didn't know all the details—Leo hadn't wanted to tell her everything—but the talk of corporate espionage and the hint that someone was setting him up for embezzling from their business had Elle very concerned for their safety.

Anyone who was willing to go as far as Leo had described—well, she knew that he wouldn't have left if he'd believed his boys were in any danger, but what if he was wrong and *Liam* was in danger?

She told herself to make time to track him down that day and explain everything better to him. Make him understand.

Her entire body ached as she rushed down the path to her first class of the day. By the time she entered the gym, a light sheen of sweat covered her, and she tried to get her focus on her body and to become centered once more.

Normally, by the time the first person showed up for the class, she was back to her normal self; however, this time, a headache had started to form behind her eyes, and she was sweating far more than she was used to.

By the time class was over, the small ache in her head had turned into a full-blown migraine. She downed a couple of ibuprofen before breakfast, which seemed to have worked, until she got the call from Bob Collins.

She figured it would be best to have the rest of the Wildflowers in the office during his call and rescheduled it for half an hour later.

By the time her phone rang, all five of them were circled around her desk. Each with her own list of questions for their lawyer.

"I've gone over the information you sent to me yesterday," Bob said. "Now, I have to ask this again. Are you sure you want me to handle this case? I'm retired."

"Bob, you're all we have." Zoey poked Elle, but she waved her away. She added, "What do you think?"

"Well, like I said on the phone yesterday. It looks like you have a pretty solid case." She relaxed slightly. "But cases like these are hard to work. I mean, most of them demand the employer to prove they did no harm, not the other way around. Even if you have a dozen people who will swear under oath that this employee . . ."

"Ryan Kinsley," Elle supplied.

"That Ms. Kinsley did go off the deep end. It will be up to you to prove it wasn't due to her work environment. That is, if it goes in front of a jury. But I doubt it will go that far; still . . ."

She felt the tension rising again and actually felt her body start to shake.

"Bob, Zoey here. Dylan suggested we use his family lawyers."

"Now, that might be a better idea. I haven't stayed up to date on anything since I retired. Joe's will was one thing, but a full-blown legal action—I'm just not sure I'm ready for something this big."

"Do you know anything about Baker, Baker, and Nelson?" Zoey asked. "That's the law firm in Destin that the Costas recommended."

"Yeah, I've known Chris and Dawn Baker and their son-in-law for a few years. Good people." Bob sighed. "I'm not officially turning you girls away—you know I'd never do that—but . . ."

Elle broke in. "Thanks. If there's anything you can think of that would help us, let me know. I think . . ." She glanced around the room, and everyone nodded. "I think we'll give the other guys a call now."

"You do that. If there's anything else I can think of, I'll let you ladies know."

After hanging up with Bob, Elle pulled out the card for Baker, Baker, and Nelson that Liam had given her yesterday morning and punched in the number.

For the next half hour, she filled Jonas Nelson in on everything she could. Owen and Dylan had both contacted him directly as well.

She emailed the man her witness accounts for each instance as well as a copy of the police report for the gun incident.

"You should be hearing from my office in the next week. Ms. Saunders, if you happen to get another call from Jeff Springs or anyone at his law firm, please feel free to have him contact me directly next time."

She bit her lip and glanced around the room. She didn't know that Liam had told his brothers about Jeff's call, but obviously now the cat was out of the bag.

"I will," she said and hung up.

"What?" Zoey turned on her. "When were you going to tell us that Jeff works at Schumer and Cobbs in Pensacola?"

"I did . . ." she started, then bit her lip. "I thought I did. He's the one that called me and told me about the lawsuit." She rubbed her forehead, feeling the pain spread.

Hannah glared. "You said you got a call from him, but not that he was the lawyer suing us."

"Jeff works for Schumer and Cobbs."

"Is Jeff still in Colorado?" Zoey asked.

"He said that he moved to Pensacola a few months ago," she said.

"This sucks," Aubrey said as she started pacing the floor.

"He's the one working for Ryan?" Scar asked. "Seriously?"

"Yeah, I call BS on that. I mean, what are the odds?" Hannah asked.

Zoey stood up and started pacing now. "You know, I bet it wouldn't take someone long to hunt through our pasts on the internet and find enough skeletons and ghosts to make the rest of our lives miserable."

"You think . . ." Scar started. "You think this is just the start of her attacking us?"

"I wouldn't be surprised," Zoey answered. "I mean, crazy is crazy. Just because crazy gets arrested doesn't stop it from being so."

Elle closed her eyes and laid her forehead on her desk, feeling heated. "God, I need . . ."

"A drink?" Zoey finished.

"No." She rolled her shoulders. "Too much sugar. I've got a headache."

"You need a nap," Aubrey finished. "You probably didn't get much sleep last night after all that sugar. We all know how you feel the morning after a binge."

Elle would have rolled her eyes at her, but she was pretty sure that if she did, they would fall out of her eye sockets and roll across the floor.

She allowed herself to be tugged up the stairs and pushed onto the sofa. She closed her eyes as a blanket was tossed over her.

"If we need you for anything . . ." Zoey kissed her cheek. "You're burning up." She frowned down at her.

"I feel fine," she lied. "I just need a nap. Really."

"Okay, but I'm going to check on you in an hour."

"Thanks, Mom." Elle yawned and rolled over.

CHAPTER TWENTY-ONE

By the time Liam walked into the lunchroom, the place was cleared out of most employees. He found Aubrey sitting in a corner booth, reading a book while she sipped a cup of tea.

"Hey, have you seen Elle?" he asked, setting his plate down.

"Yes, she's upstairs taking a nap. Zoey said she had a fever."

"What?" He grabbed his plate and stood up. "Is she okay?"

"It was just a headache—we had a call with the lawyers." Aubrey watched him closely. "Go up if you want. The code to the door is five six oh seven." She smiled. "The day we all met at camp."

He nodded, then took his plate with him on the way out. He decided to get Elle something to eat; maybe they would have some time to talk things through. He was still upset that she couldn't tell him everything. After all, it was his father. His life.

Since he hadn't returned to her bed last night, he hadn't had time to finish their conversation. He knew it was petty of him to stay away, but since she was keeping something from him, he figured . . . yeah, it was childish.

He grabbed a bowl of soup and a sandwich for her and let himself into the apartment, which felt a little strange, since it wasn't just her space. He'd been up there a few times, but there had always been someone there besides Elle.

He found her sleeping on the sofa and set the food on the coffee table. He noticed it wobbled when he put the tray down and wanted to fix the old legs.

He reached down and felt her forehead and instantly knew she was running a fever.

He walked to the kitchen and found some tea. He made the tea in the coffee maker, carried it over to her, and set it on the table next to the soup.

"Elle." He lightly shook her awake. "Princess, you need to wake up and take something for that fever."

Her eyes rolled around and finally opened.

"Liam?" she asked, and he could see her eyes were unfocused.

He helped her sit up. "I made you some tea and brought you some soup. Take this first." He handed her the pill. "It's an aspirin."

"I . . ." She shook her head. "Don't want another one. I . . . had a headache."

"Yeah, so Aubrey said. You've got a fever going too." He thought about calling downstairs and having Dr. Val come up to check on her. "Does anything else hurt?"

She shook her head. "No, just tired." She sipped the tea.

"Do you think you can try some soup?" he asked.

When she shook her head, he asked, "What did you eat for breakfast?"

She closed her eyes. "I can't remember." She sighed and rested back. The cup of tea would have fallen had he not taken it and set it back down.

"Elle?" He shook her awake again. "You're scaring me."

"Liam?" She cried out in pain as her body began a spasm and shook uncontrollably as he tried to hold her still.

When she quieted, she lay in his arms, unconscious. There were dark circles under her eyes, her perfect skin translucent and discolored in places.

His eyes threatened to water, blocking the vision of her from him, so he held her tighter.

He'd pulled out his cell phone to call for help when the door to the apartment swung open, and he jerked his head to see Zoey standing in the doorway, a look of sheer horror in her eyes when she saw Elle's pale face as she finished convulsing in his arms.

"Call 911," he yelled out to her. "She's just had a seizure." He turned back to Elle and said her name over again, wishing her to open her eyes.

Zoey rushed to his side, her phone in her hands as she dialed. Then she surprised him by running to the door and yelling down. "Get Dr. Val up here. Now!"

After answering some of the dispatcher's questions, she asked, "How high is the fever?"

He didn't know.

"She just came back from the Keys," she said into the phone. "No, just a headache."

He held on to Elle as her body started to shake again. He felt tears sting his eyes as her body jerked uncontrollably in his arms. "Come back to me."

He held her even as Dr. Val tried to push him aside. She took Elle's blood pressure and checked her breathing.

When the ambulance came, he set her gently on the gurney, then followed them down the stairs. Elle's friends and coworkers stood around, helplessly watching as they wheeled her out.

When he was denied access to the back of the ambulance, Zoey took his arm.

"We're all driving to the hospital together," she said, pulling him along.

He sat in the front seat as Dylan drove them to the local hospital in silence. Aubrey sat between them, while Hannah and Scar hugged each other in the back.

Zoey sat beside them and cried into her hands. "She just had a headache."

He'd be damned if he'd let Elle go. When he walked into the hospital, he was angry. At whom, he didn't know, but someone better tell him something quick.

"We're admitting her now, and then we'll need to run tests," the nurse told the group. "Until Ms. Saunders is stabilized, and the doctor gives me the okay, you'll all have to wait."

His brother pushed him into a chair, and for the next two hours, they waited.

He felt like punching something or someone, but since the waiting room had filled up with people who knew and loved Elle, he kept his temper under control.

When the doctor finally came out, he looked around the room and asked for Elle's family.

Zoey, Hannah, Scarlett, and Aubrey all stood up. "We're her sisters."

"Very well." He motioned for them to follow him into a smaller room.

"I'm with them," he said when the nurse tried to stop him.

"He's with us," Zoey added quickly, taking his hand and pulling him into the room.

"Ms. Saunders has a rare form of meningitis," the doctor spit out instantly.

Zoey spoke up. "What?"

Hannah frowned. "That's not . . . possible. I didn't think there were any cases of meningitis in the States."

"There've been a lot more than you'd think. A few outbreaks, mostly in Washington State, but a few other isolated ones spread out. Her chart says that she just came back from the Keys . . ."

He jumped in. "Yes, Key West. Did she catch it there?"

"We'll check to see if any more cases have been reported there. Where else did you go?" The doctor made a note in the file.

Liam shook his head, then thought about it. "Just . . ." He felt all the blood drain from his brain. He fumbled for his phone and punched Carl's number.

"Carl?" he almost yelled into the phone. "Are you and Candace okay?"

"Liam?" It was Candace's voice. "Thank god. I didn't think . . . it's Carl. He's fallen ill. We had to turn the boat around and come back to the States. We just made it to the hospital. He's . . ."

"Meningitis?"

"How did . . ." He heard Candace gasp. "Elle?"

"Yes, we're at the hospital now. Where are you?" he asked, motioning to the doctor for a pen. He wrote down the hospital name and contact information, then handed it to the doctor.

"Liam, a few of our crew members fell ill. Ricky was the first. We think he was . . ." Candace paused.

"Was?" Liam asked.

"He passed away yesterday." Candace sobbed. "If Carl—"

"Don't think that." He shook his head and closed his eyes on the thought. "They're going to make it through this." He said it more to himself than for her benefit. "Keep me posted. You have my number."

"Yes." She sighed. "Keep me posted as well with Elle."

"I will. Gotta go," he said and hung up.

The doctor had left the room once Liam had given him the hospital information where Carl had been checked in.

Now he returned. "That information was very helpful. We're in touch with the other hospital." He sat back down. "We're treating her now. As I was saying, it appears we lucked out, in that it seems to be a viral meningitis. Not the actual bacterial version going around up north. She'll need to stay with us for a few days, and I'll want you checked out as well."

"Fine," Liam said. "When can I see her?"

"Not until we move her out of isolation."

"What about all of us?" Hannah asked. "Have we been exposed?"

"Most likely if you weren't exposed earlier, then it will pass you, but we can run tests on all of you before you leave."

"Elle runs a major resort. What about the guests?" Hannah asked.

Liam hadn't thought about that, and his heart sank for the bad publicity this could cause the camp.

"No, the viral version usually sticks with direct close contact." The doctor wrote something else down in the chart. "To be safe, you might want to warn your guests, but I think if we can confirm that it's just Ms. Saunders who has it, then everyone else will be in the clear." He turned to Liam. "I assume you're the boyfriend."

"Yes."

"You would have been exposed on the boat—close quarters, plus additionally through direct contact."

"We shared a slice of cake last night," Hannah said.

The doctor nodded. "We'll check you out just in case."

For the next hour, they were all tested and told to wait in a different waiting room, away from the rest of the people.

He was updated on Elle's condition while they waited. They were giving her a round of steroid treatments, plus antibiotics to prevent secondary infections.

She was awake but groggy and was asking for him. Once his reports came back clean, he was shown to her room with the rest of them. So far, no one else had been exposed. They had lucked out again.

"Hey," he said, rushing to her side and taking her free hand in his. She had tubes running in her other hand.

No matter how upset he'd been at her for not telling him everything, it wasn't as important as seeing her alive and healthy. After all, she'd been right: his father was an adult and could take care of himself. Elle was fragile now as she lay on the big bed, looking pale and scared. She needed him, and somehow, he needed her just as badly.

"Hey." She smiled weakly at him. "I'm sorry . . ."

He leaned in and kissed her. "You scared me . . . us," he corrected when Zoey cleared her throat.

Zoey was standing on Elle's other side as the Wildflowers gathered around the bed. "How are you feeling?"

"Tired." She leaned her head back and closed her eyes. "Embarrassed."

"Alive," Hannah added.

Elle's eyes opened and searched his. She must have seen something in them because she asked, "What's happened?"

"Carl's sick," he added, feeling her hand jerk in his.

"Is he?" she asked, concern flooding her eyes.

"On the mend, like you, but a little slower. It took them a while to get back to the States. Most of the crew were sick. Carl's immune system has always been bad because of his . . . because of his phobias. The man spent an entire year locked in his own apartment because he was afraid of germs." He shook his head. "Candace will keep us posted."

"How is everyone else?" she asked.

"Rest. Don't worry about that now." He brushed a hand down her hair, which had been braided to the side.

"I am tired." She sighed.

"We will go." Zoey leaned down and kissed her. "Get some rest."

He sat back as the others said their goodbyes and left.

"You're feeling okay, though, right?" Elle asked when they were alone. He shook his head slowly. "You're sick?" She started to sit up.

"No, I'm physically all right." He closed his eyes and lifted her hand to his lips. "My god, I've never been more scared in my life."

Her hand escaped his, and she ran it through his hair, then nudged his chin up until he looked into her eyes. Slowly, she wiped away a tear that had escaped.

"I'm sorry." She rested her head back again, and he could see that she had used up all her energy.

"Sleep!" He leaned in and kissed her again. "I'll be right here."

"Thank you for the soup and tea."

He chuckled softly and watched as she drifted off. The sound of the monitors beeping kept him company for the next hour as she rested.

As the day shifted into evening, he sat and watched Elle. Nurses came and went, medicine in her drip was filled and replaced, and her vitals were checked every hour.

She sipped a cup of broth but pushed it away and soon grew tired of sitting up. Hannah and Scar delivered dinner to him.

"Do you need anything else?" they asked before leaving for the night.

"Tell Dylan he can bring me a change of clothes tomorrow morning. I plan on sitting right here until she can go home."

"Liam, you should go home, get some rest," Elle broke in.

He smiled over at her. "I'm not leaving your side."

She yawned. "Why am I still so tired?"

"Duh!" Scar said from the end of the bed. "You have meningitis."

"Thanks, doc." Elle rolled her eyes.

"We did sneak you something else. Isaac sent his best." She handed over a small bag. "To both of you." Scar winked.

"Please, oh, please, let it be chocolate," Elle said.

"Cookies." Liam smiled. "Double chocolate by the looks."

"There is a god." Elle fell fast asleep in front of them.

"It's the drugs they have her on," he explained to the room. "She's in and out a lot."

"Her body is fighting it." Hannah touched his shoulder. "She has a chance, thanks to you."

Scar jumped in. "If you need anything, you have our numbers."

"Thanks, for all this." He motioned to the food. "And the cookies. I'll make sure she gets one."

"Two," Scar warned. "At least."

He nodded. "She can have them all, if it will make her feel better." He turned back to Elle. "And get her out of here faster."

After they left, he sat in the room and ate dinner while watching the news on mute.

He hadn't realized he'd fallen asleep in the chair until a nurse came in to take Elle's vitals.

"Sorry, sweetie," the older black woman said. "I tried not to wake you."

"It's okay." He wiped his hands over his face. "I must have dozed off."

"You've been sitting here all evening. If you want to go and get some fresh air . . ."

"No, thanks." He shifted. "How's she doing?"

"Her vitals are returning to normal, and the fever is almost gone." She patted his arm. "She must be something really special to you."

"She is." He took Elle's hand and could feel that most of her fever was gone.

"She's one lucky lady," the nurse said before leaving the room.

"Yes, I am," Elle murmured.

"You're awake." He smiled down at her.

"Did Scar and Hannah leave?" she asked, looking around.

"Yeah." He glanced at the clock. "A few hours ago."

"Ugh, I must have fallen asleep." She rolled her shoulders.

"How are you feeling?" he asked.

"Like I could use a shower." She touched her braid. "I must look a mess."

"You're beautiful. Always." She gave him a look, making him chuckle. "Trust me, you are."

"You didn't eat all those cookies, did you?" She glanced around.

"Nope, I was saving them." He took the bag and handed it to her. "They're all yours, if you want them."

"I think there might be one or two in here for you." She shifted as she opened the bag. "There's a note in here." She pulled it out and read it out loud.

"'Elle, from everyone in the kitchen, get better soon.' I never thought . . ." she started but stopped.

"What?" he asked when she didn't continue.

"I never thought that I would have such a wonderful extended family," she said, handing him two cookies.

"You're not only a great boss but a good friend to most everyone who works under you. There's no doubt in my mind that you're going to beat whatever Ryan throws in your direction."

"I hope so, because this lawsuit is just her next move, and we have to be ready for whatever else she conjures up." She bit into a cookie. "God, but as long as we have Isaac, I think we'll survive the storm."

He chuckled, then bit into his own cookie and agreed.

CHAPTER TWENTY-TWO

"I can walk up the stairs myself."

But still, Elle wrapped her arms around Liam's shoulders as he lifted her into his arms.

Even though she felt weak, she was pretty sure she could have made it up to the third-floor apartment by herself.

"With me here, you don't have to. Besides, this is a lot more fun." He shifted her in his arms and brought her in for a kiss. "And, I get perks."

She smiled and relaxed as he carried her up the rest of the way.

When they walked into the apartment, her friends were there, gathered in the living room, waiting for them.

"What's all this?" she asked, seeing that the sofa had been made up with extra blankets.

"Your quarters for the next few days. You'll be under our watchful eye. One of us will be with you at all times," Zoey said, glancing around the room.

"I've got first shift," Hannah said as Liam set Elle down gently on the sofa.

"I have a thing . . ." He frowned down at her. "I would . . ."

"Go." She smiled up at him, then pulled the pillow out from behind her back and adjusted it. "I'm quite comfortable here, being pampered." She glanced over at Hannah. "As long as there's wine."

"No wine," Hannah said. "Doctor's orders. At least until these are all gone." She wiggled Elle's pill bottle.

"Fine." Elle groaned and asked, "Chocolate?"

"That I can do," Hannah agreed and disappeared into the kitchen.

"Go." She waved everyone else away. "Let me get my rest." She knew everyone had places to be and things to do. "Go run our business without me."

"I'll be back with lunch," Liam said before leaning in and kissing her. "Don't go anywhere."

She smiled. "I'm staying put. Unlike everyone else, I love getting pampered when I'm sick."

"I'll remember that." He kissed her again and then left with the others.

"Here we are," Hannah said, walking back into the room with a plate of brownies and a huge glass of milk on a tray.

"My hero." She smiled and leaned back, feeling tired from just the short trip from the car to the base of the stairs.

"You're tired already," Hannah said, sitting down next to her.

She lay back and took several deep breaths, feeling too tired to even eat a brownie. Then she glanced over at Hannah. "Have you heard from Owen?"

"No." Hannah frowned. "Why would I?"

"I just thought . . . we all did, that . . ." Elle sighed. "You know."

"Just because you and Zoey have found happiness with a Costa man doesn't mean I would. Besides, Owen and I are too different. It wouldn't have worked out."

"If you say so." Elle took a brownie, deciding to at least try to eat something. "If I keep eating like this, Liam won't be able to carry me up the stairs soon." She wiggled the brownie.

"That was the sexiest thing I've ever seen." Hannah took a brownie for herself. "I can only dream of a man carrying me up a set of stairs, Rhett Butler–style."

"It was pretty romantic." She sighed and then sipped her milk. "God, he's so . . . perfect." She set the glass down. Even with their disagreement about his father's whereabouts, he'd never been anything but kind and patient with her. It must have been extremely frustrating to him that she'd known something that could have eased his concerns but hadn't told him. "I mean, he didn't leave my bedside once. Who does that?"

"Someone who's in love," Hannah answered.

"Love?" Elle frowned down at her hands. "I . . . are you sure?"

Hannah chuckled. "I myself may have never experienced the emotion before, other than with you guys, but yeah, I'm pretty sure he's in love. By the look in your eyes, so are you."

"I can't be." She shook her head, knowing that she wasn't worthy of his love. Not when she was still hiding something so major from him. Something that could very well help get his father out of danger, or deeper into it. She should tell him everything. Damn the consequences.

Maybe he could help his father discover who had it out for them. Who was setting him up and stealing from them. But she didn't want Liam to be in any danger, and Leo had made it very clear that if they knew . . . they would be. "I . . ." She turned her thoughts to her history with Jeff and all the mistakes she'd made because she'd believed he'd been the one. "No, I'm not ready again."

"Yes." Hannah rested her hand on her leg. "You are. And, more importantly, he's the one for you. It's obvious, and if you weren't fighting off a major illness, you'd see it too."

"I can't . . ." She closed her eyes.

"Rest." Hannah took her feet and pulled them up onto the sofa, then covered her with a blanket. "Everything will get easier tomorrow."

"You should call him," she said before closing her eyes.

When she woke, Liam was there, waiting for her to open them again.

"Feel better?" he asked with a smile.

"Some." She stretched. "I could probably go for some food."

"I can arrange that." He picked up his cell phone. "Burger?" he asked, glancing up at her.

"Sounds perfect." She rested back on the pillow.

When he set his phone down, he moved the chair closer to her. "The food should be here shortly."

She wanted to ask him who was bringing it but decided it didn't matter.

"How are things at the camp?"

She'd been curious about how things were running. To be honest, if she'd felt a little stronger, she might have tried to take a short walk downstairs to check up on the place herself.

"Your friends and your staff have got everything handled." He handed her a drink of water. "Trust them."

"I do." She sipped from the cup. For the first time in two days, she felt hungry—really hungry—and she wondered how long it would take the burgers to get there.

He reached over and took her hand in his. "I'm so sorry about leaving you the other night. I should have . . . returned to you. I would have seen that you were sick and done something about it sooner."

"You were upset," she said. "You had every right to be. I'm keeping something from you. Something about your family that I shouldn't have the right to . . . but I made a promise and . . . it's important. I can't tell you why, but you need to trust your father on this."

He shook his head. "That's just the thing. I can't. I mean, Dad has done some pretty crazy stuff in the past few years. If I could trust him"—his eyes locked with hers—"I would."

"Then trust me," she said and tugged his hand closer until he was leaning over her. She needed to protect him, even if his father wasn't around to do it himself. Again, she figured she could be truthful about some things. "I don't understand everything that's going on, or where your father is right now, but I do know enough to realize that it's very important I keep what I do know to myself."

He rested his forehead on hers. "I do trust you." He sighed.

They sat holding hands in silence. In a few minutes, Zoey and Scar walked in with a bag of burgers and fries. Just as she'd been thinking she couldn't wait any longer for food.

"How's it going?" she asked Zoey, hoping for more detail. After a quick update from both, she felt more relaxed than before and dug into her burger.

"We should all be so lucky as to get a week off from work," Scar joked.

"I'm not taking a full week," she said, trying to make her voice sound strong, but she ended up sounding more like she was whining.

"You are; the doctor . . ." Liam started, but she narrowed her eyes at him, causing him to chuckle. "We'll see how you feel."

"I think if I get a little more rest today, I can be up tomorrow. Maybe not full force, but at least well enough to deal with some paperwork. Have we heard from the lawyers again?"

"No, but they did say it would take them about a week to go over everything," Zoey said. "Let's allow them to do their job and not stress about anything just yet."

"Everyone thinks it's total BS what Ryan is doing," Scar said. "More stories of how she acted are surfacing."

"Like what?" she asked, leaning forward.

"Here's my clue to cut out." Liam leaned in and kissed her. "There's a band playing tonight, and Britt needs help at the bar."

"Thanks for lunch," she said.

"Aubrey's bringing up dinner for you later." He kissed her again, then whispered, "See you after. Get some rest."

"I will. How's Carl? Have you heard anything else today?"

"Candace called me earlier. He's out of the woods," he said with a smile. "He'll be stuck in the hospital for a few more days, but they think he's past the roughest part." Then he disappeared out the door.

"That's good news," she said to Zoey.

"Yes, it was a shame about the man who died."

"What?" Elle sat up. "Who died?"

Zoey frowned at her. "I thought Liam told you . . . the employee on the boat. The one who infected you. He didn't make it."

Her heart sank, and she fell back against the sofa.

"I thought . . . Liam was probably trying to protect you from the bad news."

"I'm not upset at him," she said and rubbed her forehead. "I'm just tired."

"Get some rest, then." Zoey stood up. "I'm on watch until dinner."

"Thanks." She pulled her legs up and tucked the blanket around her again as Zoey cleared the mess from the coffee table.

She hadn't realized how close to death she'd been. Sure, she'd felt like crap, but she'd had the flu plenty of times. Even though she knew meningitis wasn't something to joke about, the worst she'd felt was just after she'd arrived at the hospital, when the doctors and nurses were poking her with needles.

"Zoey?" She glanced over at Zoey, who was sitting across from her, reading a book. "How bad was it?"

"What?"

"I remember passing out when Liam came up with the soup, but that's it . . ."

"Sweetie." Zoey set her book down. "You had four full-blown seizures. Your eyes rolled to the back of your head, and they thought at one point that your heart had stopped."

"What?" She sat up a little. "I . . ."

"Easy . . ." Zoey came over to hug her, and Elle heard her breath hitch. "You're safe now."

"I didn't know." She closed her eyes and felt tears building. "I thought . . ."

"You scared the crap out of us. All of us." Zoey held on to her tightly.

"I seriously need a drink now."

Zoey chuckled. "Maybe just a little." She walked over and poured them each a small glass of wine.

"What would have happened to this place, to you guys, if . . ."

"Don't think about it," Zoey said, waving her glass. Elle noticed it was a lot fuller than her own. "But I think we would have eventually picked up the pieces and tried to continue on. Our hearts are in this place." Zoey smiled and looked toward the windows. "More than just ours. Everyone who works here is invested in making this place great. When you pitched this idea to us, I never thought . . . I thought it would be great, don't get me wrong, but I thought it would just be . . . a job. You know?"

"Yeah." Elle lifted her glass in a small toast. "It's more than that."

"Yes, it is."

"It's the place where I found Dylan." Zoey's smile changed. "The place where we're going to build our first home. He proposed."

"What?" She jerked the wine glass, and if it had been full, she would have spilled it all over herself.

"I was going to tell everyone . . . after we bought a ring, but . . ." Zoey glanced down to the unicorn ring that sat on her finger where a wedding band would go, and Elle could see her eyes grow dreamy. "Seeing as you almost died. I made an exception and told you before the others."

"I guess another toast is in order." Elle held up her glass. "Congrats."

"Now I'll have to tell the others tonight." Zoey smiled. "I'll text them and tell everyone to meet here after dinner."

While Zoey pulled out her phone, Elle thought about Hannah and Owen.

"Has Hannah talked to you yet?" she asked. "About Owen?"

Zoey frowned. "No, there's something else going on there. I don't know what, but . . ."

"Let's get her drunk," she suggested.

"You sneak!" Zoey accused with a laugh.

"What?" Elle held up her hands. "It's the only way sometimes to break that outer shell of hers."

"I'll arrange everything." Zoey stood. "You need some more rest."

"I'm tired of being tired." She pulled the blanket back around her.

"You sound like you're five," Zoey joked. "Sleep. I've got some scheming to do."

The next time Elle woke up, she convinced Zoey to let her take a bath, so long as she left the bathroom door cracked open so Zoey could make sure she hadn't drowned.

Elle washed her hair and, more importantly, shaved her legs for the first time in days. It felt wonderful to pull on a fresh pair of yoga pants and a clean tank top.

When she stepped out into the living room again, the coffee table was full of food and drinks. Hannah and Scar were already there; they were just waiting for Aubrey to get the party started.

"She had some issues down at the pool house," Zoey explained.

"Anything . . ." Elle started, but she stopped when everyone turned to her with the same look on their eyes. The look that said, "Not your problem."

"Okay, geez." She held up her hands. "I get it. I'm off duty for now."

Less than ten minutes later, Aubrey rushed in. "Okay, seriously, I'm sorry." She picked up a full glass of wine and downed it like it was grape juice. "There, now I'm caught up." She sat down in a chair and put her feet up. "What are we talking about?"

"The Costa men," Zoey supplied. "Dylan has gotten a few updates from Owen since he left camp."

"And?" Aubrey prompted, seemingly unaware of Zoey's brief glance at Hannah.

Zoey said, "The phone call to Elle was a fluke. They had word that he'd been spotted in one of his buildings in London, but after that . . . he just disappeared again." Zoey turned to Elle. "You haven't heard from him again?"

"I only found my phone the other day with the stuff I wore to the hospital . . ." She pulled it out of her pocket. "No new calls."

"Where could he be?" Zoey asked. Elle could hear the frustration in her tone.

"I'm sure he has his reasons for staying out of touch," Elle added, causing all eyes in the room to turn to her. She didn't know exactly where he was at this moment; Leo had given her a clue where he'd been when he'd called her. He'd told her a basic outline of what he was going through, why he was hiding, but he'd confided in her and made her promise, for his safety and for that of his sons, not to tell anyone. Including her best friends. Did that mean that he believed someone was watching them? She shivered at that thought. As much as she wanted to tell her friends everything, she would never put them in danger.

"What do you know?" Hannah asked.

"Me?" She sipped the rest of the half glass of wine she'd been allowed and thought for a moment that she could trust her friends, but then she remembered Leo's words: "Not even your Wildflowers. The walls have ears, and this is the most important secret you'll have to keep in your entire life. Lives depend on it." Swallowing the answers down, she answered, "Nothing."

"You're lying." Zoey sat up straight. "Why?"

She glanced around. "I promised I wouldn't say anything. Besides, they're not my secrets to tell."

Aubrey jumped in. "Secrets? He told you where he was?"

"No." She shook her head. "Not that—well, except that he had been in Europe at that time. I doubt he's still there." She thought about

Leo being spotted at one of his London buildings. He could have easily called her from there and moved on after.

"What is going on? This is their father we're discussing. And, oh, yeah," Zoey said sarcastically, "he's been missing for more than six months."

"No, he hasn't," Elle said. "He's been . . . busy, yes, but not missing. Just because he didn't check in—"

"How would you have felt if Joe had left without a word for six months?" Zoey asked.

Elle hadn't thought of it like that before. It would have killed her knowing her grandfather had disappeared and that someone might know more about where he'd gone. But this wasn't her grandfather. This was Leo—what he'd told her about his reasons for disappearing had made sense and scared her, especially now, since she had fallen for Liam. "He made me promise." She knew she sounded like a child.

Hannah poured herself some more wine. "Is there anything you can tell them and us?"

"He's not missing. He's doing . . . something important, and . . ." She thought about it. "He'll be back by the end of next month."

She didn't want to scare her friends by telling them that lives depended on her keeping this secret. She'd doubted Leo's story at first and still didn't know if it was true, but she just couldn't chance it—not if it meant that Liam could be in danger.

Hannah stood up, taking her glass with her. "Why couldn't you have just told them that?"

"Because, I—"

"Don't say *promised*." Hannah turned on her. "Owen left because . . ."

Everyone was silent.

"Because I didn't, couldn't, tell him about his father?" Elle filled in.

"Well, yes." Hannah waved her glass.

"He would have left anyway. He was planning to before Elle got the phone call," Zoey said.

"Yes, but . . ." Hannah drank again. "Because of that call, he believed he could . . ." She set the glass down. "I don't know, find him faster."

"You're mad at me?" Elle said, feeling her heart aching.

"A little, but . . ." Her friend's eyes scanned hers, and then she watched as Hannah relaxed. "I get it. You can't tell. You were always good at keeping promises."

"If I could tell you . . ." She looked around the room at all her friends, her family. "Believe me, I would."

"I'm not mad at you." Hannah rushed over to her side. "Not really. But I am pissed at Owen." She sat next to her. "That bastard left me without even saying a single word to me."

"Are you okay?" Elle asked, taking her hand.

"I'm pissed," Hannah said, standing back up.

"So, have you called him and told him yet?" Zoey asked.

"No." Hannah shook her head quickly. "No way."

"Why not? In this day and age, you don't have to sit around waiting patiently for him to come calling. Go." Zoey waved her glass again. "Not right now, but tomorrow. Go to Destin and show up at his office building and demand he talk to you."

"What would I say?" Hannah sank down on the edge of the sofa. "'Hey, you didn't say goodbye to me'?"

"You should go and conveniently bump into him," Aubrey suggested, earning her looks. "What? It happens all the time in the movies."

"Cheesy movies." Scar shook her head. "What about going to him under the pretense of giving him more information about his dad?"

"I have an idea." Zoey sat up slowly. "Elle, you have an appointment with the lawyers next week, right?"

"Yes, I was going . . ." She frowned. "Their office is in Paradise Investments' main building—downtown Destin." She turned to Hannah. "Since I haven't fully recovered from my bout of meningitis, I think I'll send a representative from the camp instead."

CHAPTER TWENTY-THREE

"You did what?"

After lunch, Liam had found Dylan swimming laps when he'd shown up at the pool bar.

"I sold my condo." Dylan smiled up at him.

"That soon?" He edged closer to the pool, wishing he had time for a dip. The summer heat had hit full force that day, and already he had sweat dripping down his back. It was just past noon.

He chuckled. "I got full price too."

"Where are you going to live?" he asked.

"Here, stupid." Dylan splashed water in his direction.

"In the cabin?" He shook his head.

"No, now we can start building our own place." Dylan pulled himself out of the water.

"But I thought . . ." What? That he'd changed his mind? "That it would take longer."

"What about you?" Dylan asked. "You're planning on sticking around here." He dried his hair with a towel, then shook it like a dog for good measure. "Planning on gaining a few new roommates?"

He shook his head, but the tree house popped into his head. A plan formed. "What are you doing for the next few days?"

"What do you have in mind?" Dylan sat on the edge of a pool chair.

"Some manual labor." He pulled out his phone. "I've got a couple buddies that owe me." He started sending text messages to a few of his local friends.

"What do you have in mind?" Dylan asked again.

"Elle has a tree house. It would be nice to turn it into something . . . better and maybe bigger before she's back on her feet."

Dylan was silent for a while. "Have you talked to Aiden about this?"

"Good idea. I'll message him." He added a new text and got one back almost immediately. "He's meeting us over there now. Seems like he's eager to do something special for Elle while she's down."

"Lead the way," Dylan said, pulling on his shirt and tugging on his shoes.

"Don't you want to change first?" He nodded to his brother's flip-flops.

"Show me what you're thinking first, then I'll go change." Dylan slapped him on the shoulder.

He stopped by the bar and filled Britt in quickly.

"Go. I've got this tonight. You do what you need to." She waved him away. "Elle deserves something nice after what she's been through."

He walked with his brother down the pathway and met Aiden at the base of the tree house.

"I'm thinking we can take the next few days to make some improvements," he told them.

"Fixing this place up was on Elle's radar," Aiden said. "Elle didn't want to siphon any funds from the camp, so all I could do was fix the stairs."

"We won't be spending any of the camp money," Liam said. "I've got this covered myself."

"What kind of improvements are you thinking?"

"What did Elle have in mind?" he asked.

"I brought the plans . . ." Aiden started to pull them out.

"Let's head up; we can talk about them in the space. I've done some drawings too." He pulled the stairs down.

Dylan looked up at the tree house. "I've been by this area a dozen times in the last week. I never knew it was even here."

"That's what Joe wanted for Elle. A place she could disappear to when things got too . . . much," Aiden said.

"You knew her grandfather?" Liam asked the other man as they started up the stairs.

"Yeah, he was my second uncle . . . or whatever . . . my grandmother was his sister," Aiden answered when they stepped into the cabin. "Elle and I are second cousins."

"I didn't know that." Liam looked at the man now. There were similarities—the blond hair and blue eyes—but for the most part, he never would have guessed the connection.

"Nice," Dylan broke in as he glanced around the tree house. "Good space."

"Yeah." Aiden smiled. "Here's what I was thinking . . ." He laid the plans out on the small table, and Liam spread his out next to Aiden's.

Less than two hours later, half a dozen men were working on clearing everything out of the tree house and beginning the gut. The supplies to start building the extension were due to arrive first thing in the morning. Aiden had shifted around the supplies meant for the next cabin to go to the tree house instead. He'd replace the order for wood, which would delay the cabin's construction by a few days, but Liam thought it would be worth it.

He figured at the rate they were going, with a few more days working like they were, the place would be done.

"Where do you need me?" he asked Aiden after taking a break to check on the sleeping Elle.

"We can't hoist the new floor beams until the truck gets here tomorrow, but you can cut out where the door will be for the new room." He nodded upward. "The saw is already up there. I've marked where you'll cut."

"Sounds good." He looked around.

"None of this would be possible without your friends." Aiden motioned toward the crew. "I guess it pays to have friends who own their own building companies."

Liam chuckled. "Yeah, they're really Owen's friends, but I helped them out one summer. So they owed me."

"They'll be welding the new floor joists on site. Rob says the metal will arrive tomorrow. He thinks they can even replace the stairs going up to the roof with aluminum-framed stairs as well. They'll curve around the tree this time, taking up a little more space. Your drawings really helped this entire process. Elle said you had a few other ideas for tree houses?"

"Yeah." He glanced up at the frame hanging up in the air. "It helped to have a good solid frame in place already."

"Joe didn't cut corners," Aiden said. "On anything. The electricians should be here tomorrow. As well as the plumbers."

"About that. We had a thought . . . I'll show you. Come on up." Liam motioned to him, and Aiden followed him up the stairs.

The tree house was totally gutted. Even the small kitchen was bare. Wires and plumbing stuck out from the walls. The only things still in place were the toilet and shower.

"We're going to cover all of the walls with reclaimed wood like you suggested. Except in the bathroom and kitchen—we'll patch those stucco cement walls and slap a fresh coat of paint on it. Which got us thinking . . . since we're building a new room, for the bedroom, there's enough space here for a tub along this wall. The windows won't be here until the day after tomorrow, which gives us plenty of time to hoist a Jacuzzi tub up here," Aiden said.

"Can the structure support it?" Liam asked.

"Rob seems to think so. He's the engineer, so . . ." Aiden glanced around. "Then, we'll separate the kitchen and bathroom instead of this space being one giant room. You'll have a nice kitchen with a sitting area and the privacy of a full bathroom."

"Do it." Liam smiled as he looked around the space.

They were making a lot of changes in the old cabin: new wood-paneled wall coverings and hardwood flooring, along with fresh paint. The old fridge would be replaced with a full-size one, and the old kitchen cabinets had been yanked out, and new ones would be arriving in two days. But he questioned whether the new extension would be done in time.

Rob and his crew claimed they could have it all done in less than five days. Liam just had to figure out how to keep Elle away until everything was finished. The way he figured it, with the help of her friends, they could keep her busy and away from the tree house long enough.

For the next hour, he cut a massive doorway in the existing tree house. A crew of seven people, including his brother Dylan, worked around the place, preparing it for the new extension that would be hoisted up in two days.

They were building the skeleton of the new addition on the ground; then they would finish the rest once it was up in the air.

"We might have a problem," Aiden said shortly before dark.

"What?" He knew things were running too smoothly so far.

"I got a call. Elle is awake and wanting to come stay here while she recuperates." Aiden ran his hands through his hair.

"What are we going to tell her?" Liam started pacing. They needed at least five more days to finish everything.

"I don't know." Aiden sat down on the bench, then stood up quickly. "It stormed two nights ago."

"Yeah." He frowned. "So?"

"So, I could come to her and tell her that a tree limb went through the roof of the place and that I'm repairing it."

"Good, that could work."

"Okay, so . . ." Aiden glanced around. "What do I say if she wants to inspect it?"

"Tell her no."

Aiden laughed. "You don't know Elle that well."

"Sure, I . . ." He sighed. "Damn, you're right. Okay, so we need to enlist her friends to help us keep her away."

Half an hour later, Liam sat next to Elle as Aiden explained about the damaged roof on the tree house.

"Oh no!" Elle tried to stand up. "I want to . . ."

"Nope," Zoey broke in. "You're supposed to be resting. Not climbing a ladder to look at a damaged roof."

Elle's eyes narrowed at her friend.

"I haven't had the place inspected yet. We don't even know if there was any structural damage," Aiden added. "Until someone looks at it, no one is going up there."

Elle fell back against the sofa cushion.

"Besides, we need you here. I need you to help me get everything ready for my meeting in the morning," Hannah pointed out as she sat down with a laptop. "See, I still haven't got all of this worked out yet."

By the look on Elle's face, he knew they had avoided a disaster for one day.

The following day, Aubrey sent him a 911 text.

She's dressed and wanting to go for a walk by the treehouse.

He dropped everything and showed up at the apartment.

"You're up?" he asked, handing over a tray of brownies. "Isaac sent these over for you."

"Oh, how nice, but I was hoping to go for a walk," she said, slipping on her tennis shoes.

"I'm starved. Why don't you sit here with me while I have some food?" He sat next to her and held out a brownie.

"Okay," she said between bites. "It's just . . ." He leaned over and kissed her.

"I've missed you and thought"—he waved at Aubrey behind his back to leave them alone—"we could be alone?"

He smiled when the apartment door clicked shut.

"Oh, okay." She relaxed in his arms when he kissed her and instantly felt himself respond to her softness.

He knew she was too weak to do too much physically, but he figured he could enjoy a little and maybe get her to relax enough to take a nap after.

Hoisting her up, he carried her toward the hallway.

"You do have a room here?" he asked, his lips running down her neck.

"Yes, this one." She motioned to the door.

When he stepped in, he glanced around the small space quickly.

"I haven't changed it since I was sixteen," she said, biting her bottom lip.

"I like it," he said, setting her down gently on the bed. She moved up on the mattress as he pulled off her shoes. "God, I've wanted you . . . I don't want to hurt you."

"No." She held her arms out, and he went easily into them. "You won't."

He settled next to her, covering her soft mouth with his own.

"What did you do to your hands?" she asked, pulling away slightly; she took his hand in hers and frowned down at his palms. He'd been running his fingers under her shirt, over her skin.

He glanced down at his hands and noticed the new blisters from working on the tree house.

"Benches," he said. "Remember, I'm building some." When he kissed her again, she relaxed and tugged his shirt off.

"God, I just love the look of you."

"My turn." He helped her remove the soft tank top she'd been wearing and then the rest of her clothing. "Perfection." He ran his fingertips over her skin and smiled when she arched into his hands.

"God, I need . . ." She tugged on his pants, causing him to laugh. "You." She almost growled it out. "Liam, now, I need you."

"You're too weak," he argued. But she tugged his zipper down and gripped his shaft, causing his eyes to almost cross.

"Elle." Her name came out as a warning.

"Liam, I need . . ."

He didn't let her say anything more; instead, he nudged her legs wide and covered her pussy with his mouth. She was too weak for too much physical activity, but he figured he could at least give her this.

Using his mouth on her, he felt her building and knew that after, she'd rest and forget about taking a walk.

He had never experienced anything as wonderful as Elle convulsing on the tip of his tongue. He doubted he'd ever taste anything as sweet as her. How could he ever live without the feel of her next to him?

He finally realized he'd been fighting a battle he'd been destined to lose. He'd fallen hard and fast for Elle, which meant he could either run away, like his father and Owen tended to do, or he could face it head on and own up to it. Which meant telling Elle. More importantly, showing Elle. That tree house needed to get done. And soon.

CHAPTER TWENTY-FOUR

Elle woke with a start. It took her a moment to realize that the absence of noise had woken her.

"Damn it." She groaned when she realized she had fallen asleep again. Her body was still vibrating from what Liam had done to her after dinner.

It had been three days since she'd returned home, and so far, she hadn't stepped foot outside the apartment once.

Every time she pulled on her shoes, someone was there, convincing her to stay put. Or, Liam was there, wanting to please her until she drifted off in a state of after-sex slumber. Not that they had had full sex since she'd gotten sick. No, instead he'd just pleased her until she passed out.

Not that she was complaining, but she really did want him even more now. Somehow, what he was doing to her had built up a need stronger than anything she'd ever felt before.

She glanced around the darkened room and realized instantly that she was alone. What would it take for her to sneak out of her own apartment?

Glancing at the small window, she frowned. It was still fully daylight out, which meant she'd been asleep for less than an hour.

She tried to figure out the best way to escape. She'd attempted to sneak out the third-floor window once when she was fourteen. She'd gotten a broken arm for her efforts. She wasn't willing to chance that again. Not now, when just showering still drained her of all energy.

She pulled on her shorts and shirt, slipped on her shoes, and figured she could tiptoe out of the place if she had to.

When she opened the bedroom door, she listened for a few moments before determining that she was either alone in the apartment, or whoever was in the living room was reading quietly.

She sneaked down the hallway, peered across the corner, and noticed that the living area was empty. Glancing over to the kitchen, she was surprised to find that it too was empty.

Not wanting to miss her chance, she rushed across the room and quickly stepped through the doorway.

She took a deep breath and rested her back against the door; then she glanced down the stairs, trying to get a look at the main lobby.

How was she going to get past Julie?

Just then, she heard the phone ring downstairs and moved closer to get a better look.

"Yes, I'll go check to see that it printed. Give me a minute," Julie said. Elle moved closer and watched Julie disappear into the small room that housed the printers off the back of the lobby desk area.

She almost tripped and fell rushing down the stairs but managed to catch herself on the railing before she tumbled down the flight.

She was around the corner and out of sight of the front desk before she could take another breath. Trying to relax, she counted her heartbeats until they settled down. Then she smiled as she made her way toward the back door. She stepped out into the evening air and took several deep breaths, enjoying the fresh air. The night was a standard sticky Florida night, but she loved it. Loved that there was already a bead of sweat building up between her shoulder blades.

She'd never make it in prison, she thought as she started walking down the pathway. What she wanted was a nice long walk, but she could already feel her energy draining, and since she desperately wanted to see the damage to her tree house, she made her way across the campgrounds on a mission.

The sun was sinking lower in the sky, casting shadows everywhere, but the lights along the pathway kept her company. She was happily surprised when she didn't bump into any guests along the way. She wasn't fully ready to chat with anyone about her illness yet.

Stopping at the base of the tree, she searched in the dying light for the rope for the stairs; finding it, she tugged on the rope.

She knew that Aiden didn't want her to go up yet, since he'd told her earlier that day that the inspector would be looking at the place tomorrow. But, she figured, she could stand on the landing and peer in the windows if she had to.

It had been eating at her knowing that the place Joe had built especially for her had been destroyed.

Would it be a total loss? She hoped not.

She smiled at the sign that Liam had made for her that hung just outside the door. No matter what shape the tree house was in, she was determined to rebuild it.

Turning around, she glanced over the water as the last light from the sun disappeared over the horizon. Glancing up, she watched a shooting star streak across the sky and smiled.

Wishes. She'd made so many in her life. Some had come true; some she had forgotten. It took her a moment to weave a new wish in her mind, and she quickly closed her eyes and sent it up to the heavens silently.

After turning back around, she braced herself for the worst and twisted the doorknob.

What she hadn't expected was a roomful of people screaming "Surprise!" at her.

She squealed and covered her heart with her hands.

"My god!" She glanced around the small space, packed with the people she cared the most about.

Zoey and Dylan were there, holding on to one another, while Hannah, Scar, and Aubrey all smiled brightly and laughed. Aiden was there as well, sipping a beer as if he'd been dragged along for the ride.

Her eyes moved around, and she noticed Liam walking toward her, a glass of champagne held out for her.

"Welcome home," he said, leaning in and kissing her.

"What . . ." It was then that she actually looked around.

"We knew the moment you were left alone in the apartment, you'd sneak out," Hannah said as Elle looked around the space.

"All we had to do then was set out the bread crumbs," Zoey added.

Everything had changed inside the small space. The walls were covered with warm wood paneling, making the entire place feel larger.

The bed was missing from across the room; in its place was a corner-booth dining table. Soft cushions sat on the bench seats, with colored pillows for the backrest. The windows were new: they were longer and stronger and had built-in blinds. She could tell that they were the tinted windows she and Aiden had looked at before.

A small white sofa sat facing the windows, with what looked like a long wooden homemade coffee table sitting in front of it with a massive wood bowl on top. Even the flooring was new, along with several area rugs that matched some of the beautiful new landscape paintings that hung on the walls.

When she looked over at the bathroom area, she saw a new circle mirror that sat in front of a beautiful metal bowl sink. The old countertop had been replaced with warm wood countertops, and even the cabinets were new, in a dark shade of brown.

The shower walls had been repainted a warmer color. She was a little shocked to see a huge bathtub where the kitchen table used to be, and a new small wall separated the bathroom space from the kitchen. Even the kitchen cabinets and countertops were new. She laughed at the full-size fridge that sat at the end of the small kitchen area.

"You . . ." She frowned, her friends moving aside while she looked around. "Where's the bed?"

Liam chuckled, then motioned to a bookshelf. "Go on, pull it."

"The bookshelf?" She shook her head as she followed him over to the wall. The shelves were filled with her books. The ones from her room. How had he sneaked those out of her bedroom, and why hadn't she noticed they were gone when she'd left earlier?

"Here," he said, taking her hand and laying it on the edge of the bookshelf. "Pull."

She did and soon had the bookshelf opening out smoothly. She held her breath as she stepped into a whole different room.

A massive king-size bed rested on a raised platform in the middle of the room, flanked by two large windows. A beautiful wood dresser sat on the wall not filled with windows.

"You . . . built a new room?" She shook her head. "How?" She turned back to him. "You did this while I was sick?"

He smiled. "We did it." He motioned to her friends. "With a little more help."

She glanced around again, then noticed a huge painting of a stork that hung above the bed. Her eye was instantly drawn to the creature and the signature in the corner.

She stepped away and moved closer. "Yours?"

He nodded. "I thought it was time I stopped hiding it and let someone else enjoy my stuff."

"It's beautiful." The painting was full of bright colors, the stork full of life.

Then he motioned to a framed sketch hanging over the dining table.

"I . . . did one special piece for you. I'm hoping someday to have enough time to paint it, but for now . . ."

She walked over and saw the five Wildflowers at the tender age of ten smiling back at her. Tears rolled down her cheeks at the innocence in each of their eyes.

Her friends walked over to her and wrapped their arms around her.

"I love you all," she whispered.

"You deserve a place of your own," Zoey said. "Just like you've given us." She moved back over and took Dylan's hand.

"I can't believe you did all this." She turned to her friends. "Thank you, everyone. It's more . . ." She felt her eyes water again. "I . . ."

She walked around and quickly hugged everyone once more.

"Do you like it?" he asked, taking her in his arms as tears flowed down her cheeks.

"It's more than I . . ." She started to repeat her words but then closed her eyes and felt the tears rolling down her face and wiped them with the back of her hand. "Thank you. Everyone."

"The upstairs balcony is fixed as well," Aiden said. "There are new stairs . . ." He motioned toward the sliding glass door with the empty beer he'd been holding in his hands. "Head on up."

She stepped out on the balcony and wiped more tears away. She glanced up at the new aluminum staircase that led around two trees and up to the rooftop.

When she stepped up, she found a table sitting in the middle of the space. Candles burned in glass jars; a large vase of flowers sat in the middle of the table. Overhead, hanging string lights made the entire space glow, giving it a magical feeling.

Two silver-covered platters rested on the table, with a bottle of champagne chilling next to them.

"This is all so . . ." She turned to see Liam standing there, smiling at her. "Amazing."

"I hope you don't mind, but I know we didn't get to eat earlier." His smile turned almost wicked. She remembered what he'd done to her earlier that afternoon when he'd shown up at the apartment claiming to be there for dinner. Her smile grew and matched his.

"Your fault," she broke in.

"And well worth it," he added, taking her hand in his and walking her over to sit at the table. He pulled out her chair and held it for her. "I had Isaac whip us up something special and thought we could enjoy it up here."

"Everyone . . ." She glanced back toward the stairs as she sat down.

"They've all taken the hint and gone home." He sat down across from her. She watched him pull out the bottle of champagne and fill up her glass.

"How did you get this all done so quickly?" she asked after taking a sip. The bubbles made her smile even more. She was concerned her face was going to be permanently stuck like this. No wish she ever could have come up with could have been this amazing.

"We called in a few favors. And help." He shrugged and reached over to pull off the cover of the food.

A huge juicy steak, along with Isaac's twice-baked potatoes and fresh veggies, filled the plate. She felt her stomach growl.

"We have a bedroom." She smiled and held up her glass.

He lifted his and tapped it against hers. "We have a home, for now."

She felt her heart skip. "Yes, we do have a home." She leaned in and set her glass down. "We will need a new sign."

His eyebrows shot up. "We will?"

"Sure. It's no longer just Elle's Hiding Spot." She glanced around. "It's Elle and Liam's Tree House."

"It's a good thing you know someone who's good with his hands."

She laughed. "Yes, it is," she said, cutting into her steak.

His smile slipped a little. "So, this is okay, then?"

"What?" she asked between bites.

"You, me, here?" He shook his head. "My brothers are going to keep looking, trying to find something more about where Dad went, but for now, I'm going to stay right here, if that's okay with you?"

"Yes," she answered almost too quickly. Then she suddenly felt stupid. "I mean, that is, if you want . . ."

"Elle." He reached over and took her hand in his. "I've wanted to be with you since the first time I saw you looking down at me through the windows." He smiled. "The first time I saw you fall on that pretty little ass of yours."

She laughed. "I tripped."

"Right." He laughed with her.

"You tend to do that to me," she said, picking up her glass and hoping the champagne would help soothe the emotions that were boiling inside her.

"What?" he asked, his eyes glued to hers.

"Make my knees feel like rubber," she said.

His smile warmed her heart. "I couldn't even begin to describe what it is you do to me," he said softly.

Biting her lip, she decided nothing had ever felt more important to her than what she would say next.

"I love you, Liam."

There was a moment of silence, and she realized that she felt like a weight had been lifted from her chest after saying the words.

His smile grew, and for a moment, she thought his eyes glimmered with tears. "I love you too."

Her heart soared. Her wishes had come true.

"What now?" she asked.

He stood up and gathered her in his arms. "Whatever it is, whether we stick around here in this place or build our own home near the campgrounds, we'll do it together." He kissed her, and she felt her heart almost burst in her chest. "Which reminds me." He leaned back and pulled out a small box from his pockets.

She held her breath as he frowned down at it. "Zoey gave me this . . . to give to you. She told me to give it to you tonight, that you'd know what it meant." He held it out. "I didn't look, but I think I know what it is."

She relaxed slightly and took the box from him and opened it slowly; then she smiled down at the unicorn ring. The stupid thing was laughing at her as she slipped it on her finger.

"She said that now, she has a different one to wear. So it's your turn to have this," Liam said.

She met his eyes. "Yes, it is my turn."

He pulled her closer to him and kissed her until her knees buckled. "This is how I imagined it would be. How it would feel like," he said, then leaned in and placed a soft kiss on her lips. "Just like this, with you."

"I . . ." She shook her head. "I never imagined having someone, something, this . . . perfect before."

He chuckled. "I'm far from perfect."

"No." She took his face in her hands. "You are—you're perfect for me."

He nodded. "I never imagined I'd fall in love with a princess. Never thought I'd fall in love, until you came along. I love you," he said again, causing her heart to flutter.

"I love you." She reached up and kissed him. "You're everything I ever wished for and more."

He kissed her as the hot summer breeze floated through the treetops and the branches and leaves swayed in the summer night's wind.

ABOUT THE AUTHOR

Jill Sanders is a *New York Times*, *USA Today*, and international bestselling author of sweet contemporary romance, romantic suspense, western romance, and paranormal romance novels. With over fifty-five books in eleven series, translations into several different languages, and audiobooks, there's plenty to choose from. Look for Jill's bestselling stories wherever romance books are sold.

Jill comes from a large family with six siblings, including an identical twin. She was raised in the Pacific Northwest and later relocated to Colorado for college and a successful IT career before discovering her talent for writing sweet and sexy page-turners. After Colorado, she decided to move south, living in Texas and now making her home along the Emerald Coast of Florida. You will find that the settings of several of her series are inspired by her time spent living in these areas. She has two sons and has offset the testosterone in her house by adopting three furry little ladies that provide her company while she's locked in her writing cave. She enjoys heading to the beach, hiking, swimming, wine tasting, and playing pickleball with her husband,

and of course writing. If you have read any of her books, you may also notice that there is a love of food, especially sweets! She has been blamed for a few added pounds by her assistant, editor, and fans . . . donuts or pie, anyone?

You can connect with Jill on Facebook at http://fb.com/JillSandersBooks, on Twitter @JillMSanders, and on her website at http://jillsanders.com.